Clearwater

Rihannon Baker

Cover Art By Elia Peligrini

ISBN 9798373676557

For Skye, who cried for these characters

Love you, Bestie

Chapter One

I fucking hate storms, he thought to himself as he paused at the turn.

Thunder rolled in the distance, and lightning flashed in his rear view mirror. The roads were wet from the plentiful rain that had fallen over the past week, and he hoped that this would be enough to prevent the lightning strikes from starting any fires in the forest.

Davis Chevalier turned his pick-up truck down the right-hand turn, a sign on the side of the road announcing that Clearwater was only 2 miles away. He wound the window down and inhaled the fresh scent of rain and dirt and sequoia trees, whose immense branches blocked out whatever light had fought its way through the clouds, making the road so dark he had to put on his lights.

Home, he thought to himself, a feeling tugging at his stomach that he did not want and had not felt in some time. Not much had changed, except that maybe the trees seemed taller and more oppressive now. The road had been resurfaced, but otherwise, it was the same road he had driven a million times.

He caught sight of himself in the rearview mirror. Did he look any different? It had only been 5 years, but he felt a different person. If the trees had grown taller, he was sure there was a change in him that he could not see. Sequoias changed slower than people did.

Thunder rumbled again, this time loud enough for him to hear it clearly over the engine, and raindrops began to tumble through the leaves onto his windshield. He wound his window up, and ran a hand through his sandy blond hair. He needed a haircut. His mother would probably try to accost him with a pair of clippers. Davis had spent a good deal of his childhood with a cold and stubbly head as his mother had insisted she was not going to maintain his unruly head of hair, thank you very much. The hairdresser in Anchorage that he'd most recently visited had not done the best job, and now he was looking rather shaggy.

Fitting for a lumberjack, he thought to himself with a wry grin. Lumberjack. That's what his father had called him when he first took the job with the logging company. "You chopping down the trees yourself?" His father had asked.

The forest began to clear, and the rain beat down harder as the town of Clearwater appeared down below him. It had barely changed at all. The buildings on Main Street were still green, and the roadside was packed with trucks and jeeps as usual. The fire station had been rebuilt, and a brand new engine was parked outside, the paint still glossy. Up on the ridge he could see the response helicopter perched at the emergency response centre.

As Davis rolled down Main Street, a few people turned to look at the bright yellow pick-up. One or two people waved as they seemed to recognise him. He stopped at the red light at the end of Main Street, and Sandy Geller, the owner of the flower shop, stopped directly in front of his truck as she crossed the street, despite the rain, and stared at him, slack-jawed.

"Hi Sandy," he waved, although he knew she could not hear him. The light turned green and the car behind him honked, jostling Sandy from her surprise, and she scurried to the other side of the road.

Davis continued, taking the turn left up towards the ridge, and his parents' house. The potholes in the road were still there, the recent rain having washed the gravel across the road, kicking up under his truck and hitting the chassis with a loud ping.

The white picket fence glowed against the dark trees, impossible to miss, signalling home. He pulled into the drive. The front porch had been painted, and the little blue house looked fresh with the white trim. Flowers in hanging baskets swayed and danced in the rain and the breeze that had sprung up. His mother had always been immensely proud of her flowers.

Davis killed the engine, and jumped down from the cab as the rain intensified. He grabbed his bag from the backseat, and headed up the porch steps as his mother threw open the door.

"Baby boy!" She exclaimed, throwing her arms wide. Though her son was now a good 2 feet taller than her, Patricia Chevalier still insisted on calling him her baby boy. It had embarrassed him as a teen. Now he found it sweet.

"Mom," he wrapped her in a big hug, his 6'7" frame having to almost bend double to put his arms around her, "you look amazing!"

Patricia laughed. "Oh honey, bless you for saying so. I'm just getting older like the rest of us." She took a step back. "Oh let me look at you." She looked over her son's face with a warm smile. "You look good. Handsome as always. I'm surprised you're still tan after all that time in Alaska."

"They still have sun up there you know!" Davis heard his father's voice drift from the den.

Patricia rolled her eyes. "Come on, come inside out of this rain." She ushered her son in, as a flash of lightning preceded a deep roll of thunder above them.

Davis sat down to take off his boots, and his father rounded the corner. Paulson Chevalier was a sturdy man, and while Davis stood taller than his father for many years now, Paulson still towered over his wife. He had become thicker around the waist over the years, but he still looked strong. He shook Davis's hand after he rose from the bench seat, Davis noting that his father's grip had not weakened a bit with age.

"Welcome home son," he said with more emotion than Davis expected, "it's good to see you."

"Sorry it's been so long, Dad," Davis apologised, "just work and... you know."

Pauslon nodded. "I know, son. Life gets away from you sometimes." He shifted from one foot to the other. "Can I get you a beer after your journey?"

Davis nodded. "Yeah, thanks Dad."

They walked into the kitchen, which smelled like Davis's childhood, and his stomach began grumbling. He'd been on the road for over a week, travelling from Anchorage all the way down to Northern California, and he hadn't had a proper home-cooked meal in longer than he cared to remember. His mother went back to stirring a pot of something on the stove, and his father waved a hand to the table for Davis to sit down, and placed a bottle of beer in front of him.

"So, how's the job going?" Paulson asked his son.

"It's been busy, the wildfires have definitely become crazier over the years," Davis replied, rolling his fingers around the top of the beer bottle before taking a sip.

"Wouldn't you do better as a firefighter rather than a consultant?" The disdain that coloured the last word made Davis flinch internally.

"Paulson," Patricia warned from the stove, not looking up from her cooking, "leave the boy alone."

Pauslon sniffed and shrugged, but said nothing, taking a long swig of his beer.

"And how have things been here?" Davis asked, attempting to be jovial. "Any major changes I should know about?"

"Patrick took over the bar," Patricia said, turning to lean against the counter, "and the Hendersons left town, because their daughter moved to Arizona and had a baby. The school got a new gym. And you probably saw the response centre up on the ridge? That's new."

"Hardly new," Pauslon interjected. "It's been there 3 years now."

"Well, it's new to Davis," Patricia said, tucking her blonde curls behind her ears with a defiant flick. She began to serve up the meal, and Davis took a deep, appreciative breath.

"Is that tomato chicken?" He asked, too focused on his mouth watering to feel silly to call the dish by such a childish name.

His mother smiled and nodded. "Only the best for you, honey," she beamed as she placed the steaming plate of chicken cacciatore and fried potatoes in front of him.

Davis eagerly began to eat, when his mother cleared her throat, and Davis saw his father eyeing him with displeasure. Davis quickly put down his cutlery, and they all bowed their heads as Paulson said a prayer.

"Been on your own for too long," Paulson muttered after he finished saying grace. "Forgotten your manners, son."

"So, how long will you be in town for?" Patricia asked quickly, a brilliant smile on her face.

"They contracted me for 2 years, but it could be longer." Davis replied, the delicious food warming his belly and telling him, without doubt, that he was home. His mother had always been the best cook; although he was sure most people though that of their own mothers.

"So what are they wanting to do down here?" Paulson asked.

"The company has acquired logging rights to some the land bordering the national park, and they need a security engineer to oversee the new operation." Davis tried to read his father's expression, but the man avoided Davis's eyes and continued to eat. "The wildfires have made them pretty nervous, especially the ones down south a couple of years back."

"Oh they were terrible, the footage of that poor woman trying to save her horses!" Patricia exclaimed. "It made my heart hurt."

"So, you gonna stay here or find a place in town?" Paulson asked.

"I thought I'd try to find my own place." Davis loved his parents, but he didn't know that he could go back to his cramped childhood bedroom for the long-term. His father's nod of approval told him that he, at least, would welcome his grown son not taking up space in the family home.

"Of course," his mother smiled, "you're a grown man, and you need your own space." She got up to refill Davis's plate. "Does Grace know you're back?"

The name hit Davis like a ton of bricks. Grace. Grace Weaver. Grace with the red hair and the eyes like iron. Davis had pushed her from his mind completely, sure that she had gone off to college and was now living somewhere in the city. Surely Grace hadn't stayed in Clearwater. She'd hated it here.

"She's a park ranger now," Paulson told him. "Does a good job too. Her father's still a bastard. How that girl didn't turn into a boy under that man's roof is a mystery to me."

Patricia sighed. "Bob Weaver is a broken man."

Paulson snorted disdainfully, and Patricia gave him a disapproving look. "Oh come on now, Paulson, he went through a lot. Losing his wife so young, and then..." She quickly trailed off and pasted a wide smile on her face. "Who has room for dessert? I made Pecan Pie!"

"That sounds amazing, Mom, but I might grab a shower first." Davis rose from the table. "If that's OK?"

"Of course sweetheart, your room is made up and fresh towels are in the bathroom." His mother began to clear the table, and brought her husband another beer.

Davis wandered down the hallway to his bedroom, the family photos smiling at him from the walls in the half-darkness. His parents had torn up the old carpet and polished the hardwood floors, which creaked underfoot. He clicked on the light in his bedroom, as lightning struck outside and thunder cracked overhead, the storm moving much closer now.

His room had not changed much since he had moved out of home many years before. His mother kept everything meticulously clean, and the room smelled of the floral fabric softener she'd used since he was a child. He smiled at the checkered sheets on his bed. Some things just never changed.

Davis peeled off his clothes, which had seemed to shrink during the long drive. Everything was tight and uncomfortable, his muscles ached and he was suddenly very tired. He stepped into the ensuite and turned on the water, waiting for the hot water to kick in, which always seemed to take an age out here. Finally, he stepped under the steaming stream, and it felt like balsam.

After his shower, he changed into loose sweat pants and a t-shirt. The rain was bucketing down outside, the thunder rumbling almost constantly nearby. He padded down the hallway barefoot, back to the kitchen, to find his mother sitting at the kitchen table with a mug between her hands. "Your father headed to bed," she told him, "you know him, early riser and all. Would you life a coffee?"

Davis nodded as he sat down, and his mother placed a steaming cup in front of him. "Would you still like dessert?" She asked.

"No, Mom, I'm fine. I'll just have the coffee and head to bed."

"No problem," she smiled, "we can have it tomorrow. You must be exhausted after your drive. Such a long way."

Davis stirred cream and sugar into his mug. "The first three days were fun, and the scenery was amazing. But then it just became -"

"Lonely?" His mother offered.

Davis shrugged. "I guess. It's just a long way."

"I bet. Your father and I took a road trip to Mexico once and that was more than enough for me!" They gave each other a warm smile, and she reached across the table to squeeze his hand. "It's good to see you, baby. I missed you a lot."

"I missed you too, Mom. Thanks for a great welcome home."

"I'm sorry I mentioned Grace," Patricia looked apologetic, "it was silly of me."

"I can't believe she's still here, she hated Clearwater."

"Well," Patricia shrugged lightly, "she loves it now. She's out there in the park, zipping around on her ATV, like it's a calling. You would never think she'd done anything else."

"She always wanted to get out of here." Davis mused, warming his hands on his mug.

"I don't think she really had that option with her father." The contempt in Patricia's voice surprised Davis. His mother rarely spoke ill of people. "Especially after..." She trailed off and looked at Davis, then shook her head. "Anyway, let's not talk about that. You're here now, and everyone will be thrilled to see you. You should head over to the bar and see Patrick."

"I will, Mom. I have a few days before the boss gets here, so I'll try and catch up with a few people." He drained his cup, and went to put it in the sink. He walked over to his mother and gave her a kiss on the head. "Good night Mom, sweet dreams."

She gave his hand a squeeze. "Good night, baby. Sleep tight."

Davis gratefully collapsed onto his bed. The rain was beating against the window behind him, and the thunder had subsided. His muscles relaxed, and an image of Grace swam before his eyes as he drifted off to sleep, her long red hair flowing behind her like fire, beckoning him to follow her.

Come on, Davis! You chicken?

Dreams of dark forests and towering flames chased Davis from his sleep. It must have been late, the sun already sat high in the sky and streamed in through the gaps in the curtains. The house was quiet, meaning his father had already left for work, and his mother would probably be running errands or outside gardening.

His stomach was growling, so he stretched and rolled out of bed. He'd not slept well, despite his exhaustion. He put it down to winding down from his long trip, trying hard to stifle the memories of the nightmares that had plagued him all night.

In the kitchen there was a note from his mother: *Headed in to town, will be back later on. Plenty of eggs and bacon in the fridge xxx.* He put on the coffee machine, and fried himself three rashers of bacon and two eggs. As he cooked, he checked his phone. An email from his boss, saying he'd be in Clearwater by the end of the week. Davis was grateful for the break from work, even if was only a few days - he felt he'd either been on the road or working for the past 12 years.

As he sipped his coffee and ate his breakfast, he mused over how it would feel to see everyone again. He wondered if he would still feel unwelcome, whether he would still feel the scornful looks burning into the back of his neck as he walked down main street. He'd barely kept in touch with anyone - not out of malice or laziness, but out of sheer guilt. He hadn't been able to face it. Perhaps those people wouldn't understand, and he imagined a few of them would be, rightly, pissed off.

And then there was Grace... As quickly as the thought formed in his head, he stamped it down. He pushed his breakfast away and took a deep breath, his stomach suddenly a iron weight inside him. No, he wasn't going to go there. He was still processing the fact that she was still here, after years of being sure - and certainly, hoping - she would have left like she always wanted to, and achieved all the things she'd always talked about when they were kids. "Clearwater," she'd say, scrunching up her noise, "more like Shit Creek."

After he'd cleaned up the kitchen and changed into a pair of jeans and a white tee, he headed out. He wasn't sure Patrick would already be at the bar, but he thought he'd try anyway.

Main Street was busy as always, and people stared at him as he got out of his big yellow pickup and walked down the sidewalk towards Doherty's. No one said anything to him, which didn't bother him a bit. There were also no scornful looks, and he decided perhaps people had just become better at hiding their disdain. *Or maybe you're just being paranoid?* He thought to himself, giving a passerby a friendly smile which was easily returned.

The front doors at Doherty's were closed, but when Davis went down the side alley, he saw the service doors were open, and stepped inside, his heavy footsteps echoing on the hardwood floor. "What you want?" He heard a voice call from the storeroom.

"I dunno man, is the beer still shit?" Davis called back.

Patrick popped his head out of the storeroom. "You sneaky bastard, what are you doing here?" He broke into a wide smile. "How long have you been back?"

"Just got in last night."

Patrick gave Davis a bear hug. Patrick was almost as tall as Davis, and a good 50lbs heavier. Davis had been the high school quarterback, but Patrick was the left tackle. "Good to see you, man!" Patrick released Davis from his crushing hug, and gave him a shake. "Been too fuckin' long between visits though!"

Davis began to apologise, but Patrick waved it away. "Nah, forget it. Can I get you a drink?" He began to head to the bar.

"Just a coffee if you have some."

"Ooh, onto the hard stuff these days huh?" Patrick laughed. "Come on, got some hot and fresh. Take a seat." He gestured to the bar stools.

Davis sat and Patrick presented him with a large cup of black coffee. "So," Patrick began, leaning on the bar, "I had heard a little rumour that you were back for work?"

"That's right," Davis confirmed, "got a new contract with the company, and they wanted to move me down here."

"Had enough of being up there in the cold, huh?"

Davis shrugged. "Alaska was fine. Cold, but fine." He grinned. "Nah, it was time to move on. And when they offered me this, I thought, why not?"

"Oh yes, Clearwater, why not indeed," Patrick said with a grin, rolling his eyes and pouring himself a coffee. "Well, a lot has changed since you left, man."

"I heard you and Shelley got married," Davis said, smiling.

Patrick shifted on his feet, and an uneasy smile resting on his face. "Wow, you really didn't call home much at all, huh?" He looked up at Davis's puzzled face. "Shelley, uh, she was diagnosed with breast cancer 2 and a half years ago. Aggressive shit, the fast-moving kind. It moved to her brain, and, uh, she passed away 6 months later."

Davis felt his stomach drop. Patrick had been his best friend. They'd grown up together. And his wife had died, and Davis hadn't known. "Holy shit. I am so sorry," he told him, "I - fuck. How fucking awful. I am so sorry, man."

Patrick shrugged. "It was rough, but I had to keep myself going for my kid."

"You and Shelley had a kid?"

"Yeah," Patrick nodded, a proud look on his face, "Kayley. She's 3, and she's just, man she's so great." He raked a hand through his unruly dark hair. "She's so smart. She blows my mind every day."

Not only had his best friend lost his wife, his best friend had lost his wife shortly after becoming a father, and had been raising a little girl on his own ever since. Davis hung his head, staring at his clasped hands on the bar. "I let you down, man. I'm so sorry. I should have been here for you."

"Ah, it's alright, life happens. The community really came together for us." Patrick assured him. "Grace threw a fit when I said I'd have to put Kayley in daycare, said she wouldn't allow it." Patrick laughed as he crossed his arms across his chest, gazing off into the distance, lost in recollection. "She packed that baby up and strapped her to her back, took her up into the park with her, man they gave her so much shit, carrying her diaper bag full of nappies and formula. But she didn't care. She still takes her out with her all the time, I think Kayley thinks Grace owns the park or something." He laughed again, and cast a glance at Davis, who hadn't yet looked up from the bar, the mention of Grace's name placing a vice grip around his stomach yet again. "You see Grace yet?"

Davis shook his head, trying not to show how the mention of her name had derailed him. "No, not yet, I doubt she'd be thrilled to see me in any case."

"Ah, time heals all wounds." Patrick gave him a warm smile. "You should go see her. She's up at the emergency response centre most mornings." He pushed himself up off the bar. "Anyway, my friend, I have a huge delivery coming in soon and I need to make some room in this storeroom."

"Can I give you a hand?" Davis offered.

Patrick waved him away. "Nah, got it all under control. You go and explore or relax or scamper or whatever it is you logging fellows do." He waved as he rounded the bar to head back around to the storeroom. "We'll catch up soon! Good to see you, Davis!"

Out on Main Street, Davis headed back to his pick-up. He paused as he put the key in the door, and looked up to the ridge. *Grace is up there most mornings.* He wrestled with himself for only a moment, then swiftly reminded himself that seeing her was the last thing he needed right now. Patrick's revelations had left him feeling even more guilty than he had that morning.

Once in his truck, he realised he had nowhere he had to be. He could, indeed, scamper and explore as Patrick had so jovially suggested. The thought brought a smile back to his face, and as the sun was shining brightly as midday approached, he felt it would be a waste of a day to be sat inside. He reversed out of his space, and began to head south, out of town towards the entrance to the national park.

The roadsides weren't bare like they had been 5 years ago. The trees had recovered, and with all the recent rain, the foliage was lush and green. As the road rose up the mountain, the canyon came into view, and Davis could see the river raging down below. Last time he had seen it, it had been barely a trickle, carrying nothing but dead trees and ash downstream.

He crossed the suspension bridge that led to the park, and suddenly he was under towering sequoias and redwoods. He wound down his window and breathed in the fresh, crisp air. Summer always had a particular smell, no one could convince him otherwise, and today it was drifting on the breeze. And thankfully, today there was not a hint of smoke.

He took a right down towards the first lookout point, the road bumpier than he remembered it being. He pulled up just below the visitor information centre, which was closed, and jumped down out of the truck. Two squirrels chased each other around a towering redwood as he walked by. The view from the lookout had also changed since he'd last seen it - no charred tree stumps and smoking ground. Everything was green, and the sound of the river below was a dull roar.

On the horizon, dark clouds were gathering, heralding the arrival of another storm that afternoon. It was verging on being hot now, the sun beating down from directly overhead. He walked a little further along the fence line, when he heard an ATV thundering along the main track above. His heart stopped for a moment, expecting Grace to round the corner at any moment. Someone zoomed past, but through the trees all he could make out was flailing blonde hair. He exhaled. *Get a grip,* he told himself.

He started to amble back to the truck, feeling thirsty and deciding to head back to his parents' place. Patricia would probably be home by now. He should see if she needed anything done around the place while he had some free time.

He drove back down through town, deciding to stop at Sandy's Flower Shop and get his mother a gift. As he walked through the door, ducking his head through the low entrance, Sandy let out a strange, strangled gurgle from behind the counter, and the three other people in the store turned to stare at him.

"Davis!" Sandy exclaimed, coming around from behind the counter. "I thought it was you when I saw you yesterday!" Her eyes ran up and down his chest and shoulders, and he regretted wearing a tight t-shirt instantly. "You look wonderful, young man." She purred, and Davis pasted a tight smile on his face.

"Great to see you too, Sandy." He responded, trying to ignore the two other women who had begun to circle behind him, also staring him up and down.

He'd been told by past girlfriends that he was a handsome man, and he'd been popular with the girls in high school. He always put it down to his height more than anything, but it seemed there was definitely more to it than just being tall. He was suddenly keenly aware of how broad he was compared to the slight woman beside him.

"What can I get you today?" Sandy took his arm, guiding him to a pedestal display of various flower arrangements. Sandy had won awards for her flowers, and displayed all the medals proudly in the front window. "Your mother just *loves* peonies," Sandy continued, "unless of course we're getting them for another special lady?" She gazed up at him, giving him a wink and a knowing smile.

"Oh no, just some flowers for Mom, no, uh, special lady in my life right now," Davis responded. He could practically feel the ears of the other women in the store pointing in his direction.

"Hmm, such a shame." Sandy responded, plucking a bunch of pink peonies from the display and taking them to the counter. "A handsome young man like you shouldn't be on his own. It's just not right." She deftly wrapped the bouquet in pink crepe paper, and tied a lighter pink ribbon around to keep everything in place. "Twenty dollars, honey," Sandy offered the bouquet to him with a warm smile. "And tell your mom I said hi."

Davis paid, and nodded his thanks. "Take care, Sandy." He nodded at the other women as he left the store, aware that their eyes continued to follow him all the way back to his truck.

His mother was unloading groceries from the trunk of her car as he pulled up into the drive. "Hi honey," she waved, "just in time to give me a hand!"

Davis got out of the truck and handed his mother the flowers - "Oh honey, thank you!" She gushed. "My favourite!" - and got all the bags out of the trunk in both hands. "Lucky me having a big, strong son!" Patricia laughed as she opened the door ahead of him. Davis placed all the bags on the kitchen island and began unpacking as his mother placed the flowers in a vase.

"So what have you been up to this morning?" She asked.

"I went and saw Patrick at the bar."

"Oh good!" She smiled widely.

"He told me about Shelley." Davis went on. "And his daughter."

Patricia's face dropped. "Oh I know, that was really, really awful. Poor Shelley." She shook her head sadly, gently arranging the flowers. "She had this tiny baby, they were so happy, and then finds out she's sick. Life isn't fair."

Davis considered asking his mother why she never told him, but stopped himself. *You weren't here,* he reminded himself. "And then I went up to the lookout by the visitor centre," he went on, "looks like a storm's coming."

"Oh yes, it's been so humid today," his mother agreed as she began to pack away boxes and packets in the pantry, "it wouldn't surprise me if a storm hit. Do you want tacos or roast chicken for dinner?"

"Tacos would be great, Mom," he responded, "when will Dad be home?"

His mother shrugged. "Who knows? They wound his duties back somewhat after all the rebuilding was done, and now he spends most of his time sitting in the office gossiping. I swear, men say we women gossip, men are worse than a knitting circle when they get together!"

Paulson had worked in construction for as long as Davis could remember, it was why they had moved to Clearwater when Davis was just a baby. Paulson would often be gone for days at a time, but as he got older he'd found the work more difficult. The last wildfires had provided the company with a plethora of work, but it seemed now even his bosses were aware of the fact that the man, though still strong, was perhaps not as able as he had once been.

Patricia put on the coffee machine, and sat down at the table, gesturing for Davis to come and join her. "It's nice to have someone at home," she smiled and took his hand. "I've missed our talks."

"Me too Mom," Davis held his mother's tiny hand with both of his giant ones, "I am really sorry I didn't come back to visit all this time."

"You need to stop apologising for that, a lot happened before you left." She sighed. "I know people won't always understand why we react the way we do, but I know you suffered terribly after the fire. What happened to Billy -" she stopped, and took a deep breath. "A lot of bad things happened, and I don't think anyone should be judged for how they reacted afterwards." The coffee machine had stopped bubbling, and his mother rose to pour them both a cup.

"I let a lot of people down," Davis said.

"Oh no you haven't," Patricia insisted.

"What about Patrick?" Davis asked. "With Shelley and everything -"

"Things happen honey, and they would have happened if you were here or not." Patricia sat back down opposite him. "Maybe some people won't see it that way. But on the other hand - how many people tried calling you? Did anyone try and talk to you about how you felt?" She stirred a spoon of sugar into her coffee. "The people who leave will always be seen as the ones who abandoned everyone, the ones who ran away. But life isn't that simple. Just because people stayed doesn't mean they helped. Or that they cared." Her face darkened for a moment, and Davis considered pressing her further, but before he could, she brightened and looked up. "Anyway, enough of that. Did Sandy accost you when you went to the flower shop?"

Davis laughed. "She definitely seemed to, uh, appreciate my presence."

"Well, she would, handsome man like you in her shop, she'll tell everyone she sees about it." She laughed, when the distant rumble of thunder interrupted her, and she looked up. "Oh shoot, I wanted to put the new roof on the chicken house today, I noticed there was a leak when I collected the eggs this morning."

Davis jumped up out of his chair, grateful to have something to keep him busy. "No problem, Mom, I can get that done."

"You're wonderful," his mother beamed, "everything is in the shed, honey."

"Don't worry, I remember!" He called over his shoulder as he headed out.

"Don't get that nice shirt dirty!" He heard his mother as he headed down the porch steps, and shook his head, smiling. Did mothers ever change?

He peeled off his t-shirt and got to work removing the old, rusty iron roof, which had only been lightly nailed on. His mother had clearly been responsible for all the home maintenance for some time, and he was annoyed that his father, who worked in construction of all things, had left things like this to his wife. Patricia wasn't incompetent, but things like this? His father wasn't around enough, and never had been.

The sun continued to shine as he worked, the humidity rising to an almost oppressive level, and soon beads of sweat began to form on his forehead and neck. It was going to be another hot summer. Even if all this rain kept up, he wondered if it would be enough to ward off a severe fire season.

The old roof removed, he began to work on putting on the new one.

You're good with your hands, right Davis?

The sudden memory was a jolt, and the drill whined as he missed his mark. He shook his head, willing the images of Grace's face away, but there she was, on a hot day, like this one, lying naked by the lake, staring at him.

"You're good with your hands, right Davis?" She lay on her back in the sand, arms stretched above her head. She turned to stare at him. He'd seen her naked before, but his breath still caught in his throat as she lay stretched out before him, and he tried to hide his arousal.

She turned on to her side. "Well, are you?" She ran a hand down her chest, over a pink nipple, and grinned devilishly. "You're not embarrassed are you?"

He shook his head, feeling cold despite the pelting sun. His heart was beating out of his chest. He didn't know why he suddenly felt so nervous, while she was so confident.

"Shame," she said, rolling back into the sand. "I just thought today would be such a good day to lose one's virginity." She giggled, then looked back at him.

"I - I don't have a condom with me," he replied, attempting to sound casual.

She shrugged lightly. "I'm on birth control. And it's not like we've been with anyone else." She gazed back at him. "I mean, only if you want to..." Her voice trailed off, and the question hung in the air between them.

He moved over to her side, gently cupping one of her breasts. They weren't small, but his huge hands made them look tiny. She did not take her eyes off him as he began to explore her body, gently caressing, sometimes eliciting a small jerk or gasp.

She reached down and took a hold of him, and the feel of her hand on him took his breath away for a moment. "Jesus, Davis," she giggled quietly, "you sure are packing, huh?"

"Am I too big?" He asked, concerned, then instantly felt like an idiot.

She shook her head and bit her lip, and put her other hand on his shoulder, pulling him towards her. "No, I just want you now," she whispered. He tried to keep his weight off her, afraid he would crush her, but she wrapped her arms around him and kissed him passionately. She tasted sweet and salty at the same time.

She reached down and put her hand around him again, guiding him to where she wanted him. He gently eased into her, and she gasped. Her skin was still cool from the water, but inside she was hot and wet. She held him tightly, her legs entangling with his. He moved slowly, not wanting to hurt her. "Is this OK?" He asked.

She nodded. "You can do it harder."

Oh this felt so good. She was warm and tight. He wanted to move faster but was afraid he would come too quickly, and he wanted her to enjoy it too. He'd heard the girls at school talk about boys who came too fast - the One Hit Wonders, they'd joked - and how disappointing they were in bed. He didn't want to let Grace down.

Unable to hold back, he moved harder against her, pleased as she moaned. His body felt electric, and she raised her legs to his waist. He felt himself sink into her deeper, and he thought his eyes would roll back in his head. He'd dreamed of this moment for so long, all those nights alone in his bed where nothing but his fantasy and his hand had been there to keep him company, and now it was actually happening.

"Oh god," he gasped as the electricity in his body made him tremble. His thrusts became faster, sweat forming between them, her skin no longer cool against his. She arched her back, pushing her breasts into his chest, and he dug his face into the crook of her neck and shuddered as the white heat in his groin exploded deep within her. She shook gently as he held her, her breath fast against his cheek.

He propped himself back on his elbows and looked at her face. She was smiling contentedly. "Was - was that good for you?" He asked, uncertain, breathless. She nodded.

"That felt really good," she sighed, throwing her arms back above her head.

He withdrew from her carefully, and lay beside her on his side. "But did you -"

"Come?" She giggled. "No babe, but that's OK. It felt good anyway." She gazed at him. "And for you?"

He smiled, and she laughed out loud. "It felt real good," he responded, gently stroking her cheek. "But I want you to enjoy it more."

"It was our first time, babe," she raised herself to his mouth and kissed him, "no rush." She lay back down in the sand, and closed her eyes, stretching her body in the sunlight. "Not a bad place for a first time, huh Davis?"

Thunder rumbled overhead, and Davis looked up to see the sun had disappeared and the dark clouds had rolled in. He finished securing the new roof, and as he began to pack up the tools, a light rain began to fall. The drops on his skin cooled him down - not just the work had caused his body temperature to rise. The memory of Grace holding him, lying beneath him...

He gave himself a shake as he walked back to the house. "Going to shower Mom!" He called, bypassing the kitchen and heading straight down to his room. He felt with embarrassment the bulge in his jeans, angry at himself. It almost felt dirty, a grown man being aroused by a teenage girl, even if it was his own memories fuelling how he felt.

Once in the shower, he turned on the cold water, dousing himself and chasing away the feeling of Grace's warm skin against his. He washed away the sweat and the memory, emerging into the bathroom still feeling tense, his skin still hot despite the cold water.

The smell of cooking wafted down the hallway, and Davis could hear his mother singing along loudly to the radio. He took a deep breath to steady himself, the image of Grace's face fading slowly. He dressed in sweatpants and a t-shirt, thunder rumbling loudly overhead as he walked down the hallway to the kitchen.

"Thank you so much for getting that done, honey," she called over her shoulder from the stove, making herself heard over the music from the radio. She wiped her hands on her apron and turned the music down, then retrieved a beer from the fridge and handed it to him. "I probably didn't do a great job of it last time, if I'm honest."

"Why didn't Dad do it?" Davis asked, clicking the lid off the beer bottle and taking a cooling swig. He didn't usually drink during the day, but today he was grateful for it.

Patricia shrugged. "He's... He's busy. And I think he's a bit lost without his usual duties at work." She sighed. "It's not easy getting older, you know."

Davis had never really considered the age gap between his parents, to him it was normal. But his father had married his mother when she'd been barely 21, and Paulson had been 38. Davis had heard whispers amongst the women in town that it had caused a huge scandal - indeed, he'd never met his maternal grandparents as they'd cut Patricia off when she had fallen pregnant. And now, while Davis's mother still gave off a youthful, active vibe, his father seemed to be an old man.

"Dad still shouldn't leave all this stuff to you, Mom," Davis tried to hide the irritation in his voice.

Patricia ignored him, and gave him a bright smile. "Why don't you go down to Doherty's tonight? It's free pool tonight, so there should be a few people there you know." She saw the hesitation on Davis's face. "Go on," she said gently, "you need to stop worrying so much."

Chapter Two

Loud music and the sounds of people laughing spilled out of the bar and onto the street as Davis locked up the truck. He passed some young women standing around outside, talking and smoking, a few of them smiling at him flirtatiously when he met their eyes. He nodded and smiled, trying to be friendly, but kept walking. Once inside, he saw Patrick behind the bar, serving beers and smiling widely as he chatted to his patrons.

The place was as packed as Davis remembered it being, since it was the only bar in town. People milled around the pool tables, some women were dancing by the jukeboxes, and the usual leering male patrons watched them, nursing large glasses of beer.

"CHEVY!" Someone called out across the din, and a tall, wiry man with short cropped black hair approached him, grinning. "What the fuck are you doing here?"

"Tyler," Davis smiled and accepted the man's handshake, "good to see you."

Tyler Hayden had started on the fire crew the same year as Davis. He'd trained with a crew in Malibu, but moved up north to take a position in Clearwater once he realised a fireman's salary didn't go far in southern California. They'd become good friends, and Davis had always enjoyed working with him.

"You back to join the crew?" Tyler asked hopefully.

Davis shook his head. "Nah, I'm still working with SNA, doing fire safety engineering. They got a logging permit for the land between here and Jolie, so, here I am."

Tyler's face dropped a little, but the smile remained. "Nice. Anyway, let me buy you a beer." They walked to the bar together, more calls of "Chevy!" and a few fist bumps meeting Davis as he passed, mostly old fire crew mates, and a few people he went to high school with. No one seemed put off at the sight of him, and he felt himself relax. He'd gotten himself worked up over nothing.

"Davis!" Patrick exclaimed as Tyler and Davis reached the bar. "Good to see you here."

"Two beers, Mr Innkeeper," Tyler said in an exaggerated British accent.

"Coming right up guv'ner," Patrick replied in his own bad British accent, and Davis couldn't help but smile.

"Cheers, man," Tyler said as Patrick placed their glasses on the bar.

And then Davis heard the laugh. It was unmistakable, high, tinkling like crystal over the noise in the bar, the laugh that he knew belonged to her. He turned and scanned the room, searching for the flowing red hair. But he couldn't see her.

"You OK?" Tyler asked.

Davis nodded. "Yeah, just, uh, thought I recognised that, uh, that voice." He shook his head and took a sip of his beer. "It's so strange being back."

"I bet!" Tyler agreed. "Everything changes but everything stays the same."

Davis turned back to look at the room, sure it had been her laugh. He must be going mad. At that moment, a blonde in tight jeans and a black tank top approached the nearest table, pool cue in hand. Her sandy hair tumbled down her back to her waist, and as she flicked it over her shoulder and turned to the man beside her to laugh and smile, Davis's heart stopped.

The blonde was Grace.

Tyler followed his gaze. "Oh, shit," he whistled, "I guess you haven't seen her yet, huh?"

Davis tried to respond but could only shake his head.

"Be careful man, you keep staring at her like that, and that cue might end up across your head," Tyler joked, raising his glass to Patrick, "you got a strict no fighting policy right, Pat?"

"Sure do, unless a man gets his ass handed to him by a pretty lady, then she gets drinks on the house."

Tyler feigned outrage. "Sexist policies, why sir I am shocked." He laughed and turned back to Davis. "Just be cool. You look like you've seen a ghost." He clapped a hand on Davis's shoulder.

Davis pulled himself together and gave them both a smile. "Just shocked that she's a blonde now, y'know."

Tyler squinted as he looked back at Grace. "Hasn't she always been blonde?"

At that moment, Grace went to take her shot from the opposite end of the table, and as she leaned down, she looked over the table edge and spotted the three men staring at her. Her face dropped instantly. She went back to her shot, which she missed, and said something that Davis was sure was a curse word. She gave her cue to the woman beside her, gesturing to the bar, and walked directly over to them.

She was beautiful. The blonde hair made her grey eyes look even darker, and she had a tan, something she'd never had when she was younger. The black tank top was almost scandalously tight, barely covering her belly, and Davis felt a deep tug watching her hips sway as she walked towards them.

"You boys lost something?" She asked. Patrick laughed and made his way down the bar to serve the other customers.

"We were just wondering if you'd always been blonde," Tyler said, leaning back on the bar. "Just wondering."

"I was born a redhead." Grace told him flatly. She looked up at Davis. Grace wasn't short, but she was still almost a foot shorter than Davis. "Hello," there was no emotion in her voice. "I see you're back in town."

Davis nodded. "Yeah, for work." He was overwhelmed. What could he say to her? "You look great."

"Thanks." She was impossible to read. "So do you, but you always did." Was that a compliment or an insult? "Still working for that logging company?"

"Uh, yeah. They got a new contract for here in town -"

"Yeah I know," she leaned on the bar, her arm brushing against his, "Paddy, a tequila please!" She called down the bar, and Patrick raised a hand in acknowledgement. She turned back to Davis. "SNA have been trying to get a contract to log in the park, now they have the land beside it, probably only a matter of time."

"I just do the fire safety," Davis said weakly, feeling more and more like a fool every time he opened his mouth.

"Well, at least their investment is in good hands," she said, a sarcastic smile on her face. Patrick brought her tequila shot, and the sight of Grace's tongue licking the salt from her hand sent a bolt of desire directly to Davis's groin.

Get a fucking grip.

Grace downed her tequila shot and stuck a piece of lemon in her mouth, sucking slowly. She saw Davis watching her, removed the lemon and licked her lips. "Memories?" She cocked her head to the side.

Fucking hell. Davis shifted on his feet and attempted a jovial smile. Grace wiped the edge of her lips with a finger and leaned against his chest as she put the shot glass back over the bar. He tried to breathe normally but was sure she could feel his heart beating wildly.

"Good seeing you," she said quietly. He could feel her breath against his face, cool and fresh. She turned on her heel and swayed her hips back to the pool table.

Tyler burst into laughter. "That girl is a fucking *tease*," he shook his head and took a swig of beer, "hot and she knows it. Fucking lethal."

"Does she have a boyfriend?" Davis asked.

"Not anymore," Patrick answered, having rejoined them. He leaned on the bar and lowered his voice. "She was with some relative of the Stephens family for a while, but he got into drugs and disappeared or some shit. No one really knows what happened, and Grace won't talk about it."

"Drugs?" Davis was shocked that Grace would get involved with a drug dealer.

"Well, it started innocently enough I guess," Patrick went on, gazing over at Grace as she took another shot - and sank it - at the table. "He inherited money and invested it in a marijuana plantation somewhere up here in the mountains. But then there was a police bust and they found he'd been cooking meth or something. Some hitchhikers had disappeared and they found them on his land, I dunno man, it was a fucking mess and he disappeared with some of Grace's shit, and she never heard from him again."

"So I guess that means my man here has a chance," Tyler playfully punched Davis in the chest.

Davis laughed and shook his head. "I think I messed up that chance when I left town," he willed his voice to stay light.

"Aw, nah, don't say that. Girls never forget their first love, right?" Tyler said in a tone much more sincere than Davis expected.

Patrick cleared his throat. "I think she has enough on her plate with her Dad being an asshole." His face darkened.

"Once an asshole, always an asshole," Davis agreed.

"He actually chased us off his property last fire season when we had an evacuation order," Tyler told them both, "like, with a double barrel fucking shotgun. He's crazy."

Davis and Patrick looked at each other knowingly. Bob Weaver had been an asshole since his wife had died, when Grace and Billy had only been small. Everyone in town hated him, but had never said it out loud because, well, a man who'd lost his wife and was alone with two small children deserved sympathy right? Many a night, Patricia had arrived at home with Grace and Billy asleep in the back of her car when Bob had lost his mind, gotten drunk and started ranting and raving, the neighbours calling Patricia instead of intervening themselves.

"How anyone thought it was a good idea to leave those kids with him, I'll never know," Patrick sighed. "I think about my little girl and I just - nah. They deserved better."

He doesn't mean it, man. He just wants the best for me. The sudden memory made Davis's eyes sting. *He just misses my Mom. It's OK, they don't even hurt anymore.* He inhaled sharply and pushed himself away from the bar. "Gentlemen, I think I'll turn in for the night." His voice cracked slightly as he tried to keep the smile on his face. "We should do this again sometime."

The two men waved him off with big smiles, and Davis cast a look over at Grace as he left. She was watching him, her face unreadable. He smiled and waved, but she didn't move, her steely eyes simply watching.

Back in the truck, he leaned over the steering wheel and exhaled. *I should never have come back here.*

The sounds of screams and roaring flames jolted Davis awake, and he had to orient himself for a moment before he realised it had been a dream. He was bathed in sweat.

Fucking nightmares. They didn't happen as regularly anymore, but when they did, they were vivid and left him with a sick feeling for the rest of the day. He'd seen a therapist for a few years, and that had helped him a lot. But the nightmares still crept in, and seemed to have increased since he'd returned home. Too many memories. Too many ghosts...

He showered and dressed in jeans and a black t-shirt. His wet hair dripped water down the nape of his neck. He really needed a haircut. He'd head down to the barber's and see if they could take him.

His mother was in the kitchen, cooking bacon and eggs, and his father was sat at the table reading a paper. "Good morning," Paulson said without looking up, "nice to see you still get up before midday."

Davis ignored him and gave his mother a kiss on the cheek. "You want some breakfast, honey?" She asked.

"Sure, did you need help with anything?"

"No no," she shook her head, smiling sweetly, "just sit down." She cracked more eggs into the skillet. "How was Doherty's?"

"Yeah it was good to see some people."

"Was Grace there?" His father asked from behind his paper.

"She was," Davis answered curtly, "we said hello."

"Beautiful girl, Grace Weaver. Shame no one can tie her down." Paulson sniffed.

"Perhaps she doesn't want to be tied down," Patricia pointed out.

Paulson put down his paper. "Every girl wants to be tied down, they just won't admit it." Davis resisted the urge to roll his eyes. "And maybe if you -" he pointed at Davis, "hadn't left town, she'd be happy and we'd have some grandchildren by now."

Davis was taken aback. Grandchildren? His father really was struggling with his age.

"Now, Paulson, that's enough," Patricia placed a plate of eggs, bacon and buttered toast in front of her husband, "Grace and Davis were childhood sweethearts, who knows if it would have lasted."

Paulson snorted, but said nothing and began to eat his breakfast.

Patricia ran a hand through Davis's wet hair as she put his food down in front of him. "You need a haircut, honey," she commented, "Mr Kraus should have some appointments today." She poured herself a cup of coffee and joined them at the table.

Paulson finished his food, and rose from the table without saying a word. He pulled on his trucker's cap, and left the kitchen. A moment later, they heard his truck start up and pull away down the drive.

"Is he like that a lot?" Davis asked his mother. She met his eyes and sighed.

"Like I said, it's not easy getting older. Aunt Dora wrote this morning, Tiffany had her fourth baby last night, a little girl. I think your Dad just… feels his age. His brothers and sisters all have grandchildren, and he doesn't." She shrugged. "He'll be 70 before too many moons, and I think he's scared of missing out."

Davis wanted to tell his mother his dad shouldn't be an asshole simply because he was discontent, but he bit his tongue. Patricia loved Paulson, he'd been her first and only love, and she would defend him no matter what.

"We won't be like them, will we?" She whispered into his chest, her fingertips flexing across his bare and sweaty skin. "I don't want to be like them when we grow up."

He tried to catch his breath and concentrate through the euphoric haze of his subsiding orgasm. "What are you talking about?"

"Our parents. Your parents. Our fathers." She looked up at him, her eyes fixing him with an intense stare. "Please don't ever be like them when you get old. I don't want to be married to some grumpy old asshole who just yells at everyone all the time."

"Baby, I'm nothing like my father," he assured her, pulling her close.

To his surprise her body started to shake, and he felt hot tears on his skin. He sat up, looking at her face, stroking her cheek. "Grace, what's happened? Has he hurt you?"

Her shoulders shook with sobs, and she covered her mouth with her hand.

"Grace," he took her hands in his, "what did he do?"

"Nothing," she said finally, " he just... He's so mean." She covered her face with her hands. "He's so mean. I hate him so much."

"Baby, we're going to get out of here as soon as we can," he said gently, looking into her eyes. "You and me. We're getting out of this town. I promise."

She sniffed, and nodded. "He found my birth control pills," her breath caught in her throat, "and he called me a whore."

"Fucking asshole," Davis growled through gritted teeth.

"I told him they were for my period," her cheeks flushed and her eyes fluttered up to his, "and he told me I was dirty."

"I'll kill him."

"No," Grace exclaimed, "I don't want you to be like him. I don't want you to think hurting people is the answer." She began to cry again, and he wanted to slap himself for even saying the words.

He pulled her into his lap, and held her as she sobbed. "I swear to you, Grace," he whispered, "we're getting out of here."

"So, you're going to get a haircut today then?" His mother's voice broke through his daydreaming.

"Yeah I need one, need to look good for the boss I guess," Davis laughed dryly. "Mom, do you know anything about the guy Grace was with for a while? Patrick said he got in trouble with drugs?"

His mother leaned back and clasped her hands on the table. "Oh he was bad news. I don't know much of the story but, oh I saw him and I thought to myself, this kid is trouble. I don't mind tattoos but I'm sure this kid had a swastika on him somewhere. I never understood why Grace took up with him."

"So what happened?"

Patricia raised her hands and shrugged. "I have no idea, honey. Grace doesn't really talk to me much anymore," she said, a hint of sadness colouring her voice. "Sarah would know, maybe ask her."

Sarah Morgan was Grace's best friend, and had been since childhood. Sarah had stayed friends with Grace even as Sarah became more popular, head of the cheerleading squad, and a track star. Grace had been something of an outcast, but everyone seemed to know it was her father that held her back, it wasn't that she didn't want to belong.

"Why would Sarah tell me anything?" Davis crossed his arms across his chest.

"Because she always liked you," Patricia said meaningfully. "And she cares about Grace. No matter what happened, everyone knows what you and Grace meant to each other."

Davis sighed. "And where would I find Sarah?"

"She owns The Coffee Pot now, took it over from her aunt. Go see her, and talk to her."

Tiny bits of hair scratched Davis's neck as he walked down the street. The new haircut was great, and he felt much better and less shaggy than before, but the tiny loose bits of hair that the barbers never quite managed to sweep away had worked their way into the neckline of his shirt, and now they just itched.

He considered heading home to have another shower, but decided to go to The Coffee Pot first. He found himself intensely curious about this drug dealer Grace had gotten involved with, and hoped Sarah would talk to him. Not that it was actually any of his business.

The Coffee Pot was a very small cafe, with only two tables outside and 8 inside. Sarah had redecorated since she'd taken over, and instead of yellowing wood, the interior was now painted white, and decorated with red accents. Davis liked it much better than the ageing 80s decor.

He walked in and took a seat, and Sarah came zipping out from the saloon doors that led to the kitchen. As soon as she saw who it was, she smiled and tilted her head to the side. "Well, I'd heard you were back and here you are." She sat down opposite him and shook her head. "Davis Chevalier, you look fantastic."

He gave her a wide smile. "You look pretty good yourself." He'd always liked Sarah. They'd been good friends, and had only grown closer through Grace. Everyone had always pegged them as getting together at some point - the head cheerleader and star quarterback trope never seemed to die - but he and Grace had been a couple, and Sarah had championed them from the start.

She did look great, her once-long black hair now cut to shoulder length, her blue eyes bright behind glasses, and her olive skin smooth and showing no signs of ageing at all. She reached across the table and ran a hand through his hair. "Seen Mr Kraus, huh?" She nodded her approval. "So, what brings you to my fabulous establishment? Heard about my famous blueberry pie?"

Davis laughed. "I hadn't but now I am intrigued." He leaned forward on his forearms. "I actually wanted to talk to you about Grace."

Sarah raised her eyebrows. "You come to me, expecting me to bare the secrets of my best friend?" She leaned back and crossed her arms across her chest. "Brazen, Chev. Daring."

He shrugged. "I heard about this drug heist story, and I, uh, I worried about her."

"Oh, yes, Hal," Sarah's lips set in a hard line. "And had you considered asking Grace about all of this? Or did you come straight to me?"

"My Mom sent me actually." Davis admitted sheepishly, and Sarah burst out laughing.

"Ah Patricia, she never partakes in the gossip but she'll tell you where to get it!" Sarah regarded him carefully for a moment, then nodded. "OK, you buy a piece of pie and a cup of coffee and I'll tell you all about it."

"Deal."

"So," she began, as she set the enormous piece of pie and dainty cup of black coffee down before him, "what do you know? I guess it's not much of any sense because no one in this town listens but everyone talks, so?" She looked at him expectantly.

"I was told he came into town with strange tattoos and a bunch of money, and he invested in a weed plantation, but the police found him cooking meth with some lost hitch hikers, and he disappeared."

Sarah nodded and rolled her eyes. "As I thought, half the damn story." She took a deep breath. "OK, so, do you remember Whalan Stephens? That weird old guy with the huge house that owned that farm down past Mammoth Lake? We used to toilet paper his house at Halloween because we were horrid little kids who though he was creepy?"

Davis nodded.

"Well," Sarah continued, "he died about a year after you left. Took like a week for anyone to even notice he was dead, because why would anyone notice? It's not like he came out of his house, like, ever. Anyway, after he died, there was this whole kerfuffle about who would inherit the house because no one even knew he had any family. Turns out, he had a brother who'd died, but not before he'd produced a son, who had himself produced a son, Hal. And so they blew into town to size up their inheritance." Sarah shook her head and looked out the window. "I still don't know what the hell Grace saw in him. His name was Whalan too, because for some reason rich people can never come up with their own names and just recycle the same one for every kid they have. This one was Whalan Stephens the fourth." She looked back at Davis and rolled her eyes again. "I mean, why? It's not even a good name, it's not even his *Dad's* name! I never understood it. Anyway, Hal hated it too which is he why went by Hal."

"Was he as creepy as his uncle?" Davis asked.

"Oh yeah. I mean - he wasn't - *ugly*," she emphasised the word, "but he was creepy. Tall, pale, kinda wiry but muscly too. Covered in tattoos. Someone said he had a swastika tattoo but, I dunno, I never saw one, and Grace wouldn't sleep with a nazi."

Davis swallowed hard at the thought of Grace being with someone like that, some weird, wiry rich boy covered in tattoos. *She's not your property man,* he told himself angrily, *you didn't exactly live like a monk after you left.*

"Anyway," Sarah went on, "I don't even know when they officially got together, but they went up to the snow cabin one weekend, and after that they seemed to officially be a couple. Hal moved in with her and - that was that. How's the pie?" She asked suddenly.

"Oh," Davis took a bite of the pie he'd almost completely forgotten about. "It's really delicious."

Sarah looked pleased. "Told you. It's famous. Anyway," she drawled, "so they were a thing. He never really hung around with us when Grace did, but he wasn't, like, unfriendly. Just creepy. And Grace seemed happy so no one really said much. Maybe we should have. I dunno." She stared at the table. "It just seemed like, they were OK, y'know?"

"So where do the drugs come into it?" Davis asked.

"Well," Sarah gazed back out the window, fiddling with the ties on her blouse, "so, Hal inherited half of Whalan's estate. That was what the will said, 50% to his Dad and 50% to him. So he had a LOT of money. His Dad left town after the house and farm sold, Hal stayed with Grace. We all thought it was kind of strange that they stayed in her tiny apartment. She'd finished college, and we thought, well, they'd move away somewhere. But they stayed. She started working for the park, and I just kept thinking, why were they still here?"

Davis knew how badly Grace had wanted to leave. Not just one, but two men had let her down, and left her in this town. She deserved better.

Sarah turned back to him. "So, one day she comes in here crying. The police had been by her place, asking if Hal was there. Some girls had been spotted hitchhiking down near Mammoth Lake, and they'd gotten into a truck that looked like Grace's, which Hal used a lot. He'd been seen driving it that day, et cetera and so on. So Hal's not there and they ask Grace to tell him to come to the station when he gets back. When he gets home and Grace tells him the police were looking for him, he flips out, he's furious that she didn't cover for him. Like, how was she supposed to know? And Grace is not the kind to lie to police. So she comes in here crying, and tells me that the farm down past Mammoth Lake *didn't* get sold, at least not the whole thing, just the house and the surrounding 12 acres. The rest Hal had turned into a weed farm. There's so many of them up here in the mountains, he seemed to think it was a great thing to sink his money into. Which, y'know, great way to make money while you're living rent-free in your girlfriend's tiny apartment right?"

"Wait, he didn't even pay rent?" Davis asked incredulously.

Sarah shook her head. "Nope. Hal said it was because he was working towards their future. Personally I think it had nothing to do with that and that he was just a freeloader."

Davis had no issue with weed, he'd smoked it himself to deal with anxiety a few times. But for a guy to sink his money into a weed farm instead of making a better life for himself and his partner? That didn't sit right with him at all.

"So did the hitchhikers show up?"

Sarah nodded emphatically. "Oh boy did they ever." Her eyes widened. "In the worst way. The police ended up raiding Hal's farm when he didn't show up at the station, and they found these hitchhikers working there. And not only that -"

The bell on the door rang as two women walked in. "Hi girls!" Sarah welcomed them, rising from the table. "The usual?" She went to the espresso machine and prepared their order, chatting to them in her usual easy, friendly manner.

Davis's protective instincts were in overdrive, and he felt deeply conflicted that now he had the urge to protect Grace, when he'd left her here 5 years ago. *I can't leave. Not now. Not after what happened.* Her face as she had said those words to him...

He should have insisted she come. Or he should have stayed. But instead he'd run away.

The two women left and Sarah rejoined him at his table. "I still see pie, Chev." She pointed at his plate. "Now, where was I? Oh right, the sex slaves."

Davis's eyes widened. "The *what*?"

"So when the police showed up, they found the hitchhikers. Hal had picked them up, and offered them jobs at his plantation, picking and packing and whatever else you need to do to marijuana to sell it, I dunno." Sarah shrugged. "I've never smoked. But it turns out, Hal had a little issue with labour laws. And also his dick. He'd not been paying them in money, but in food and board. And also blackmailing them for sex. They'd run away from bad homes, and he threatened to call the police on them and return them to their families if they didn't sleep with him and his buddies."

"Wait," Davis tried to sort all this information in his head, "why would the police care about -" He looked at Sarah in horror, realisation hitting. "They were minors?"

Sarah nodded emphatically. "Oh yeah, fifteen years old."

"Oh my god," Davis raked his hands through his hair. "That fucker."

"Yep. And it *still* gets worse. The police keep looking through the property, and found some caravans where it seems Hal was inspired by Breaking Bad or some shit, and he'd been cooking up meth. I mean, obviously that's not worse than blackmailing abused and distressed minors for sex, but... Man it just added to the fucking pile. Grace was *devastated*."

"So where was Hal in all of this?"

Sarah shrugged. "Gone. He just, I dunno, went underground or something. He reappeared one night while Grace was asleep, and took off with her grandpa's rifle. He left a note that said something wimpy like 'I'm sorry' or some shit, meaningless basically after he'd just broken her heart and robbed her. I'm guessing he headed to Mexico or something, I mean that's where all the criminals go, right? The poor Mexican people deserve better than all our shitstains."

Davis leaned back in his chair, hands behind his head, and exhaled. "Wow. Poor Grace."

"Yep," Sarah agreed, "it was fucking horrid, and her Dad made it worse by blaming her for 'losing'-" she made quotation marks with her fingers in the air, "the precious family rifle. It was meant to go to Billy, but obviously he could't give it to him anymore, so he very begrudgingly passed it on to her, and my god, the rage when Hal stole it."

"Does anything ever not make Bob Weaver angry?" Davis asked, frustration straining his voice.

"It got so much worse after Billy was gone," Sarah mused sadly. "When he was still around, they bore the brunt together. But after that, Grace just... She had to deal with it alone. And being a girl, I mean... I dunno." She sighed. "It's just sad. Grace is the best person. She didn't deserve all this."

Davis became keenly aware of heat rising in his shoulders, accompanied by the old, familiar pang of guilt. The itching of the loose hairs stuck in his shirt suddenly became unbearable. He jumped up from the table, startling Sarah.

"Is everything OK?" She asked, alarmed.

"Yeah, sorry, uh," he laid the money for his order on the table, "I just need to get back, my Mom needed something picked up and I forgot about it."

"Oh, OK," she looked at him suspiciously. "I mean, it was great to see you."

"Thanks for telling me about - all this." He gave her a quick hug, and hurried out the door. He strode down the street, the anger and guilt rising into his chest, and he felt the intense desire to hit something.

Everyone had let Grace down, everyone had left her alone, whether they meant to or not.

It took all his willpower to stop him speeding down Main Street as he headed home. The house was empty when he arrived, and he went straight for the shower, the warm water soothing the itch on his skin and the sick feeling in his stomach. He leaned against the shower wall with both hands, letting the water run over the back of his head, and focused on his breathing, like the therapist had told him to do.

Breathe. Just breathe. She's OK. Whatever happened, it was bad. But she survived. She's here. And she's OK. You're both OK.

He got out of the shower and dressed in shorts and a t-shirt - the afternoon had become almost unbearably hot - and stretched out on his bed, staring at the ceiling. His phone beeped, and an email from his boss had come through. He'd be in town the next day after all.

Good, Davis thought with relief. Finally, back to work. Too much free time had given him too much time to think. He needed distraction, he needed to be busy, he needed to stop thinking about Grace and Hal and Bob and Billy and the whole sad situation. Work was exactly the solution. It always had been.

"Davis, oh god, please don't tell my Dad."

"Shut up, man, we'll get you out of there. The water drop will be here any minute."

"I'm so sorry, Davis, I should have listened to you."

"Billy, shut up. You're going to be fine."

"Please don't tell my Dad, man. He'd be so fucking ashamed of me." Sobs started to come through the radio. "Fuck. Fuck.. It's so hot. I don't wanna die."

"You're not going to die, Billy. Shut up. The water drop will be here, any minute."

"I don't want to die."

"Any minute, Billy. Just hold on."

More sobs. "I want my Mom."

"Billy, just -"

"I don't want to die."

"They're coming."

"I don't want to die."

Chapter Three

"Are you OK honey?" Patricia asked as she poured Davis another cup of coffee.

He looked up at her, and smiled weakly. "Yeah, just - had a bad night."

"OK," she said slowly, not sounding convinced, but she didn't push him. "Well, back to work today, huh?"

"About time," Paulson said into his coffee cup, "too much free time isn't any good for a man."

Patricia rolled her eyes so Davis could see, and gave him a smile. "Too much work isn't much good either." She told him pointedly. She poured coffee into a thermal cup, sealed the lid and handed it to Davis. "There you go, for the road, honey. Jolie is a bit of a drive."

"Thanks Mom," he checked his phone, "speaking of which, I should go, or the boss will beat me there." He rose from the table, and gave his mother a kiss on the cheek. "I'll be back this evening. Have a good day." He glanced over his shoulder. "Bye Dad."

Paulson raised his cup in acknowledgement, but said nothing as his son left.

The morning fog had not quite lifted as Davis pointed his truck east along the mountain road, heading towards Jolie. His boss, Craig Hayden, had wanted to see the outermost point of the logging operation, which lay against the edge of the national park, and was therefore one of the areas of most concern when it came to the fires.

Davis switched on the radio as he drove, trying to lift his mood. The nightmares had plagued him again, and he'd felt too ill to stomach any breakfast that morning. He took a sip of the coffee his mother had given him. The sky was purple and orange as the sun rose, the fog swirling along the ground and looking almost blue in the morning light.

He got to the site just as Craig pulled up. "Good morning, Davis!" He called from his shiny blue truck. Craig always seemed to have a brand new, shiny truck every time Davis saw him, which thankfully wasn't all that often. Craig liked to act like he was "Very Involved" in every aspect of the company, but really the thing he liked most was the money it earned him. Davis still found it mystifying how one could get rich from something like chopping down trees, but since he was paid well, he didn't ask any questions.

"Found your way back from Alaska?" Craig said jovially, shaking Davis's hand.

"I always manage to find my way home," Davis replied.

"Ah, like a good dog." Craig laughed heartily at his own joke, and turned to survey the trees before them. "My god these are impressive." He exclaimed, running his hand over the bark. He turned back to Davis. "So, how's the fire season looking this year?"

"If the past years are anything to go by, we should be concerned," Davis saw no reason to sugarcoat things.

"But we've had all this rain!" Craig gestured to the wet ground.

"Sure, but we also had 5 years of drought before that." Davis said. "The bark beetles have killed off hundreds of thousands of trees, so there's plenty of tinder. And all these storms mean lightning."

Craig's brow was furrowed. "Well that all sounds very concerning. We need this to go well or we'll lose our bid for the further logging." He looked at Davis pointedly, as though he had any influence over the fires, or the weather.

"We'll do everything we can to make sure things go smoothly. The new machinery we discussed is much safer than what we used previously and -"

"Oh and it's so much more expensive." Craig waved his hands dismissively. "I don't think the investors will go for that."

Davis looked at him in surprise. "But we had talked about the new machines being lower risk than the machinery we used up north. We need to try and avoid the chance of human error in starting fires."

"Our team are experienced, and I know you have all the risks in hand," Craig assured him. "The old machinery will do fine. Like you said, the biggest risk is lightning."

"Sir, with all due respect, I never said -"

"You used to be a firefighter, right?" Craig interrupted him.

"Yes, uh yes. I was."

"I heard you were one of the youngest chiefs they had up this way?"

Davis sighed. "Yes, sir, but only because -"

Craig reached up and clapped his hands on Davis's shoulders. "Then I know we'll be just fine. You're the best. And I only hire the best." He gave Davis a knowing wink. "Now, let's go over where the operation is best to start."

Her hands raked through his hair, his head between her thighs. She moaned and arched her back as he licked and sucked. "Oh god, Davis. Oh my god." She cried out.

He ran a hand up her belly to her breasts, finding one of her nipples and pinching it gently between his fingers. She gasped and threw her head back. He felt her legs begin to shake around him.

"Oh fuck," her breath hitched in her throat and he felt her pulsating against his mouth as a deep moan escaped her.

She shuddered and shook for a while, her forearm across her face. "Oh my god Davis," she said quietly as he lay down beside her.

"I guess I don't need to ask if you came this time," he teased.

She laughed behind her arm. "No, I think that was pretty obvious."

He leaned over and teased her nipple with his tongue, and she jerked away, grinning. "Oh my god don't, I feel like I'm going to explode."

"What a way to go, huh?"

She put her arm down and gazed at him. "Where did you learn to do that?" She asked as she snuggled into him.

"I just... did." He smiled as she laughed into his chest.

"You're just instinctively good at oral? OK, good story."

"No, I just... I just listened to you, and did what seemed to feel good for you."

"Well, you're a good listener."

They lay in each other's arms for a while, when she looked up at him, an uncertain smile on her face. "Do... do you want me to..." She glanced down at him, his arousal evident.

"Oh, I didn't do it so you would-"

"No, I know," she said gently. "I just, I want to do things for you too."

"You do plenty for me, baby. You don't have to do that."

She put her hand around him, and he inhaled sharply. "Do you want to -" Her hand began to move up and down his shaft.

"Yes," he gasped, "yes I want to."

She climbed on top of him, and eased herself onto him, giving a little moan. She felt hot and sweet and slick, and he dug his fingers into her hips as she began to move them in a circle. "Does this feel good?" She whispered.

"Yes, yes it does." Oh god, she felt better than good. He focused on his breathing, letting the feeling build, not wanting to come too quickly.

Her breathing quickened as she moved, and he watched delighted as her breasts bounced, the sight sending his arousal into overdrive.

She began to grind against him, giving little moans as she did, and her cheeks flushed red. She threw her head *back, grinding harder and gasping, and he felt her tighten around him. She collapsed onto him, trembling.*

He grabbed her around the waist and deftly flipped her onto her back, thrusting into her quickly. "Fuck, oh fuck." It was his turn to swear as goosebumps broke out across his shoulders, and he felt himself shudder and release inside her.

"I'm sorry I came so fast," she said as they lay beside each other a while later, once their breathing had quieted and the sweat had cooled on their skin.

He laughed. "Are you serious?"

She laughed too and covered her face with her hands. "It just felt so good."

"Good!" He cried, pulling her hands away and kissing her. "It's meant to feel good."

She stroked his cheek and smiled at him. "I love you."

"I love you too." Hearing her say it still got him, a gut punch of the very best kind, every single time.

"We'll always be like this, right?"

"Well, maybe not exactly like this. There might be times where we actually wear clothes and not just fuck all the time."

She swatted at him and he grabbed her wrist laughing, and kissed her again.

"Yes Grace, we'll always be like this. Always."

He'd been so caught up in his thoughts that he hadn't checked how fast he was going. *Shit.* The lights flashed in his rearview. He pulled over to the side of the road, watching as the cruiser pulled up behind him, the red and blue lights flashing on its roof.

The officer approached his window. "Chevy?" The officer smiled at him, taking off his sunglasses.

"Logan?" He smiled at the man in uniform, recognising his old schoolmate. "You're a cop now?"

"Yep, moved out to Jolie last Fall." Logan shook his hand. "And you're back in Clearwater?"

"Uh yeah, just got back. Working for SNA, they have logging permits here and they hired me as the safety consultant."

"Great, great." Logan nodded amicably. "Now, I know you know you were going too fast."

Davis nodded. "I know, I wasn't paying attention. Bad night's sleep and I wasn't concentrating." He raised his hands. "I should know better."

"Hey, the bad night's sleep will do it to you," Logan agreed, "I got newborn twins at home, I'm a zombie half the time."

"Congratulations, man. Not on the lack of sleep of course."

Logan grinned. "Thanks, they're pretty cute. Just tiring." He stood up straight and looked back at his cruiser. "OK, well, look. I know you're responsible, being a firefighter and all, so I'll let you off with a warning." He looked back at Davis sternly. "Take care of yourself though, yeah? Don't want to read about you ending up off a cliff because you were driving tired."

"Oh for sure, I will." Davis nodded. "Thanks Logan, it won't happen again."

Logan raised a hand as he walked back to the cruiser. "Take care, Chevy."

As Davis pulled away from the curb, he felt his anger at himself rising. This endless fantasising about Grace, remembering all the times they'd been together, it was distracting. She had had a life since he'd left, had other boyfriends, just as he had had other girlfriends. Grace would always be special, because she was his first. But that's all it was - a special memory of his first times.

The road rose up alongside the canyon. He wound down the windows and put on the radio, grounding himself in the moment. He had to head to the site office to oversee the delivery of the equipment. He couldn't believe Craig hadn't listened to him, and was keeping the old machinery. The new machinery was safer and easier to maintain, meaning there was less build-up of potentially flammable material. For a man who had a new truck every 5 minutes, Craig sure didn't seem to understand the value of good machinery. Sarah was right - rich people were mostly stupid.

Davis pulled up to the site office, and jumped down from the truck. The workers were busy assembling all the equipment, and he waved to them as some shouted a greeting.

He swung the door to the office open, and came face to face with Grace.

"Hello," she smiled at him sweetly. Her blonde hair was pulled up in a high ponytail, and she was wearing her khaki ranger uniform. Her sleeves were rolled up, revealing her toned forearms. The freckles across her nose were visible under her tan.

He froze and found himself unable to speak for a moment. "Uh, hi. I mean, um," he shuffled around her and put his paperwork down on the desk. "Can - uh, can I help you with something?"

She plopped herself down in the chair on the other side of his desk. "I had a call about some illegal fires being spotted this morning. I came down to check, and make sure your crew weren't doing anything stupid."

"We're not in the park," Davis pointed out, sinking into the creaking office chair on the opposite side of the desk.

"No, but close enough to be of concern, Davis." Grace responded matter-of-factly. "We've already had 4 fires this season and I would prefer it if we didn't have any more." She glanced to her right out the small, barred window. "Those machines look a little dirty and worn out. Are they fire-safe?" She gazed back at him, fixing him with her steely eyes.

"The boss has deemed them fit for service," Davis didn't like the way the words sounded as he said them. "We'd discussed newer machinery but it was decided that it wasn't necessary."

"You're the safety engineer," Grace said, leaning forward on the table. "Do *you* deem them to be fire-safe?"

Davis hesitated. "I - I think they've served us well until now, and the crew know what to look out for. There'll be a safety briefing before work starts to get everyone back up to speed, and I'll be overseeing the beginning phases in each section myself, just to ensure the crew know what they're doing." He gave her a reassuring smile, which she did not return.

"You were a good firefighter, Davis," she told him, "I hope you're good at this job too."

He suddenly became aware of her scent in the hot, cramped office. She smelled of pear and jasmine. Her ranger uniform made her look almost like a girl scout. Her cheeks were rosy. Being outdoors a lot seemed to do her good.

"I'm very good at my job," he replied, his voice low.

She leaned back and cocked an eyebrow. "Are you flirting with me?"

The question knocked the wind out of him.

She leaned forward on the desk on her crossed arms. "Davis, I have the same memories you do, you know." She told him. "And I know those things can be hard to let go of sometimes. But I think we're both different people now. Right?"

He nodded, his mouth dry.

"So, I think it would be really nice if we can be friendly with each other, but also know that those times are gone."

"Are you still mad at me?" He blurted out, instantly chastising himself.

She shook her head. "No. I was mad for maybe the first 6 months. And then I was just sad, for a real long time. Losing you and Billy basically at once was -" she broke off and bit her lip. "It fucking sucked." She said finally, her grey eyes the colour of an impending storm.

He bowed his head. “I’m sorry Grace.”

“I don’t need your apologies, Davis, not anymore.” She rose from her chair. “I don’t want to rehash the past. I just want to move on. I don’t want it to be awkward to see you around in town. We can be friendly, right?”

“Absolutely, yes.”

“OK, great. Have a good day, Davis.” And she was gone, the sound of her ATV disappearing into the distance.

Davis threw himself into his work for the rest of the day, determined not to think about Grace or their interaction from that morning. By the time the sun was hanging low in the sky, the trucks had pulled out and the workers had finished work for the day, he was exhausted.

He drove home along the mountain road, squinting in the glaring evening sun. As he pulled up in the drive, a message came through from Patrick. “The Grants have an apartment free, up on Freeville Rd. Swing by the bar and I’ll give you details.”

Excellent, his own place would be a great start.

His mother was, as always, in the kitchen, serving up dinner to his father. “Oh hi honey,” she smiled as he entered. “How was work?”

“Tiring,” he said, sitting down at the table, stifling a yawn. “The first few days are always just a lot of running around and doing checks.” Davis turned to his father. “How was your day, Dad?”

"Fine," Paulson answered, cutting his steak and not looking at his son. "Nothing much of anything happened, so, it was fine."

Patricia set a plate of steak, mashed potatoes and peas and carrots down in front of Davis. "Eat up, son, you must be starving. Did you even take any food with you?"

He realised at that moment that he'd not eaten all day. "No Mom, I didn't."

"You'll lose all that muscle if you don't eat right," his mother chided him, "big boys need their food."

He laughed. "Big boys, huh?"

Paulson snorted from the other side of the table. "What does he need muscle for in his job?"

Davis said nothing and began to eat. Patricia chatted away about her day, having gone to the salon to get her hair done, running into people downtown, who was doing what and where. Davis tried to listen and seem interested, but he found he was bone-achingly tired by the time he'd finished his meal. After helping his mother clean up - his father had already disappeared - he said goodnight and headed to his room to shower and sleep.

The hot water on his shoulders was soothing, and he realised how tense he'd been all day. As his muscles relaxed, he focused on the words Grace had said to him that morning - they could be friendly when they saw each other. There didn't need to be any awkwardness.

He dressed only in boxers for sleep, the night not cooling much from the day. He collapsed onto his stomach on the bed, and fell asleep almost instantly.

"Why are you wearing sunglasses?"

She said nothing, but her lip trembled.

He felt anger rising in his gut, and reached out to gently remove the glasses from her face.

"Please don't," she whispered, her voice thick with tears. But she didn't try to stop him.

The bruise around her eye was angry, and fresh. He gritted his teeth, and she put her hands on his chest. "Please, Davis, don't do anything, it'll make it worse."

"If I kill him, he can't hurt you anymore."

"Stop it!" She was sobbing now. "Please don't talk like that, he's not worth it."

"Grace, we have to go to the police."

"And then what." She looked at him helplessly. "I go into foster care? I never see you again?"

"Grace, come on, we can work that shit out. The man is beating you up." Realisation washed over him. "Where's Billy? He hasn't been at school."

She sobbed even harder. "He went after him with a bat. I tried to stop him."

"Grace, what the fuck? Is he OK?"

She nodded. "I think so. He will be."

"Grace this has to stop, he can't do this to the two of you."

She collapsed against his chest, and he held her tightly as she cried.

"What are we going to do?" He asked once her sobs subsided.

"Nothing." She replied quietly. "Nothing. There's nothing to be done."

"He's going to kill one of you one day."

She nodded. "I know."

Her resignation shocked him. "Fucking hell, Grace. What the fuck are we going to do?"

The one bedroom apartment would suit him just fine. It was a basic but cosy little log cabin the Grants had used as a holiday rental for some time, but since the fires business hadn't been the same. It was small, but large enough for one person, and it had a fireplace which he looked forward to using in the cooler months.

Freeville Road was quiet, just off the main road out of town. He looked out onto trees, and he could just about hear the river in the distance. His mother dug a dining table and two chairs out of their garage for him, and Sarah offered him the sofa in her basement that no one was using. He'd brought some basic kitchen items down from his place in Alaska, but he didn't have a bed.

After two nights of sleeping on an air mattress on the floor, he'd had enough. It was a bright Saturday morning, and Davis drove down to Mammoth Lake to buy a bed and mattress. It was hot, and summer had well and truly arrived. As he drove down the mountain, he smelled smoke in the air. Fire season was definitely here.

He picked a simple wooden framed bed at the huge furniture warehouse, but decided to splurge on a memory foam mattress. He loaded the flat-packed frame and the rolled up mattress into the bed of his truck, then walked down main street to find a kitchenware store, where he picked up some utensils, a skillet and some more bowls and plates.

As he strolled back to his truck, the scent of barbecue wafted down the street, and his stomach grumbled. He'd again avoided breakfast after a night of bad dreams, and he'd already noticed his jeans hanging looser on his hips. It was no good to not look after himself. He needed to eat better, and start working out again.

He sniffed out the barbecue place, and enjoyed a large lunch. Some people had a lot of trouble being on their own, but it didn't bother Davis much. He'd had some friends in Alaska, but generally he'd kept to himself and had gotten used to his own company. Eating lunch alone was no big deal.

A man walked past the barbecue joint with a German Shepherd. *A dog would be nice though.* He'd always wanted a dog, but his father was dead against any sort of pets. His mother had had to fight to get the chickens, pointing out they weren't pets but a food source. *You can play football if it gets you into college.* Davis rolled his eyes at the memory of his father's words. Everything with his father had to have a purpose. Just enjoying something wasn't enough.

After he'd eaten, he walked back to his truck, when an antique store caught his eye. He wasn't much for home decor, but a few things to make it feel more like home rather than a dorm room couldn't hurt. He wandered in, and was greeted by a friendly "Hello there sir!" From behind the front counter. "After anything special?" The shopkeeper asked.

"No, just having a look around, thanks," Davis raised his hand in greeting, "got a new place and trying to make it feel like home."

"Ah, we have some really nice things here for that, sir," the shopkeeper gestured around him. "Let me know if you need any help."

Davis wandered around, looking at the large assortment of enamel wash basins, old tools, and wooden furniture. The back wall had a large display of guns, which he began to walk past, as he had no interest in displaying guns in his house. But something caught his eye, and he stopped short, doubling back. High-shine wooden handle with ivory inlays. A silver butt and trigger. One long shiny single silver barrel. It was unmistakable. He'd seen that gun before.

It was used by my ancestors in the great war. Bob Weaver had slurred to him one afternoon. *We have a proud history, and one day that gun is going to go to my son, then my grandsons.*

"Excuse me, sir," Davis called the shopkeeper over, "could you tell me something about this gun?"

"Certainly," the man smiled as he walked over, "ah yes, that's a beauty, we only just got her in. I've never seen this level of detail with the ivory before. I'm not even entirely sure it's legal." He gave Davis a conspiratorial wink. "Would you like to have a closer look?"

"Oh no, that's OK. You said it only just came in? Do you remember what the person who brought it in looked like?"

The shopkeeper furrowed his brow. "Now let me see," he rubbed his chin, "I believe it was - yes, he seemed to know his guns. Young fellow, I think about 25?"

"Lots of tattoos?" Davis asked.

The shopkeeper shook his head. "No, clean-cut, blonde fellow. I think he was even wearing a suit? I'd not seen him around before. I gave him a good price for it and he seemed pleased, not that he looked like he needed the money judging by the car he was driving."

"What kind of car?"

"A Bentley. Don't see them often around here!" The shopkeeper gave him a wide smile. "So, would you like to purchase it?"

"Could I put it on hold while I think about it?" Davis asked, offering a $100 note. "I'd hate for it to sell in the meantime."

"Of course," the shopkeeper pocketed the money and took the gun from the rack. "I'll keep it out back for you. We're open til 6."

Davis headed outside and dialled the police station immediately. "Hello, I need to report a suspected stolen item."

Davis left the police station in Mammoth Lake with his head full of questions. He'd signed a statement as to how he had recognised the gun and what had led to him reporting it stolen. The police said they would contact Grace to identify it.

Why would the gun be pawned now, 2 years after it had been stolen? Had Hal stayed in the state? In the immediate area? With an arrest warrant for sex with minors and major drug offences and god knows what else on his head? It seemed highly unlikely. And who was the well-dressed man in the Bentley who'd sold it to the antique shop? Did they know it had been stolen in the area? That was incredibly risky. It all made no sense.

He headed back up the mountain to Clearwater, the hot afternoon air heavy with the promise of yet another storm. The smell of smoke had cleared, but with more lightning strikes imminent, he was sure there'd be another fire that afternoon.

He passed a load of RVs on his way back, and remembered school had broken up for the summer. Tourists, all heading to the park. More fire danger, he mused. They'd seen it every year, illegal campfires, tourists ignoring the fire safety warnings, glass bottles left behind to start a spot fire that soon turned into several thousand acres and a major emergency.

He pulled up in front of the apartment, and found a basket full of fruit and vegetables waiting for him. "Happy Housewarming! Sarah xxx". He smiled. She was a good friend. He carried all his purchases into the apartment, and set about getting his bed ready and unfurling the mattress. He listened to the radio as he worked.

Just as he finished the bed frame, there was a knock on the door. It was his mother, holding a large covered casserole dish. “Hi honey!” She grinned widely as she handed over the dish. “I made you a lasagne, so you don’t starve to death.” She walked by him into the apartment, surveying everything carefully. “Well this is just fine. Not bad at all.”

He walked to the kitchen to place the dish in the fridge, and put on the coffee machine. “Yeah, I really like it,” he said over his shoulder. His mother joined him in the kitchen and looked out the window.

“Ooh, a nice view too.” She turned and leaned on the counter. “So, how was Mammoth Lake?”

“Well, it’s funny you should ask…” Davis regaled with his mother with the find of the rifle, her eyes becoming wider every second. By the time he was finished, her hand was covering her mouth.

“Oh my god,” she exclaimed, “this is all so bizarre!”

“I know,” Davis nodded, “why would anyone pawn the gun after all this time?”

They each took a cup of coffee and sat down at the dining table together. “Is the person who pawned it known to the police?” Patricia asked.

Davis shrugged. “I have no idea, they didn’t tell me.”

“I mean,” Patricia leaned forward on the table, gazing off into the distance, “good clothes and expensive car, I would suspect that that is one of the drug kingpins, or whatever it is they get called these days. But why would *he* pawn the gun? Isn’t that dirty work for cronies?”

Davis shrugged. “I guess so. I just wonder where this Hal Stephens has ended up in all of this.”

"He was bad news." Patricia shook her head. "I guess you know more than me after speaking to Sarah." She held up her hand to stop him as he started to reply. "No, no, I don't need to know. Grace would have told me if she wanted me to know. What was said stays between you and Sarah."

"Well, suffice it to say that yeah, he was bad news alright." Davis felt the anger creeping into his chest again.

Patricia took a long sip of her coffee. "I wouldn't be surprised if he showed up dead in a ditch somewhere. Getting wrapped up in that sort of mess. Who knows what's happened to him."

Chapter Four

He took off his sweaty gym clothes and headed for the showers. School started in half an hour, and he needed to get to class, he had an English test first thing.

Billy rounded the corner, already showered. He seemed startled to see him. "Oh, hey Davis."

"What time did you get here?" Davis asked him.

"Oh, just a little earlier than normal, my Dad really wants me to make track this year so I thought some extra training couldn't hurt."

Davis noticed the faint purple smattering along Billy's arms and shoulders. "You OK man? We haven't seen you much lately."

Bill shifted on his feet. "Oh just busy, you know, lots to do." He smiled and gave Davis a nod. "See ya."

Davis looked over his shoulder as he walked to the showers, and had to stifle a gasp. Billy's back was covered in angry, small, round, red scars. Cigarette burns. Billy turned back suddenly, and saw Davis staring at him, mouth agape. "Oh," he smiled weakly, "hey, I think I rubbed up against some poison ivy when I went, uh, swimming last week, it stung like a bitch."

"Billy, this isn't OK." Davis said, a lump forming in his throat, making it hard to speak. "I need to tell someone."

Billy rushed at him, his eyes pleading. He grabbed Davis's shoulders. "No man, you can't do that." The desperation in his eyes made Davis feel sick. "Please, you don't understand."

"He beats the shit out of you and Grace and I'm sick of watching it happen."

"No, you can't say anything, Davis." Billy's grip on Davis's shoulders intensified. "Please, you don't understand. He doesn't mean to hurt us, he just - He gets mad, and he doesn't mean any harm."

Davis shook Billy off. "Do you even hear yourself? He beat you up with a baseball bat for fuck's sake!"

"He didn't mean it, he's gone through a lot since Mom died -"

"Billy!" Davis roared, instantly regretting it when he saw exactly the same fear in Billy's eyes that he saw in Grace's whenever anyone raised their voice. "Billy," he said again, lowering his voice, "this has to stop. I have to tell someone."

"It'll get better once I make the team," Billy insisted. "Please, just wait til after tryouts, and when I get on the team, you'll see. It'll be better then." Billy's eyes were full of tears, but he smiled and nodded at Davis. "Please, it'll be OK by then OK? Really. Just wait and see."

Davis clenched his jaw, but finally nodded. "After tryouts," he said emphatically, "but then, if it happens again, I'm calling the cops."

Billy breathed a sigh of relief, and wiped his eyes with the back of his hand. "Great, thanks Davis. We're gonna be OK, my Dad just wants us to be the best we can be. It'll be OK." He turned and walked quickly out of the locker room, the door slamming hard behind him, the sound echoing along the tiled walls.

Bob Weaver, that son of a bitch. Hot, angry tears stung Davis's eyes. How could no one notice what was going on? Not one teacher had ever questioned Grace and Billy's injuries. The coach had never commented on Billy's long absences. Why didn't anyone care?

Davis punched the shower wall, pain shooting through his fingers and into his wrist. Grace hated displays of violence. He didn't want to be like this. But the helplessness was driving him mad.

Something had to be done. And after tryouts, Davis would stay true to his word.

Smoke hung heavily in the air as he headed down to the site office. A large fire had been burning overnight in the national park. The sun shone orange through the stifling haze, and Davis observed the distant plume of smoke with concern. This didn't look good. Parts of the canyon were hard to access, so laying containment lines would be difficult, if not impossible.

Craig's truck sat beside the site office, and Davis groaned. He was not in the mood for more safety talks in which no one would listen to him. He jumped down from his pickup, and braced himself as he approached the office door.

Craig didn't look happy as Davis entered. "This smoke isn't the best news, is it?" He asked sternly.

"No, it sure isn't." What else could he say? "The wind appears to be in our favour, and the line isn't anywhere near your trees. I think we might be in luck."

"The crew around here is good?" Craig looked sceptical.

Davis nodded. "Absolutely sir, they know this terrain like no on else."

Craig nodded, rising from the office chair. "Good. I hope you'll be out briefing the crews. Oh and can you head up and speak to the rangers, I've been trying to call them all morning and gotten no answer. I need to be updated on any park closures directly."

Davis suppressed the urge to roll his eyes. "Absolutely sir, I'll go and talk to them." As if the rangers didn't have better things to do than update a private citizen on park closures.

He headed out and did a few rounds of the crews, checking they were safe. The smoke had become thicker, and Davis knew the fire was spreading rapidly. The crew were already working with masks on, but the smoke had become too dangerous. After two hours, he called off work for the day and ordered the crews to cease operations. Craig would be pissed, but Davis wasn't interested in breaking the law or endangering workers.

Once the crews had begun to head in, Davis headed up to the national park, which seemed to still be open. He didn't especially care that Craig wanted to know about park closures, but he did want to know that everyone was safe. He kept his windows up as he drove. If the smoke kept travelling like this, visibility would get worse.

A trail of RVs were exiting the park as he approached, and he guessed an evacuation order was in place. The Firehawk helicopter buzzed overhead as he parked beside the information centre. He felt a tug, knowing his old crew were heading out to lay lines and fight the fire. *I should be out there with them.*

The ranger station behind the visitor's information centre was buzzing with activity. Two rangers on ATVs took off into the park as Davis approached. He ducked his head into the office, and saw Grace on the phone. She had her back to him, rubbing her neck as she talked.

"Yes, I understand. OK. So what kind of acreage are we looking at now? Oh god. OK, well, keep me posted. Yeah. OK. No you too. OK, bye." She hung up and sighed, leaning her head back in her hands.

"Fuck, fuck, fuuuuuck," she said quietly, clearly not realising she wasn't alone in the office.

"Everything OK?" Davis asked, giving a brief knock on the doorframe.

Grace spun around, startled. "How long have you been standing there?"

"I just got here. I wanted to check everything was ok."

"Not really. We need to close the park, and the tourists don't want to leave because they only just got here." Grace rubbed her face. She looked tired.

"How big is the fire now?" Davis asked, stepping into the office.

"About 6,000 acres. So, small compared to what we've had, but it's spreading fast. It's down in the canyon and the crews are struggling to lay containment lines, so... Yeah." She shrugged. "Not much we can do but hope."

Davis nodded and tucked his hands into his pockets, leaning back against the door frame. "You OK?"

She gave him a questioning glance. "I'm... fine."

"I just mean, uh, the whole rifle thing. I thought it may have, y'know, brought up a lot of things for you."

"Oh, right," she looked down at her hands, and fidgeted with her nails. "Um, it was weird, and unexpected. The police said they'll keep me informed, but there does seem to be suspicion that something may have happened to Hal. His father hasn't heard from him in 2 years, which is right around the time I stopped hearing from him, so... they think it may have gone not so great for him." She looked back up at Davis. "And I honestly don't know how to even feel about that."

"Were you hoping he'd come back?" The thought that Grace might still care about this guy hadn't occurred to Davis, but it was always a possibility that she would stand by him despite everything. Love made you do strange things.

But Grace shook her head emphatically. "Oh my god, no. I mean, yes for the sake of his ass being handed to him after what he did. But no. I made my peace with him not being in my life anymore, a long time ago."

"Did you know he was into drugs?" He felt a little too forthright asking questions like this, but Grace surprised him by responding without so much as a hint of reticence.

"I mean, " she leaned back on her chair and exhaled, "I knew he wanted to grow weed. I was fine with that. It's legal so, y'know? He said he wanted to help people, it was for medicinal purposes. But the meth, that was... I don't even know what gave him the idea. It's not like he needed money."

The radio buzzed to life, interrupting her. "Base we have reports of hikers up on Mt Whitney that won't come down."

"Goddammit," Grace hissed, picked up the receiver, "This is Base, got that. We'll get someone up there." She slammed the receiver down. "Goddamn fucking tourists." She jumped up and gave Davis an apologetic look. "I'm sorry, I have to go. It was - nice, talking to you." She slid out the door past him and jumped on an ATV.

"Grace wait!" He called out, following her. "You shouldn't head up there on that in this smoke, it's too dangerous."

"I'll be fine," she called over her shoulder, revving the engine.

He strode up to the ATV. "Grace, let me drive you, this is crazy. The smoke is getting worse."

She flashed him a look of anger and frustration, and she tipped her head back and exhaled sharply. "Fine," she climbed off the ATV, "up the Portal Road, you know where to go right?"

"I do." They climbed up into his truck.

At first the smoke became thicker as they followed the road towards the alpine section of the mountains. Then Davis took a turn to climb up towards the ranges, and the smoke began to clear, hanging like yellow fog over the canyon below them.

"It's gotten bigger," Grace said flatly, "they haven't been able to contain it." She sighed. "Four years at this job and it just hasn't gotten any easier dealing with fire season." She looked over at him. "I bet you don't miss this part."

"What have you done?" She looked at the acceptance letter he'd handed her. He'd expected her to be proud. But she looked furious. "You said we'd get out of here."

"Baby, this is a good thing," he sat down beside her, "a steady job, good income. I can support you through college and save some money. We've got nothing right now."

"You said that when you started the training, and now you've accepted a job up here with the crew, when will this stop?" She threw the letter on the floor. "There are no other crews hiring right now? Anywhere?" She turned her head away from him.

"The crew here are great, with the experience I'll have here, I won't just be some rookie, I'll be an experienced firefighter, I'll be able to work anywhere you want to go." He took her hand. "Baby, we have to be realistic."

She turned back, her eyes blazing. "For years, literal years, you have said you wanted to get me away from my Dad. And now you're just keeping me with him?"

"We can get a place together. I can afford that now. Just because we're here doesn't mean you have to stay in that house."

She shook her head. "I hate this town."

"Baby, I know. But if we get a place together, then that's you and Billy out of his house. Billy's training will be done

by the end of the year, and then he can go wherever he wants too."

She sighed and gave him a pained look. After a while, she leaned her head against his shoulder. "OK. We'll get a place together. I'll keep working at the store, and we'll save up some money, and then I'll go to college."

He stroked her hand. "I know it's not what we had planned, baby. But this is going to be amazing, for all of us."

"Do you miss it?" She asked. Her gaze didn't shift from his face.

"What?"

"This," she said, gesturing through the windshield at the Firehawk helicopter as it passed over them. "Firefighting."

"Oh, um, yeah, I do," he admitted. "I feel like I could be doing more to help than just supervising a worksite. My job now is, well, it's great. It pays well. But - I guess it doesn't have the same feeling that I'm actually helping anyone."

The road began to rise up towards the peaks, and Grace leaned against the window, looking up towards the trails. "I can't see anyone yet." She picked up her radio. "Chopper 1 have you spotted anyone?"

After a burst of static, the answer came: "This is Chopper 1, we haven't spotted anyone on the peaks."

"Copy that." She responded. They drove on in silence, reaching the snow cabin, which was closed up for the summer. No snow lay on the ground at this time of year, and the usually cool air was hot and dry.

"I don't like this wind movement," Davis said, looking down at the ever-growing plume of smoke. "The humidity's dropped."

Grace rounded the cabin and began to walk up the trail towards the peak. "Hello?" She called out, cupping her hands around her mouth.

Davis followed her. "Do you really think anyone's up here?"

"Mountain climbers are stupid," she responded without turning around, "they think they're invincible and also that climbing a mountain is their spiritual calling. The trail has been closed by blizzards and we've had to come out and rescue them before. They don't care that they endanger us or themselves, the mountain is all that matters." She raised her hands back to her mouth. "HELLO?" She bellowed, and sighed heavily when there was no response.

They walked on in silence up to the first rest point, which afforded them an open view of the trail ahead, and a good view of the canyon below. They couldn't see anyone.

"I guess they went back down on their own." Davis reasoned. "If the chopper hasn't seen them."

The radio attached to Grace's belt buzzed to life. "Rangers this is command, all rangers this is command, the fire has broken containment lines and is threatening to cut off the portal road. All rangers back to base immediately, I repeat all rangers back to base immediately."

Grace gave Davis a brief look of fear, before breaking into a run back down the trail towards his truck. Davis thundered after her. If the portal road was cut off, they wouldn't be able to get back down the mountain. Up here on the peaks they were above the tree line, but Davis still had no desire to get stuck on a mountaintop during a fire.

They jumped back into his truck and Davis gunned the engine. The smoke had started to rise towards them as they headed down the portal road. "Do you think it's cut us off yet?" Grace asked, her voice strained.

"No, it'll be fine." He reassured her, concentrating on the road ahead. "We'll make it back in." He glanced to the side. He could see the flames lashing the tops of the trees in the distance. The fire had gotten far too close.

The smoke became so thick he could barely see. He slowed the truck, following the line of the road carefully. He didn't want to scare Grace, but the situation was looking bad. "Grace, I don't think we can make it back down." Out of the corner of his eye he saw her head whip around to stare at him. "The visibility is impossible."

"All rangers, the fire is crossing the portal road. I repeat, the portal road is closed. If you are on the peaks, shelter in place." As the words crackled from the radio, Davis threw the truck into reverse and drove back up the trail until he could turn around, and gunned the engine back up the mountain.

"We can - we can go to the snow cabin," Grace stuttered. "I have the keys. We'll be safe there." She was afraid. Davis couldn't blame her. After what happened to Billy, Grace's fear of fires had escalated.

The smoke had started to creep up the mountainside as they pulled up beside the snow cabin. Grace jumped down from the truck and went to unlock the cabin, while Davis grabbed the fire extinguisher and fire blankets from his truck. He followed Grace inside, the acrid smell of smoke burning his nose.

The snow cabin provided accommodation and shelter for paying tourists during the snow season. There were four bedrooms with four bunks in each, and two bedrooms at the back with two twin sized beds. At the front there were two bathrooms and a large kitchenette and dining area with chairs and tables, and a lounge under the large window that looked out over the canyon.

The snow season had lasted unusually long that year, so the place had only been locked up for a few weeks. He was pleased to see two large water bottles for the water cooler standing in the kitchen, and Grace found some crackers and cookies in the cupboard. At least they had some supplies to get them through until the road opened.

Grace radioed in their location to base, then took off her boots. Since the cabin had been closed up, it was hot inside, and the air smelled musty. Grace looked out the window down to the canyon. "It always looks bad." She said quietly. "I can never just look at a fire and say, Oh that looks containable. It always just looks so... bad. And scary."

Davis stood behind her and looked over her shoulder. "The wind is getting stronger. They're going to have a hell of a time containing that."

She turned around and looked up at him. "Thank you for coming up here with me, I don't even... If you hadn't been here..." She took a deep breath and pushed past him. "Coffee?" She asked suddenly, and he could hear how hard she was trying to keep her voice even. "It's just powdered, but there's some creamer and sugar here too." She put the electric kettle on to boil.

"Sure, sounds good," Davis also kicked off his boots. It really was stifling inside. He got up to look out the window, and saw with dismay that the smoke outside had become even thicker. The sky glowed orange, the smoke dimming the light and making it seem as though the sun was setting.

Grace remained silent as she prepared the coffee for them. She put a cup on the table for Davis and sat down. "I feel so stupid," She said, gazing out the window. "Stuck up here, doing nothing."

"I know what you mean," Davis took the cup and took a sip, sitting down in the chair opposite her. "I was fine doing my job for the past few years, but being back here, it just -"

"Feels different," she met his eyes.

She gripped the pillow and moaned as she came. She was soft and warm underneath him, and her tightness around him drew him out. He shuddered and shook against her, gasping into her shoulder. She lay face down, breathing heavily. "Good morning to you too," her voice was muffled by her pillow.

He laughed as he rolled off her, onto his back beside her. "The perfect way to christen the new apartment, right?"

She rolled over and stretched out, her red hair splayed out on the pillow around her. "Well, if we get to do this every morning I do have to wonder how we'll ever get out of the house."

They'd moved into the apartment the day before. They'd sat on the floor, surrounded by boxes, eating Chinese takeout, and had not been able to stop grinning at each other. All Grace's misgivings about staying in town seemed to have disappeared.

Her father had been surprisingly pleased that the star quarterback had decided to take up with his daughter for real. Davis had to restrain himself as Bob Weaver praised his daughter for being "fine enough" to secure a man like Davis Chevalier. Davis hated how much Bob fawned over him. Davis was everything Bob wanted Billy to be. To Billy's credit, he never resented Davis for any of it. But Davis felt it was so unfair and cruel for Billy to constantly hear his own father comparing him to another man.

It was why Billy had decided to become a firefighter. Bob had pushed him and pushed him, ranted about heroics and self-sacrifice until Billy applied to the academy. Billy's GPA had dipped too far for him to consider college, thanks to his father's constant beatings forcing his absence from school. But he was doing great at the academy. Davis hoped he ended up with a crew far, far away from his father.

Grace clambered up off the mattress on the floor, and Davis watched her admiringly. "You're so fucking sexy," he said, smiling.

She tossed her hair over her shoulder and gave him a smouldering look. "I know," she grinned, "and I'm also going to be late for work if we do that again." She cast a look at his growing arousal. "And you'll be late for work too, so some restraint please, Chev."

He rose from the bed, and walked up behind her as she retrieved her clothes from a suitcase on a stack of boxes. He wound his arms around her waist and held her close. "I love you," he whispered.

She leaned her head back against him, stroking his arms gently. "I love you too, baby." She looked up at him over her shoulder, and kissed him. "I'm so glad we're here together."

"Can I ask you a stupid question?"

She nodded, giving him a puzzled smile. "I guess."

He leaned forward on the table. "Why'd you colour your hair?"

She laughed. "Oh god, umm, I dunno. I guess, kind of because of Hal? He always went on about hating blondes and hating tans." She rolled her eyes. "He hated it when I was out in the sun. He had this whole goth wannabe thing going on and loved that I was a pale redhead. So when he left, I decided to colour it, and I used fake tan just to spite him." She giggled self-consciously. "And then, I dunno, I guess I just liked it." She glanced at him. "You don't like it?"

"Hey, it's your hair. I think you look gorgeous no matter what." The words came out without him thinking, and they stared at each other for a moment. "I mean, uh," he stuttered, "you know, you're your own woman. What a man thinks about it is irrelevant, right?"

She nodded, running her fingers along her long blonde braid. "Yeah, exactly. I like it."

They finished their coffees in silence, and by the time Davis was done, sweat started to drip down his brow. The temperature in the cabin was rising, and unable to open a window, they were going to start getting very hot. He got up to put a water bottle in the cooler and flipped it on. He could see the sweat marks on the back of Grace's ranger uniform.

"I don't want to be creepy, but we should probably be wearing less clothes to try and keep cool." He glanced at the bathrooms. "Maybe you should take a shower, help you cool down."

Grace looked at him uncertainly, but then nodded. "Yeah, good idea." She got up and headed to the bathroom. Davis headed to the one opposite. The water pressure was pitiful, but the cool water trickling down his back made him feel a lot better. He washed all the sweat off, and got back into his boxer shorts and t-shirt.

Grace emerged shortly after, wearing only her panties and a black tank top. Her long wet hair hung over her shoulder, tiny drops of water running down her tanned arms. She smiled at him shyly. "This isn't awkward at all."

He laughed and ran his hands through his wet hair.

"This is probably the smoke inhalation and the heat talking, but... I've missed you." She gazed up at him. "I'm glad you're back."

Jesus. Her words caught him completely off guard. She saw the startled expression on his face and looked down at the floor, embarrassed. "Sorry, I - I shouldn't have said that," she stammered, "it was stupid."

"No, no it wasn't," he took a step towards her. Everything in him wanted to take her in his arms at that very moment, but he didn't want to be presumptuous. "I'm glad to see you too. I - I'm just happy you're still talking to me after -"

"I didn't want to," she interrupted, and smiled at her own brashness, "but when I saw you again, I just - all the old memories came back. I guess after a while the bad stuff fades, and there's just a lot of good memories left."

They stood and just looked at each other for a while, smiling. "Grace -" Davis took another step towards her, raising his hand to touch her.

A loud static squeal erupted from the radio, followed by a man's voice; "Weaver, Weaver, come in Weaver, this is base. Please advise your current location."

Grace rushed to the radio. Davis rubbed the back of his neck, frustrated. They had been so close, and now the moment was gone. "This is Weaver," Grace spoke into the radio urgently, "I am still in the snow cabin, my location has not changed."

"The fire crew have set up containment lines at the portal road, you can come back down the mountain safely." The man responded.

"Copy that, we'll make our way down." Grace put the radio down and began getting dressed. "Come on," she said to Davis, "let's get out of here before that fire flares up again."

They emerged from the cabin to find the smoke had cleared somewhat. "Wind's changed," Davis said as they climbed into his truck, "the fire should blow back on itself now, the crew have a good chance to get it under control."

They drove most of the way in silence, Davis focusing on the road and trying to ignore how close Grace was to him. His skin was tingling after their exchange in the cabin, and he knew he had to keep his hopes and expectations under control.

"My Dad still blames you," Grace said suddenly. "Sorry, this is probably not a great time to bring this up."

Davis felt his stomach tense. "I expect he does," he replied. "I suppose it's only natural to want someone to blame." He gave Grace a side glance. "And you?"

She looked out the window, her hands clasped in her lap. "I don't know," she said after a while, "Billy was following orders, you weren't to know..." She trailed off.

She still blames you. He pushed down the urge to tell her the truth. It wouldn't help anybody, and she might not even believe him. She might just think he was saying it to get her back. There was no point trying to make it right now. He'd made a promise to a dying man, and he wasn't about to go back on it.

"Billy was a good firefighter." Davis didn't know what else to say. "And I regret what happened every day."

"You know -" Grace turned to him, then slumped back in her seat. "No. Never mind."

He wanted to press her, but at that moment the fire crew came into view, approaching the truck and waving them through the thick smoke. Davis navigated past them, nodding his appreciation, and feeling again a deep pang of regret that he was not there with them. They continued on down the road, and before long the ranger's station came into view.

Davis pulled up, and Grace paused with her hand on the door. "I mean it," she didn't turn to look at him as she spoke, "I am glad you're back. But things can't go back to how they were, Davis."

"I know." His voice was flat.

"I still care about you." She threw open the door of the truck and jumped down, slamming the door behind her, and Davis was alone again. His phone rang. He saw it was Craig calling. He ignored it.

He drove on out of the park, and headed home, Grace's words replaying over and over in his mind. *My Dad still blames you. Things can't go back to how they were.*

"Tell Grace I'm sorry."

"Tell her yourself. The water drop will -"

"It won't come in time."

"Billy, just hold on."

"Tell Grace I'm sorry, and I love her."

"Billy, we're getting you out of there, just hold on."

"Please don't tell her what I did."

"Billy.... Billy, please..."

"It's so hot in here, Chev."

"Billy, they'll be here any minute, just hold on."

"She'll never forgive me. Please don't tell her. I'm so sorry."

"Billy -"

"Look after her, Chev. Tell her I'm sorry."

Chapter Five

"Did you hear about the memorial opening?" Sarah poured Davis his second cup of coffee.

"A memorial?"

She nodded. "Yeah, it's being unveiled on the 5th anniversary of the big fire. They'd wanted to do it for a while, but Bob Weaver kept insisting the font Billy's name was in was wrong, or not big enough." She rolled her eyes. "He is obsessed with Billy's hero status."

Davis took a sip of his coffee and remained silent.

"Anyway," she went on, "it's next Sunday."

"I doubt Bob Weaver would welcome me being there," Davis looked down at the apple pie Sarah had just served him. He'd lost his appetite.

"Oh," Sarah waved a hand and tossed her dark hair, "who gives a shit what he has to say?"

"I think a lot of people would take offence to me being at Billy's memorial."

"No one blames you, Davis," Sarah laid a hand on his shoulder and looked at him earnestly. "Fires are what they are. It could have been anyone who went in there. It could have been you, for pete's sake. And then what? Do you think everyone in town would vilify Billy for your death?"

Davis knew she meant well, but her words brought him little comfort. "Sarah, can I get this to go please?"

She gave him an understanding look. "Sure, Davis." She picked up the plate. "Please, just think about it."

Davis left the cafe and walked down the street. *No one blames you Davis.* No one seemed to hold any ill will towards him, it was true. No one had been unkind, no one had even been indifferent. People were generally happy to see him.

But SHE blames me, and that's what matters, he though to himself sadly. As long as Grace blamed him for Billy's death, it didn't matter what anyone else thought.

"Hey, Davis!" Davis looked up to see Patrick calling to him from the corner, waving. A little girl with golden-blonde pigtails was holding his hand. Patrick gave him a wide smile as he approached them. "Hey man, how you been? How's the new apartment?"

Davis nodded. "It's great, all going well."

"Well, we're headed to the park, care to join us?"

"Park for swings!" The little girl at Patrick's side announced loudly.

Patrick looked down at her and laughed. "Yeah, swings honey!" He looked back at Davis. "This is Kayley, in case you were wondering."

Davis crouched down and gave the little girl a smile. "Hi Kayley, nice to meet you. I'm Davis, I'm an old friend of your Dad's."

Kayley shyly hid behind her Dad's legs, sizing Davis up with her big blue eyes.

Patrick ran his hand over her head. "Come on, sugarplum, let's go to the park."

Davis walked along with them, smiling to himself as Kayley chatted to her father about the swings and the slide and the rocky-horsey at the park. Patrick listened intently and answered all her questions with enthusiasm and patience. It was surreal to see his friend as a father, but Davis could see that Patrick was doing an amazing job.

Once they got to the park, Kayley zoomed off to play with another little girl in the sandpit, while Patrick and Davis stood back and watched.

"She's a cutie," Davis commented.

Patrick nodded proudly. "She's the best," he agreed, "just, so funny and clever. She blows me away every day."

"Shelley would be proud of you, man."

Patrick tucked his hands into his pockets and shuffled the ground with his foot. "I hope so. She was a great Mom."

Davis couldn't imagine what Patrick had gone through. To lose your wife so young, and just after having a baby. "I'm so sorry," he said, though he knew the words were meaningless.

"I'm glad I had her for as long as I did. And she got to say goodbye to Kayley, write her letters and record videos for her for when she's older. We have photos of her, and we talk about her every day. Kayley has a picture of the two of them on her bedside, and every night she says goodnight to Mama." He swallowed hard, the smile on his face wavering slightly. "It's hard some days, but mostly I'm just grateful for what I have."

Patrick turned to him, his eyes slightly red. "Anyway, have you heard about the memorial opening?"

"Sarah just told me."

Patrick clapped Davis on the shoulder. "You should come."

Davis shook his head. "I doubt Bob Weaver would welcome my presence."

"Fuck Bob Weaver," Patrick's eyebrows knit together in contempt, "his son wouldn't have been on that mountain if it wasn't for him. Billy didn't even want to be a firefighter. And all Bob Weaver does is bask in the glory of his son's heroic death. Fucker." The last word was hissed through gritted teeth.

"I just wouldn't want to cause a scene when the day is meant to be about remembering Billy."

Patrick nodded. "You wouldn't be causing a scene though, Bob would," he pointed out, "and no one would listen to him. He'd get told to take a fucking seat." Patrick turned back to seek out his daughter in the playground, who was still playing happily in the sandpit. "I mean it, man. You should come."

"Grace still blames me," Davis blurted out, feeling foolish.

Patrick chuckled. "Don't be stupid, no one blames you."

"She told me herself."

Patrick turned to him. "She did not. I don't believe that for a second."

Davis shifted on his feet. "She told me she can't be with me, that too much happened and that things can't go back to how they were."

"That doesn't sound like she blames you to me."

"She mentioned that her Dad still does."

Patrick snorted. "Of course he does, because admitting he pushed his son into a dangerous job that killed him would be way too much self-reflection for an abusive piece of shit like Bob Weaver." He sighed. "But that doesn't mean Grace blames you. She puts too much weight on what her Dad thinks, for whatever reason, but... I can guarantee she doesn't blame you."

Patrick crossed the playground to check on his daughter, leaving Davis to think about what he'd just said. At that moment, Kayley jumped up from where she was playing and ran across the grass, arms wide open, yelling "Graciiiiiiiiieeeeee!"

Grace came running across the park, and Davis couldn't help but notice how pretty she looked with her hair in two plaits, wearing tight blue jeans and a floaty white top with thin straps. She had her arms outstretched and a huge smile on her face. "Where's my girl?" She called, sweeping Kayley up off her feet and swinging her up over her head. Kayley squealed with delight.

Patrick walked back over to Davis, smiling. "Those two," he shook his head, "thick as thieves. Grace has basically been a surrogate Mom to Kayley. They adore each other."

Grace waved over to the two of them, and Davis watched as Grace took Kayley to the swings. The little girl chatted away, and Grace responded to everything she said animatedly.

"Grace is a natural with little kids," Patrick commented.

"Well, she wanted to be a pre-K teacher, for as long as I can remember." Davis felt a pang as he said it, knowing that yet another thing Grace had wanted had not worked out.

"Really?" Patrick looked surprised. "I had no idea. She would have been great at it."

As Davis watched Grace and Kayley play, he began to wonder just how much Grace still wanted to leave Clearwater. She seemed happier. She had deep connections, she had laid roots. She had a career, she was independent, she even had a step-child of sorts. He couldn't imagine her wanting to leave all of it behind anymore.

Grace and Kayley came running over to them, and Kayley announced loudly "Gracie take me for ice cream!" The little girl looked up at Grace adoringly.

Patrick laughed. "Ok, not a problem."

"I'll drop her back to you at the bar later, OK?" Grace said to Patrick, then gave Davis a quick smile. She hoisted Kayley onto her back, and the two of them walked towards Main Street.

Patrick turned to Davis once Grace and Kayley were out of sight. "I think you should come to the memorial. You were there that day. The crew would want you there. Billy would want you to be there."

Davis swallowed hard. "I'll think about it."

"Good." Patrick seemed content with the answer. "And just try not to beat yourself up anymore, OK?"

"Where the hell is that water drop?" He roared into the radio. Only static answered him. "Shit."

"Chev, the fire isn't holding on that line." Davis couldn't see Tyler's face behind his mask, but he could hear the worry in his voice. The fire was coming up on them fast.

"Pull black!" Davis ordered, and the crew moved back to the burnt out section of the forest. He looked around to account for everyone. "Where's Weaver?" No one knew. "Where the fuck is Weaver?" He asked again.

"Weaver!" He yelled into the radio. "Where are you?" No answer. "Goddammit, we've lost communication."

"Chev! There!" Tyler pointed suddenly. Davis followed, and saw Billy rushing up the hill towards the Campbell property.

"Billy!" Chev rushed towards him. "What the fuck are you doing?"

Billy stopped and spoke into the radio. "The Campbells refused to evacuate, they might still be in there." His voice was distorted and robotic through the weak signal.

"Billy, pull back now." Davis responded. "Right now! The property is compromised."

"What if they're in there?"

"Weaver, pull back immediately."

"There might be people in there!" Billy shoved the radio back into his belt, and took off up the hill. Davis lost sight

of him in the smoke. He could see flames lashing at the roof of the Campbell house behind the trees.

"Weaver! Pull back! That's an order!" No response. "God fucking dammit."

Tyler approached him. "The water drop is coming." He told him, pulling him back to shelter.

"Stubborn son of a bitch!" Davis raged.

At that moment they heard a roar, and an explosion. They turned to see the Campbell's roof had disappeared. There was a loud crash as the house collapsed in on itself.

"Billy!" Tyler held Davis back as he began to run towards the flames.

"No Chev!" Tyler yelled over the roar of the flames.

"Let me go!" Davis shouted, and the rest of the crew came over to help restrain him. "Billy's in there!"

The radio crackled to life, and they all froze as they heard Billy's screams.

Davis was about to go to bed when he heard a frantic knock on the door. He opened it to find Sarah standing outside, wringing her hands and looking anxious. "Patrick just rang me," she burst out before Davis could say anything, "Grace is down at the bar, falling down drunk. She went to the police down in Mammoth Lake because of something to do with Hal, and I don't know what happened but she came back and just drank like 5 bottles of tequila and she's blind drunk."

“Oh what the hell,” Davis muttered, “wait here.” He hurried back to his bedroom and pulled on jeans and a sweater, and shuffled into his sneakers. “Come on.” He said as he got back to the door. “Let’s go.”

They got into Sarah’s car. “So you have no idea what happened at the police station?” Davis asked as she drove out of his driveway.

She shook her head, keeping her eyes on the road, clutching onto the steering wheel anxiously. “No idea. She told me this morning she’d be going to Mammoth Lake to talk to them because some new information had surfaced. Then I didn’t hear from her, and she didn’t respond to my messages.”

It had to have been something serious. Grace hated getting drunk. Her Dad had spent so much of her childhood drunk, she couldn’t stand excessive drinking and she had certainly never made a habit of getting drunk.

Sarah rounded the corner onto Main Street, and pulled up outside the bar. Davis stormed in, and immediately spotted Grace hanging over a man he didn’t know, running her hands over his chest suggestively, laughing loudly. Davis met Patrick’s eyes as he crossed the room, and saw that Patrick looked worried.

“Grace, it’s time to go home,” Davis said, taking her arm.

She turned and laughed. “Oooh it’s the quarterback,” she slurred. “You looking for a touchdown? Where are you gonna take me?” She giggled and stumbled.

The man she’d been hanging over held up his hands. “I don’t know her, man” he said to Davis. “She and I were just talking.”

"Oh don't worry about him, honey," Grace drawled, turning back to the man who looked increasingly uneasy as Davis's face darkened. "He's just my ex."

"OK, Grace. Home now." He began to lead her out of the bar, Sarah following them.

"But I was just having fun!" Grace cried. "Come on, Davis, you like having fun. WOOOOOOO!" She threw her hands over her head and whooped. Davis scooped her up and threw her over his shoulder.

"We're going," he said, trying to ignore her laughter, and placing her in the back of Sarah's car.

Grace was singing loudly as Sarah started the engine. "She can't go home by herself in this state," Sarah said to him.

"Just go to my place," Davis told her, "I'll look after her." He knew Sarah had a small child at home, and he didn't want Grace waking up a sleeping household. Sarah hesitated, but then turned her car towards Fairville Road. Grace continued to sing loudly in the backseat.

They arrived at Davis's house. "Are you sure about this?" Sarah asked him, looking into the backseat where Grace was draped over the babyseat, singing and giggling to herself. "I've never seen her like this before."

Davis nodded. "She just needs to sleep it off." He climbed out of the car, opened the rear door and retrieved Grace, again throwing her over his shoulder, and carried her into the apartment. Sarah followed them, clutching her keys.

Davis placed Grace on his bed, where she lay, still singing and giggling to herself. Sarah pulled off Grace's shoes, and Davis covered her with a blanket.

"She'll feel better in the morning," Davis told Sarah, "well, maybe not better. But it'll be OK."

"Alright," Sarah touched his arm. "Thanks for this. She's a mess." She glanced back over Davis's shoulder at Grace, who had quietened down a little. "Call me in the morning, I'll bring by some breakfast." She gave Davis a smile. "I better get home."

Davis saw her out, and waited til her car had left the driveway before he closed the door. He turned and came face to face with Grace, who put a hand on either side of him on the door. "Hey handsome," she slurred. She reeked of alcohol.

"Ok," Davis said, taking her hands and attempting to move her back down the hallway towards the bedroom, "you need some sleep. You are gonna have a killer headache in the morning."

Grace fought a hand free and grabbed his crotch. "Maybe you need to sing me a lullaby so I can sleep better." She put her other hand around his neck, trying to pull him down towards her. "Don't I look pretty tonight?"

He loosened himself from her grip. "Grace, you're blind drunk," he tried to restrain her, but she was like an octopus. "You need to rest."

"Don't I look pretty?" She repeated, her eyes blurry.

"You're gorgeous. But I don't sleep with drunk girls." He put his arms around her waist and half-carried her back to the bedroom. He put her on the bed, where she began to undo her jeans.

"Come on Davis, it'll be fun," she purred. She kicked the jeans down her long legs, and sat up to take off her shirt. She lay down on the bed in only her underwear, grinning at him. "Come on, Davis, for old time's sake."

He ignored her and went to retrieve a bucket from the laundry. When he returned, she had fallen asleep. *Thank god.* He gently placed the blanket over her, and put the bucket on the ground beside the bed. She snored quietly, and Davis had to smile. She had always snored. She'd always hated it, even when he told her he was a deep sleeper and it didn't bother him.

Davis turned out the light and went out to the lounge room to sleep on the couch. He lay down and gazed at the ceiling, wondering what the hell had happened at the police station to set Grace off. He drifted into a light sleep, waking several times to check on her, each time finding her sleeping peacefully.

When he woke, Grace was still asleep. He sent a message to Sarah, telling her that Grace had slept all night and was still sleeping now. Sarah said she'd be by with some breakfast in a while.

Davis got up and put the coffee machine on, then snuck into his room and placed a towel on the edge of the bed, in case Grace wanted to shower when she woke. He checked his kitchen for Tylenol, thankful to find a packet hidden in a drawer. Grace would need it when she woke up, he was sure of it.

Sarah knocked on his door a while later, a large white paper bag in her hands. She looked tired. "Good morning," she handed him the bag, "I made a couple of breakfast burritos, and there's some almond croissants as well. I wasn't sure what you'd want."

"Thanks Sarah, you didn't have to." The smell of the food wafting from the bag was amazing. "I hope she can stomach some food this morning."

"I have to get to the cafe, but let me know how she is. I'll try and see her this afternoon." Sarah turned and waved as she headed back down the steps to her car.

Davis went back inside and heard the shower running. Grace was awake. He took the bag of food to the kitchen, and took two cups from the cupboard. He poured coffee into both of them, stirring in cream and sugar. He turned to find Grace standing in the doorway, her hair raked up into a messy bun on top of her head. Her face was bare of makeup, and he could see the light smattering of freckles across her nose underneath her tan. Her eyes moved from the floor to his face and back again. She was biting her lip. He could see she was embarrassed.

"Good morning" he held out the cup of coffee, "how are you feeling?"

She took the cup gratefully. "Like there's a jackhammer in my head, but I'll live."

He motioned to the dining table, and they sat down opposite each other. "Sarah brought some breakfast if you're hungry."

She grimaced. "Um, maybe later."

He watched her over the edge of his coffee cup. "You had us all a bit worried last night."

She looked away, out the window. "Yeah, it was a pretty stupid thing to do."

"Anything happen to bring that on?"

She tapped her foot on the floor nervously, and he saw tears well up in her eyes. "Umm, yeah, something happened." She dashed a tear away from her cheek. "I went to the police station in Mammoth Lake, they said they had news."

"About Hal?"

She nodded, and her face crumpled. "They found his body in a ditch somewhere by the Interstate down near LA. There was hardly anything left of him." She covered her mouth with her hand, silent sobs shaking her shoulders.

"Oh Grace, I'm so sorry." He wasn't altogether surprised by this news, in fact he was fairly sure this was exactly what his mother had predicted would happen. The police had raised the suspicion that something untoward had happened to Hal back when Davis had discovered the rifle.

"I feel so stupid," Grace sniffed. "Why am I crying over him? I haven't seen him in 3 years."

"You cared about him," Davis leaned forward on the table. "Even if it was over, you cared about him once, and something obviously awful happened to him. You didn't wish that on him. Of course you're upset."

"I'm so mad at him," she admitted, looking ashamed for a moment. "Why did he have to get wrapped up in this garbage? He was so stupid, and it got him killed. Now his Dad has lost his son, and for what? For money?" She took the tissue Davis offered her. "It's a waste, just such a stupid waste."

This is why Billy didn't want her to know what he did. Davis immediately quashed the thought. Not now. He couldn't think about that now. Grace was upset about Hal, not Billy.

"So last night, I got back, and I just... I just wanted it to stop hurting for a bit," she went on, "I picked up a bottle of tequila, finished that, and then I went to the bar. I don't remember much after that. Next thing I knew I woke up here. And I knew I was in your apartment."

Davis smiled. "How did you know?"

"Who else hangs their bedsocks on the night stand?" She asked, giving him a crooked grin through her tears. "It made me feel safe, knowing I was here with you." She lowered her eyes, and Davis felt his heart swell a little. She felt safe with him. Still, despite everything.

The pregnancy test lay on the table between them. She couldn't meet his eyes.

"What does it say?" She asked.

"Just wait," he replied, "it says results can take up to 5 minutes."

"I feel so stupid," she whispered.

"Stop it, you didn't do this on your own." He reached across the table and took her hand. "Hey, look at me. Look at me." She met his eyes. He could see she was scared. "We're in this together, OK? Whatever it says, we'll deal with it."

"Do you even want a baby?"

"I want whatever you want. And if that's a family with me, then I want that too. We always talked about kids."

"Yeah, but, in 10 years or something."

"So it happens a little sooner, so what?" He smiled at her reassuringly. "We can handle this."

Tears welled up in her eyes. "I was so worried you'd be mad."

"Grace, it's a baby, not a war."

She took a deep breath, and picked up the stick. "It's negative." She sighed a breath of relief. "Oh god."

"You OK?"

She nodded. "Yeah. Are you glad it's negative?"

"I'm glad you're OK, negative, positive, whatever."

She got up out of her chair and climbed into his lap, wrapping her arms around his neck. "I love you so much."

"I love you too, baby." He nuzzled her neck, breathing her in.

"My dad would have been so mad."

"You need to stop caring what he thinks."

She sighed. "He's my Dad."

"He's an asshole."

She got up and walked into the kitchen. "I wish you wouldn't say things like that about him."

"Why do you always defend him?" He asked incredulously.

"Because he's my Dad, Davis. He and Billy are the only family I have."

"And what about me?"

"Oh don't do that." She retrieved a bottle of water from the fridge, opened it and took a large swig.

"You always talk as though you have no one but him," he said, frustrated. "You don't need him anymore."

"How can you tell someone they don't need their parents, Davis? That's horrid."

"He is NOT a father, Grace. The man beats you and Billy senseless and you still want to act like he's Daddy of the Year or something. The guy's a piece of shit."

"Stop saying that about him!" She yelled.

"You think I've forgotten the nights where my Mom had to come and get you and Billy, because your neighbours called her? Your Dad would be drunk and raging again? Have you forgotten my Mother coming to rescue you from him?" Davis never raised his voice with her, and he hated the look on her face as he got up from his chair. He took a deep breath, willing himself to calm down. "I spent my whole life watching that man abuse you, watching him scare you, call you names, tell you that you were worthless. I'm sorry that I struggle with you defending him."

She was leaning back against the kitchen bench, holding on to the edge as though to steady herself. Suddenly she began to sob, her hand covering her face. Davis stepped forward and took her in his arms, holding her as her body shook against his.

"Baby, I'm sorry," he whispered into her hair. "I'm sorry I yelled at you."

She continued to cry. He berated himself for all the years he spent as an angry teenager, swearing he would protect her, that he would take her away from her Dad, that he would kill that son of a bitch Bob Weaver. And what had he done? Nothing. All he'd done was get mad that a sad, scared little girl still loved the only father she had ever known.

"I still remember your Mom coming to get us," Grace said as Davis put out the food Sarah had brought. "When my Dad got drunk and started yelling, I remember your Mom pulling up in her old blue Buick, and bundling us up in the back. She always had cheese and peanut butter crackers." She smiled at the memory.

"I remember us making couch beds on the floor with all the couch cushions," Davis said, and she looked up at him nodding.

"Yeah, you always used to set them up with towels and stuff, and we'd drink cocoa and watch cartoons." She picked up an almond croissant and sighed. "I don't talk to your Mom enough. We used to be close."

"She's always there," he assured her. "She'd love to see you."

"I guess - I guess when you left, I felt like I had no right..." she trailed off, and took a bite of her croissant. "She was going to be my mother-in-law -" her eyes flashed to his for a moment, "I mean, I guess she would have been one day. And when we broke up, that connection was gone."

Would you have left if she had been pregnant? He frowned at the thought. Would he have abandoned his child? Just how deep did his selfishness run? He had to accept that now; he'd left because he was selfish. And because he had talked himself into feeling a level of guilt that he shouldn't have. Just as Grace had convinced herself she no longer had a right to the relationship with a woman who had essentially been a mother to her all her childhood. They had both sabotaged their own lives, in a way.

"Sarah told me about the memorial opening," Davis said tentatively.

Grace looked up at him, and tilted her head. "Would you come?"

"Would you want me to?"

The silence hung heavily between them for a moment. Grace shrugged. "I think Billy would want you to be there. He idolised you."

"But would *you* want me to? I won't go if you don't want me there."

She bit her lip. "Davis, I stopped blaming you for what happened a long time ago," she began, not looking at him, "I understand the nature of your job and that you had to make tough calls. And Billy knew the risks. Firefighters die, it comes with the territory." She picked apart the croissant in front of her. "People would probably think it was odd if you weren't there, now that you're back. And I don't have a problem with you being there. Just stay clear of my Dad."

They continued to eat in silence, neither of them finding the words to continue the conversation. So much remained unsaid. It was just too late.

"I should go," she said when she was done. "I should go see Sarah and apologise for last night."

"Here, I'll drive you."

"Oh no," she waved him off. "No, I'll walk. It'll do me good to get some fresh air. It's not that far."

He wanted to protest, but felt that would be fruitless. She pulled on her ballerina flats, and he escorted her to the door. She hesitated as she went to leave, and turned back to him. She gazed up at him with her steely eyes, and he felt all the heaviness of the memories that lay between them. He wanted nothing more than to kiss her, but he knew that he couldn't.

"Thank you for looking after me," she said simply.

"Anytime. Always."

Her face crumpled a little at his words, and she gently stroked his cheek. The feel of her hand took his breath away.

And then she was gone, down the steps and out onto the road, heading down the hill into town. And he was left alone in his doorway, watching her walk away, the feel of her hand still on his skin, and the aching feeling in his stomach almost bringing tears to his eyes. Grace. His Grace. There was so much still between them - but it simply wasn't enough.

Chapter Six

Thunder rumbled as he pulled up to his parents' house. Dark clouds rolled in overhead, heavy with the promise of rain. Light shone from the front windows, illuminating the flowers hanging from the porch. His mother threw open the door as he killed the engine. "You sure do bring the weather with you, honey!" She called, waving as he approached.

"Should have called me Thor," Davis joked, giving his mother a kiss on the cheek.

"Come on in," she motioned to the front door, "I tried a new Moroccan recipe I found on Pinterest, and I need your honest opinion, because your father is of no help."

Davis chuckled as he followed his mother to the kitchen. His father was in his usual spot, his nose in the paper, a cold beer standing on the table in front of him. He acknowledged Davis's greeting by simply raising a finger from the paper, and saying nothing.

Patricia urged her son to try the bubbling, aromatic stew on the stovetop, which was delicious. She beamed as her son declared that it tasted wonderful. "Oh I'm so thrilled. I always wanted to try Moroccan food, and just never got to it." She went to retrieve a beer from the fridge for him.

"Moroccan food is just French food, isn't it?" Paulson asked from behind his paper.

"Morocco is more of an Arabic country, Dad," Davis informed him, "they were a French colony once."

Paulson sniffed. "By the smell of that food I can see why the French left."

Davis's eyes shot to his mother. He saw the hurt flash across her face, and anger welled up in his chest. "Why do you have to be such an asshole?" The words tumbled out before he could stop himself. He'd never spoken to his father like this. He and his mother had accepted his father's cynicism and disconnection for years - "You know how your Dad is," his mother would say - but he'd had enough.

Paulson dropped his paper and gave his son a look of sheer disbelief. "What did you just call me?"

"You heard." Davis met his father's gaze, furious. "She's proud of the meal she cooked and you can't help but be an asshole about it. Why do you do that?"

"Davis -" Patricia took a step towards Davis, "honey, it's OK."

But Davis went on. "She's been here, every day, for years, taking care of this place on her own, cooking your food and bringing you your beers and fixing the fucking chicken coop because you're not here to do it for her."

"I've been working hard, son, to give your mother everything she needs." Paulson snarled.

"She needs a husband who looks after her, not one who leaves her alone all the time, who never lifts a finger around the house, and who mocks her fucking cooking."

"Watch your language!" Paulson hissed at him.

"Davis, please," Patricia laid a hand on her son's shoulder. "Let's just enjoy a meal together."

"You talk down about Bob Weaver being an abusive asshole," Davis continued, fury coursing through his veins, "just because you don't hit Mom doesn't make you any better than him."

Paulson's eyes widened, and Patricia gasped. "Get out!" Paulson roared, rising from the table.

Davis rose to meet his father's gaze but did not move towards the door. "You talk down to her, you belittle her, and I'm sick of it."

"Get out of my house!" Paulson yelled again. He began to move around the table towards his son, but Patricia rushed at him, holding him back.

Davis turned and stormed out. He could hear his mother's pleading tone as she tried to talk her husband down, growing fainter as Davis stomped across the porch and out into the yard. Thunder rumbled loudly overhead, and rain had begun to fall. He paused for a moment as the ice-cold drops ran down his face. He was breathing heavily, and he felt dizzy and nauseous. He'd never stood up to his father before.

I need a drink. He jumped into his truck and gunned the engine, heading for Patrick's bar. When he pulled up, Main Street was quiet, and the bar was mostly empty. Patrick was behind the counter, and smiled as Davis approached.

"Hey man," his voice was jovial, but his eyebrows knit together as he examined Davis's face. "You OK?"

"A whiskey, please," Davis's voice was gravelly.

Patrick looked concerned as he poured the whiskey into a lowball glass, and pushed it towards his friend. Davis downed the whiskey in one gulp, the alcohol burning his throat. He gritted his teeth and inhaled sharply. "Another."

"I think you need to tell me what's going on before I have to call Sarah again telling her one of her friends is falling down drunk in my bar," Patrick said, crossing his arms across his chest.

"Fight with the old man," Davis replied, his voice full of scorn, "he was being an asshole to my Mom and I told him so." He laughed bitterly, running his finger along the rim of the empty glass. "Y'know, Grace was always scared of me ending up like him."

"I think she probably meant her own father, not yours," Patrick pointed out.

Davis shook his head. "Nah man, she meant mine too. She saw what a miserable, disconnected old man he was, and she was terrified I'd be just like him." He sighed. "Why are they like that, man?"

Patrick shrugged. "Our fathers thought it was enough to put food on the table and a roof over our heads," he rubbed the side of his neck pensively. "I mean, I'm a dad myself now, and I definitely see the mistakes our parents made. It really puts a lot of things in perspective. And for you -" he looked back up at Davis, "you came back in with a fresh set of eyes. This isn't your Everyday anymore. You see things in a way you didn't see them before. And you're not a kid anymore, so you call them out."

"Why does she put up with it?"

"Are we talking about Grace or your Mom now?" Patrick raised his eyebrows at him.

"Both. Either. I dunno." Davis mumbled.

"Love," Patrick shrugged, "it makes us do weird shit. I was always raised that family comes first, and you repair things that are broken, you don't throw them away, blah blah blah. If you pair that kind of thinking with an abusive situation where you've been told you're nothing without that person, and that everything you have is *because* of that person, well…" He shrugged again. "This is the result. Unquestioning loyalty, despite being treated like shit."

Davis slumped down into a bar stool. "Things really can't ever go back to how they were, can they."

"I don't think we would really want them to." Patrick leaned on the bar. "How would we know that we've learned and grown if everything just stayed the same?"

"You've really taken this whole philosophical bartender role seriously huh?" Davis jibed half-heartedly.

Patrick gave him a quick grin. "Helps me sell the hard stuff," he joked, and shook his head. "Nah, I think… I think when I lost Shelley, it gave me a new perspective on things. When Nancy Weaver died, and left behind those two scared little kids, no one was willing to call Bob out on the way he treated them. I didn't want to be like that. I didn't want my kid to suffer because I was in pain." He paused, lost in memory for a moment, before he went on. "I remember talking to Grace about it, about how Kayley deserved a good life, and how I couldn't give her that if I was broken. So Grace helped me, looked after Kayley when it all got to be too much for me, helped me have that space to process everything I was feeling, so I could be a better father."

"But Bob Weaver had that help," Davis countered. "My Mom was there for him every step of the way, watching his kids, swooping in to take them whenever he had a breakdown. And what did he do? He got drunk."

"Well then I guess it comes down to Bob Weaver being a selfish asshole. He probably wasn't a very different man before Nancy died." Davis considered Patrick's words for a moment. Before Nancy had died, Bob had probably been exactly like Davis's own father. Through the buffer of his wife's own sweet nature, no one had seen Bob's bad behaviour as anything more than a normal man of his generation. "After Nancy died, that facade was gone but he just had an excuse to be the way he was, and he drank more, and that got excused, and he hit the kids, and that got excused. And the more it got excused, the more it became normal."

"Grace said I should come to the memorial for Billy, because Billy would want me there." Davis's voice was flat.

"She's right, Billy loved you." He leaned in close to Davis. "My friend, you need to stop beating yourself up. I know what happened up there. The crew talk. I hear it."

Davis looked at him with shock. "They told you?"

"They all struggle with what happened to you after Billy's death, but their loyalty to you means they won't break their promise. But don't think they find it easy to lie. They respect you, you were their captain that day."

"Billy just wanted his Dad to be proud."

"Billy would want *you* to be happy."

"It would break Grace's heart." Davis gave Patrick a pleading look. "I can't tell her, I just can't."

Patrick shook his head. "I told you, man. Love. It makes you do weird things sometimes."

Davis pulled up outside his apartment, raindrops tracing haphazard patterns down his windshield. Davis sat slumped over the steering wheel watching them for a while, Patrick's words weighing heavily on his chest. His head felt fuzzy. The adrenaline of the confrontation with his father had worn off, and the whiskey had done it's job. Now he just felt oddly disjointed and a little lost.

A small red car he didn't recognise was parked over by the trees. As he walked up the stairs to his apartment, he saw movement out of the corner of his eye. Grace was at the top of the stairs, waiting outside his door, anxiously clutching her keys. Her hair and clothes were wet, clinging to her skin.

"Is everything OK?" He hurried up the stairs. "Grace, what happened?"

Without a word, she threw her arms around his neck, her keys jangling as they fell to the ground. Her mouth found his, and after his shock subsided he found himself kissing her back, pulling her close to him. His head was screaming at him to stop, to push her away, to find out what was going on. But the feel of her against him, the heat of her mouth, her hands running through his hair - it was too much. His resolve melted away, and there was just her. Nothing else.

As she pressed against him he was reminded she was soaked through from the rain, and shivering. "Let's get you inside," he whispered, "you're freezing." He unlocked the door, pulling her inside after him. He pulled her wet dress up over her head, and held her close to try and warm her. Her lips found his again, and she tasted fresh like lemonade on a hot summer's day.

She pulled on the back of his shirt, yanking it up over his head. Her skin against his was cold and soft. Her back was against the wall, and he leaned over her, breathless. "Grace, what are we doing?"

She wrapped herself around him. "You're taking me to bed," she whispered. He picked her up, her legs around his waist, her lips on his neck, his jaw, his earlobe. He carried her to the bed and they collapsed together, her hands undoing his jeans, seeking him out, her hand finding what she was looking for.

Oh god. Her touch was icy and firm, her hard, cold fingers wrapped around him. He was hot, almost throbbing in her hand. He shuffled his jeans down his legs, groaning as her hand began to move on him. She let him go so he could remove her bra and panties, letting them drop to the floor. She pulled him back to her, wrapping herself around him again, kissing him, her hands flexing on his back. He felt his arousal hard against her thigh.

"I've missed you so much," she breathed against his mouth.

"Grace, I think we should -"

"Don't talk, please, just don't talk anymore," she pleaded, her eyes going a darker shade of grey, " I just want to be with you, like this." She kissed him, and pulled him closer with her thighs. She reached down to grab him again, and he groaned against her lips. She guided him towards her, and he was unable to withstand. He sank into her, and felt her tightness and warmth around him, holding him perfectly, sweetly, like they were made for each other.

She moaned, her hands on his back, grabbing his ass as he began to move inside her. She felt like heaven, like a place he'd never left but had been dying to return to. Her skin warmed up against him, her cheeks flushing pink as her breathing quickened. Her hands were urging him to move faster, harder, but he held back, not wanting to let go of this feeling, not wanting to lose this moment with her, within her, just feeling her against him.

"You feel so good," he whispered. She arched her back, her hands gripping the bedhead behind her, her breasts on full display for him. She was a beautiful sight, her tanned skin soft and smooth, her rosy nipples glowing and hard.

He ground harder, feeling her stretch for him, and she threw her head to the side, muffling her cries with her arm. He felt his climax growing, trying to hold off, not wanting to let go just yet. She raised her hips, and he felt her legs tremble around him. She shuddered and moaned his name, holding him, tight and wet. He could hold back no longer, and groaned loudly as he felt himself release within her, his hands finding hers against the bedhead, his arms shaking, their fingers entwined.

He leaned his forehead against hers, not wanting to move, not wanting to leave her. "I love you," he whispered, without thinking, without caring. He had to say it, he had wanted to say the words since he had seen her again in the bar that night. He meant it.

She wrapped her arms around his neck, kissing him tenderly. This is where he belonged, in her arms, with her. Nowhere else. He felt a relief wash over his body that he had not felt in years.

Finally they parted, and rolled onto their sides. She was enveloped in his arms, her back against him. She smelled of pears and jasmine, her hair was wild. She was beautiful.

"So what brought that on?" He whispered after a while, his fingers tracing tiny circles on her chest.

He felt her squirm as she giggled. "Does it matter? You seemed to enjoy it."

"Yeah I enjoyed it, it was just very unexpected."

She ran her fingers along his arms. "I guess... I guess... I dunno." She sighed. "All the old feelings just came back, and I didn't want to push them away anymore." She rolled onto her back, and gazed at his face, raising a hand to stroke his cheek. "I just wanted to be with you again. It's never been like this with anyone else, not like how it is with you."

"Same for me," he said, planting a kiss on the tip of her nose.

"Were there a lot of girls in Alaska?" She asked him, snuggling against his chest.

"No, not really. Just a few. And you?"

"No, not really. Just Hal and besides that, no one really." She looked up at him. "I think I was always just waiting for you, even though I didn't want to admit it. I knew you'd come back one day."

"I should have come back a lot sooner."

"Yeah, but you're here now."

"I should never have left."

"Davis, the past is done. But we have this," she put a hand on his chest, "this here, now. Us. And I don't want to let go of that again."

The morning light flooded Davis's bedroom, blinding him as he woke, blinking. Had it been a dream? He turned to find Grace beside him, fast asleep, her hair shining in the bright sunshine. She lay on her stomach, the light illuminating her golden skin. She was there, he hadn't dreamed it. He reached over and traced the line of her spine with his fingers. She stirred, her eyes fluttering open. She squinted at him, then smiled and closed her eyes again.

"Good morning," she murmured. He leaned over and kissed her shoulder. His hand ran down to her back to her butt, and she giggled. "Don't you have to be at work?"

"I could call in sick," he replied, kissing her neck. "I could do with a day in bed."

She rolled over and kissed him. "It's that bad is it?" She teased, nipping at his lips. "An entire day in bed? That sounds pretty serious."

"And you?" Her body was warm against his, his arousal pressing against her hip. "Don't you need to get to work too, Miss Park Ranger?"

She pulled a thoughtful face. "Oh, hmmmm. I *am* feeling a little under the weather, maybe I should stay in bed all day too." She ran her lips along his jaw. "I wouldn't want to get anyone sick." She pushed him onto his back and climbed on top of him, coming down on him, hot and wet. He groaned as her tightness held him. She circled her hips, small gasps escaping her lips.

He gripped her thighs, watching her move, her breasts bouncing lightly, her hair wild around her shoulders as she rode him. She leaned forward, grinding against him, and his hands found her nipples, kneading them between his fingers, making her moan.

She threw her head back, her fingers flexing and clawing at his chest. Her movements became faster, and he pushed himself up on one arm to meet her, his other arm around her waist, holding her close to him as she began to tremble. "Fuck, oh fuck," her voice was shaky as he nuzzled her neck, feeling her tense around him.

She let out a loud moan, her body slick as she writhed on top of him. He gritted his teeth, his head against her neck as he felt himself move inside her, the electric ache in his body building and then releasing, spilling within her. He tilted his head back, gasping. The heat between them was at once unbearable and unbreakable, neither of them wanting to move away. Her thighs slid against his as she wrapped herself around him, their bodies drenched in sweat. He ran his hands through her long hair, holding her close to him.

Davis's phone rang at that moment. "Ignore it," she said breathlessly, "just ignore it." His chest heaved against hers. He knew he should answer it, he knew he needed to get to work, but the feeling of her wrapped around him, consuming him, was too sweet to move away from.

Once their breathing had steadied, they parted reluctantly. "Well, after that I need a shower and a big breakfast," Grace smiled at him, and made her way to the bathroom. He heard the shower start, and followed her in.

"If that's how you wake me up every morning, you're moving in immediately." He joked as she washed her hair.

When they emerged from the bathroom, Davis's phone was ringing again. He saw Craig's name on the screen. "That's my boss," he explained to Grace, "I should really get that." Grace pulled a face, but said nothing as she threw a t-shirt on and headed towards the kitchen. "Craig," Davis answered, trying to sound as under the weather as he could manage, "sorry, I was in bed sick."

"Well, I hope you get better quickly because we have a meeting in Mammoth Lake this afternoon." Craig snapped into the phone. "I need you there by 1pm."

"What meeting?" Davis asked, and feigned a cough.

"A committee meeting over the logging license in the national park." Craig replied sharply. "I need you there."

"Craig, I'm really not feeling great -"

"1pm at the town hall." And Craig hung up.

Davis sighed as he threw his phone onto the bed. Craig had been lobbying for the logging rights for years. Davis had never thought it would actually come to fruition, even as the last administration threatened to turn over large chunks of the national park land over to "private management", as they called it. And now he would have to go in to a meeting and argue that SNA's practices were not just safe, but the ethically sound choice in the future of the park.

He wandered into the kitchen to see Grace leaning over into the fridge, searching for food. She wore only a t-shirt, no underwear, and the sight of her bare ass and her long, tanned legs was incredibly enticing. "Find what you're looking for?" He asked, leaning against the door frame.

She turned to him and smiled. "You need to shop more, Davis. How does a man of your size survive on this little food?" She had eggs, ham and scallions in her arms. "Omelette OK for you?" She asked, making her way to the stove.

"Amazing wake-up sex and a woman who cooks for me?" He feigned shock. "How did I get this lucky?" He stood beside her at the stove, leaning back against the counter, watching her as she began to prepare the eggs. "I have a meeting to go to this afternoon in Mammoth Lake."

"Oh?" She didn't look at him as she continued to work.

"Yeah. My boss has gotten some committee meeting over the logging in the park." He watched her face, her expression, as ever, impossible to read. "He's been at this for years. I never thought he would actually get a meeting with them."

"It's been a talking point for a long time," Grace replied as she chopped the ham. "They talked about making the national parks smaller a few years ago, because we can't look after them or whatever excuse they used." She shook salt and pepper into the bowl of eggs and whisked. "Why do you work for this guy, Davis?" She looked at him, her eyes dark. "Do you think this is the answer? You're a firefighter, you know what it takes to look after the park." She waited for his answer, and sighed at the helpless look on his face. She put the skillet on the stovetop and waited for it to heat up.

"I don't agree with it, Grace," he told her. "I think logging companies are the last people who should be looking after the park."

"But you're going to go into a meeting today and tell them the opposite, Davis." She angrily flicked butter into the skillet, where it sizzled. "I'm not happy about this, Davis."

"Grace, this is my job."

"Well, maybe it shouldn't be," she dumped the eggs into the skillet. "Maybe you should come back to the crew and actually do some good work rather than help some billionaire destroy the environment."

He didn't know what else to say to her. He watched her finish cooking in silence, and they sat down at the table together to eat. She wouldn't meet his eyes. He hated this. They'd finally reconciled, they'd had this wonderful night and morning together, and now - now his job had come between them. Again.

"I'm not lying," Tyler was incredulous. "Are you fucking kidding me?"

"We're doing this for Billy," Davis insisted.

"I'm not throwing you under the bus, Chev." Tyler's eyes were wide. "I can't do that to you. You're my friend."

"Billy was your friend too."

"He wouldn't want you to take the fall for him!"

"He begged me not to tell his father," Davis countered. "He begged me. I promised him I wouldn't tell anyone. He spent his entire life desperate for his Dad's approval. I can't do this to him. I can't -" he took a deep breath, "I can't let Grace think Billy left her alone."

"Chev come on," Tyler threw his hands up in frustration, "this is bullshit."

But Davis shook his head. He couldn't do it. Billy had begged him. "I had to listen to that man die, I listened to him screaming as he burned up." His eyes stung. "I had to listen to my friend die, and beg me not to disappoint his Dad."

"Billy ignored a direct order, and he died, and that fucking sucks," Tyler's voice rose. "He was my friend too. He was my crew mate. But so are you."

"Tyler, please." Davis choked up. He couldn't get the sounds of Billy's screams out of his head. "This is one thing I can do for him. That we can do for him. We couldn't save him. But he can die a hero."

Tyler sucked his breath in between his gritted teeth and punched the locker beside him. "This is fucked!" He yelled, and stormed out of the room, slamming the door behind him.

Davis sat down, leaning his head back against the cold metal door of the locker behind him. He couldn't let Billy down. He couldn't break his promise to a dying man. And Tyler would come around eventually.

He couldn't let Billy down.

Davis pulled up to the Mammoth Lake Town Hall, the sick feeling in the pit of his stomach growing. He didn't like being blindsided like this.

Grace had left his place shortly after breakfast, placing a brief kiss on his lips before walking out without a word. He cursed himself silently for having told her anything, but he didn't want to lie to her. Not again. This was his job.

Davis spotted Craig, pacing outside the town hall, a thick yellow binder in his arm. He waved curtly as Davis approached, his face serious, his lips pulled into a thin line. "Davis, this is important," he didn't even say hello. "We need to convince this committee that the park is too big for oversight from the national parks service." He held up his hand to silence Davis as he began to protest. "I know this is personal for you as a local boy." Davis bristled internally at the word 'boy'. "But we need to be realistic. There are millions of dead trees in these forests, and we need to be responsible." He turned on his heel and walked inside the building. Davis followed him, dejected.

They were escorted into a conference room by a middle-aged woman in a pants suit. The managing director of the park rangers, Callum Andrews, was at the head of the table, along with the mayor, Bert Rauch, and a man Davis did not know. Callum nodded at Davis - he'd been assistant coach back when Davis had been in high school. Davis gave him an unsteady smile back - he didn't like being on the other end of this table. Just as they sat down, Joseph Keller, the fire chief, walked in. He hesitated as he met Davis's eyes. Joseph had been a good boss, and Davis had enormous respect for him.

The look Joseph was giving him now made Davis feel tiny. *This fucking sucks.*

The men all took their seats, and the man Davis did not know introduced himself as Larry Hirschmann, representing the county. "So, gentlemen," Mr Hirschmann began, "as you are all aware Mr Hayden here has made a bid to overtake the management of a section of the national park between Jolie and Clearwater, that's correct, Mr Hayden?"

Craig nodded. "It certainly is. The park has several million dead trees which pose a fire risk, and I believe private management would provide relief to the fire service and the national parks services."

"Mr Hayden, you wish to log within the national park," Callum leaned forward on the table, his hands clasped, "let's not pretend this is about conservation or helping the fire services."

Craig gave him an indulgent smile. "Mr Andrews, we both know that with current conditions both the fire service and the rangers are struggling to maintain the park and keep it safe." He gestured to Davis. "One of my own workers was recently caught on Mt Whitney for several hours as a fire was unable to be contained and cut off the only road down off the mountain."

All eyes turned to Davis. "Is this true, Mr Chevalier?" Mr Hirschmann asked.

Davis took a deep breath, cast a look at Craig, and nodded. "There was an incident recently where a park ranger and I were cut off for a time. But the fire service very quickly cleared the road and made it possible for anyone still above the portal road to exit the park safely."

"Only because the wind changed unexpectedly," Craig added, and Davis clenched his fists under the table. "Had the wind not turned, who knows what may have happened."

"Mr Hayden," Joseph spoke up, his voice as deep and gravelly as Davis remembered it being, "with all due respect, the situation you described was hardly life-threatening. And the portal road was cut off for maybe an hour or two. My crew know how to handle these fires."

"The fire grew to 16,000 acres," Craig replied shortly, "I wouldn't call that a well-handled situation." Joseph's face darkened, and Craig directed his attention back to Mr Hirschmann. "We're not talking about taking power away from anyone or destroying anything, we are simply concerned that the drought has created an environment where public management must be supported by private management. I can provide the very best equipment to safely remove a huge number of dead trees, making the park and the surrounding towns safer." Craig looked around the table. "Isn't that what we all want?"

Mr Hirschmann looked at Callum, who remained silent and stony-faced, then turned to Davis. "Mr Chavelier, I believe you're a fire safety engineer, is that correct?"

"Yes it is," Davis replied, "I've been a senior fire safety engineer and advisor for various subsections of SNA for the past 5 years."

"And your safety record is, I assume, sound?" Mr Hirschmann went on. All eyes were on Davis. He felt the knot in his stomach growing.

He leaned forward on the table, knowing he was about to make Craig very angry, and possibly put his job on the line. But he had to do the right thing. "I have advised Mr Hayden several times that SNA's safety procedures need to be improved." He felt Craig tense beside him, but he went on. "SNA is using outdated machinery, and this poses a risk to the environment here."

"Have there been any incidents prior that make you say this?" Mr Hirschmann asked.

Davis shook his head. "No, but the environment here is decidedly more vulnerable. We're talking 5 years of drought. Machinery that has a higher level of build-up, running on diesel fuel, is significantly more risky in this environment."

"Mr Hayden," Mr Hirschmann turned back to Craig, "and you were made aware of this, but have done nothing?"

Craig tried to laugh amicably, but his teeth were gritted. "My machinery is of the highest standard," he said reassuringly, "it is maintained by the best mechanics in the industry, and my safety record speaks for itself."

"You have a former senior firefighter telling you that it needs overhauling," Callum spoke up. "I assume you hired Mr Chevalier for his reputation. I find it hard to believe that you would overlook his advice when he knows this environment so well, and I find it hard to believe that you think this would convince the city that the park being handed over to your private management would be a sound move."

Davis kept his eyes forward, but he felt Craig glaring at him. "Mr Chevalier is excellent at his job," Craig said, his tone slightly menacing, "but I have been in this industry for 20 years and -"

"I've been a firefighter for 35 years," Joseph interrupted, "I have seen some of the worst fires in my career in the last 10 years. I don't think you have the first clue of the challenges this environment brings with it. We have saved huge portions of some of the oldest trees in this country. And I don't need some billionaire coming in here telling me I can't manage the safety of this area when he won't even listen to a safety advisor that he hired himself." Joseph turned to Mr Hirschmann. "I'm going to be honest, this seems like a clear case of profit over safety. If Mr Hayden can't even be bothered to invest in better equipment, where else is he going to cut corners?"

Davis gave Craig a sidewards glance, and saw his boss's face had begun to turn red. Mr Hirschmann twirled a pen in his hand, considering everything he had just heard. "Mr Hayden, I have to say I agree with Mr Keller," he said plainly, "SNA have an excellent safety record, but I do find it troubling that a multi-billion dollar company won't even pay for safer equipment when dealing with a vulnerable environment. Until that changes, I can't accept any proposals for private management of the park."

"But, Mr Hirschmann, we're in the middle of fire season, this is a matter of public safety." Craig's voice had increased in pitch. Davis knew him well enough to know he was absolutely furious.

Mr Hirschmann held up his hand for silence. "The matter is closed for now, Mr Hayden. If and when you improve your safety standing, we can bring this back to the table. Until then, this meeting is adjourned." He turned to the other men. "Thankyou, gentlemen, for your time."

Craig snatched his binder from the table and stormed out of the room. Davis looked at Joseph, who gave him a brief, approving smile. Mr Hirschmann began to speak to the others, and Davis hurriedly excused himself. As he stepped out on to the sidewalk outside the town hall, Craig stomped up to him, his face now a shade of purple Davis had never seen before.

"Are you fucking crazy, Chevalier?" He yelled, ignoring the passers-by, startled by his sudden outburst. "You work for *me*."

"I am paid by you to be a safety consultant," Davis pointed out, "and you ignored my safety advice. I'm not going to make myself liable by being dishonest about the company's safety standards and level of risk."

"I pay you *very* well," Craig hissed, "and this is how you thank me?"

"I work for that pay, Craig," Davis countered, using his height to tower over his boss, to show he wasn't intimidated. "You pay me for my expertise, not to be your lackey."

"Well then, you're fired."

Davis shrugged. He had expected nothing less. "Fine." He turned on his heel and walked away.

"Did you hear me?" Craig shouted after him. "I said you're fired!"

"I heard." Davis called back, without turning around. He climbed into his truck, gunned the engine, and drove off, barely noting Craig still standing on the sidewalk, slack-jawed, staring after him.

Chapter Seven

"How do I look?" Grace emerged from the bedroom wearing a black dress with a small pattern of white flowers on it. Her hair hung in a golden cascade of curls around her shoulders, and gold hoops adorned her ears. "Wearing black felt kind of... appropriate." She gave Davis a questioning look.

"You look gorgeous." He smiled at her, putting his arms around her waist, gazing down at her. "Just perfect."

"You look pretty good yourself." She straightened the collar of his white shirt, which was tucked into tan chinos. "And you smell so good." She sniffed at his chest. "Why do men always smell so amazing."

He laughed and turned to put on his watch.

"Wait," Grace disappeared into her bedroom, and re-emerged with a red velvet box. "I wanted to give you this." She opened it, revealing a silver and gold watch inside. "This was Billy's," she told him, "I think - I think he would want you to have it." Grace put the watch on his wrist. "It belonged to my grandfather, the good one," her eyes flicked up to Davis's, "my Mom's dad. Billy got it for his 18th birthday. I hid it after he died so my Dad couldn't pawn it off."

"This is a Rolex!" Davis exclaimed, examining the timepiece.

Grace shrugged. "My Mom came from money," she explained, "not that you would know it. I guess my Dad drank most of it away." She sighed, then looked up at him. "We should go."

It was the day of the memorial for Billy. Davis's apprehension about going had almost disappeared since he and Grace had gotten back together. He felt like a new man - the past week since Craig had fired him had been one of the best weeks of his life. He and Grace had spent every day together, making love with an almost frantic fervour, a desperation to make up for lost time.

The day was sunny and hot, and as they drove up the mountain road Davis could see dark clouds on the horizon, a threat of yet another summer storm. They pulled up to the park adjacent to the emergency response centre, where two large shiny firetrucks stood. The parking lot was packed, and it appeared most of the town were there. Rows upon rows of chairs had been set up in front of the lecturn, and a large stone beside it was covered in a red cloth bearing the emblem of the Clearwater Fire Service.

"I can't believe it's been 5 years," Grace said quietly. "It feels like yesterday, and it feels like forever." She looked over at him, a sad smile on her face. "I miss him."

Davis took her hand and brought it to his lips. "I know, baby. I do too." There was nothing else to say.

They climbed down from the truck, and held hands as they walked through the crowd, people greeting them and smiling approvingly at seeing them together. Davis felt his chest puff a little, proud at having Grace by his side. He felt a little pang at his own happiness, since the day was about Billy. But he knew Billy would be glad to see them together again.

Tyler approached them, looking very official in his dress uniform. "Grace," he greeted her, giving her a kiss on the cheek. He shook hands with Davis. "Come this way, let's get you seated." He motioned for them to follow him. Davis felt slightly awkward being seated with the family, but did not want to leave Grace alone.

Bob Weaver was sitting in a chair at the front, a small crowd of people around him. Davis could hear his slurred words cutting through the noise of people speaking and cars driving into the parking lot. "My son died a hero, and I am so proud of him for that. Not once did he question his directives. He didn't think of his own safety or his life for a second. He made the ultimate sacrifice!"

Grace gripped Davis's hand tighter as they sat down. Tyler gave Davis a look he couldn't quite make out, nodded to them, and left. Bob Weaver barely noticed them, only turning when the people around him began to disband to find their own seats.

"Ah, my very own daughter and the high school quarterback," he drawled, and Davis felt his skin crawl at disgust that the man couldn't even stay sober on a day like today.

"Hi Dad," Grace said, barely looking at her father.

"I"m surprised you can even show your face here today," Bob said over his daughter to Davis, "seeing as you're the reason we're even here."

Davis kept his eyes forward, trying to ignore the rush of anger tightening up his chest. Grace kept her hand on his arm.

"Dad, we're here for Billy," she told her father quietly, "this isn't the time."

Joseph Keller was suddenly standing in front of them, and Davis rose to his feet. "Chevalier," he said, shaking Davis's hand, "good to see you here."

"Of course, sir."

"I hear you're in search of a job," Joseph went on, "you know you're welcome back with the crew any time. We need good men like you."

"Good men like him?" Bob scoffed.

Joseph gave Bob a disapproving glance, and looked back at Davis. "I mean it, son. You're welcome back with us any time."

"I'll think about it sir, thank you." Davis replied. Joseph nodded, gave Grace a warm smile, and walked away.

"The last thing this crew needs is men like you killing them all off." Bob hissed.

"Dad, enough!" Grace turned to her father. "Stop it now."

"He killed my son!" Bob yelled. Several people stopped to look. Davis looked over Bob's head and saw Tyler, his jaw set. *Don't do it.* Davis knew that look. He met Tyler's eyes and shook his head slightly. *Don't do it, man.*

But Bob wasn't done. He stood up, unsteady on his feet, and pointed at Davis with a spindly finger. "We wouldn't be here if it wasn't for this man!" Bob yelled. The crowd had fallen completely silent. People looked at each other and back at Bob. No one seemed sure of what to say or do. "My son was a hero! This man was a coward and sent my boy into a fire to his death! And now he's back in town, fucking my daughter, and everyone is fine with it! What is wrong with you all?" His eyes were wild.

Grace rose to her feet. "Dad, enough!" Tears were running down her cheeks. "Dad, please, stop this!"

Bob slapped her hard across the face, her head snapping to the side. Davis caught her as she stumbled, fury burning in his chest. "Whore!" Bob screamed. "You're a fucking whore! You're fucking the man who killed my son!"

Several firefighters rushed forward and restrained Bob, who continued to rant. "My son, my poor son, he was a hero!"

"He died because of you!"

It took everyone a second to place the voice that had suddenly risen above the din, above Grace's sobs, above Bob's raving. Davis looked up to see Tyler standing over Bob, pure rage on his face.

"Tyler, don't -" Davis pleaded, but Tyler ignored him.

"Your son died trying to impress you!" Tyler yelled at him, the white-haired man suddenly cowering as the arms of the firefighters held him down. "Your son defied an order, an order Davis gave him, to pull back. He went into a burning house, even though his superior told him not to. And then he begged Davis not to tell you because he couldn't bear the thought of you being disappointed in him."

The firefighters holding Bob began to look at each other, a look of knowing and defeat settling on their faces. Davis's heart sank as he remembered Patrick's words - *The crew talk.* They knew. They all knew. Joseph walked over, looking at Tyler earnestly. "Is this true?" He asked him.

Tyler nodded. "Billy died begging Davis not to tell his Dad that he'd defied an order. Because he knew his Dad was a sack of shit who hated him." Tyler shot Bob a venomous look. "Everyone knew. The whole town knew Bob Weaver beat the shit out of his kids, and no one ever did anything about it."

Grace covered her face with her hands and crumpled into her chair, her shoulders wracked with sobs.

"And then Billy died, and everyone believed that Davis sent his friend to his death?" Tyler went on, incredulous. He turned to the crowd, who remained silent. "You all honestly believed that Davis would send a man to his death? Davis would have been the first man to run into that house if he'd thought someone could be in there."

Joseph turned to Davis. "You ordered Billy Weaver to stand down that day?"

Davis nodded, swallowing hard. He couldn't speak.

"And Weaver asked you to lie for him?" Joseph asked. Davis nodded again.

"It's a lie!" Bob screamed, struggling anew against the arms holding him back.

"It's not a lie, you old bastard!" Tyler yelled down at him. "Now shut up!" He turned back to Joseph. "I'm sorry I wasn't honest sir. I lied too. Davis begged me to defend Billy's honour, and I agreed because Billy was my crew mate. Billy's intentions that day were heroic. He was selfless, and he was willing to die to save lives." The rest of the crew mumbled in agreement, apologising.

Davis looked out over the crowd, and found his mother's face. She was crying, her cheeks red. His father stood beside her, his eyebrows knit together and lips drawn into a hard line. His mother turned and buried her face in her husband's shoulder, and Paulson placed an arm around his sobbing wife.

Heads hung in shame, eyes darted from one person to another. Joseph turned to Davis. "Son, I understand why you did what you did." He said gently. "Hearing a man die isn't something you ever forget. You tried to protect a crew mate. I understand." He placed a hand on Davis's shoulder. "Billy Weaver was a good man."

Grace stood up and fled. Davis turned and followed her, calling after her. She didn't stop until she reached the parking lot, and she doubled over, long, heaving sobs escaping her lips. He placed a hand on her back, and she pushed him away, stumbling back. "You lied?" Her eyes were wild. "You lied to me? You let me believe you sent my brother to his death?"

"Grace, he begged me. He begged me not to tell anyone."

"You left me for no reason!" Her voice was raspy as she screamed at him. "You left me! You said you couldn't handle the shame of his death. And it was all a lie!" She covered her face again, her sobs becoming louder. "You left me here with *him*, you left me alone, and it was all over a lie!"

"Grace, I'm so sorry-" He reached out for her arms.

"Don't fucking touch me!" She slapped his hands away from her. "Don't ever touch me again! You're all the same, you're all the fucking same!" Her face was red and blotchy and soaked with tears. "You left me for no reason! You lied to me and you left! I fucking *hate* you, Davis! I fucking *hate you!*"

"Grace, please!" He took a step towards her. "I had to listen to him die, I heard him screaming as he died, calling for you, calling for his Mom." Grace doubled over again, a hand over her mouth. "I couldn't say no to him. I couldn't let him down. I couldn't save him that day, but I could -"

"You sabotaged your entire life!" Grace cried. "You sabotaged my entire life!"

"I couldn't let him down."

She straightened up, fixing him with red-rimmed, steely eyes. "But you could let me down." She bit her lip. "You let me down instead." Her voice was full of bitterness. She turned and began to walk away. "Don't fucking follow me." She said without turning around. "Don't talk to me ever again."

He watched helplessly as she walked down the mountain road alone.

The clouds overhead were an angry shade of purple-grey, interrupted by occasional flashes of lightning. Davis killed the engine and slumped in his seat, gazing up at the lights shining from the windows of his parents' house. Thunder rumbled. He sat still, paralysed, unable to move. He'd lost her again. This lie had cost him everything, all over again. *Damn you Billy.* He instantly felt guilt at the thought.

His mother opened the front door and waited. Davis willed himself to move, mechanically stepping down from his truck and walking towards the porch. He felt completely detached from himself. His mother met him at the top of the steps and gave him a hug like only a mother could give, enveloping warmth despite her tiny size. He crumpled against her and sobbed.

"Oh honey," she stroked his hair as he wept. "Oh my poor sweet boy. I know. I know."

"I fucked up Mom," he gasped between sobs.

"No honey, you didn't." She took his face in her hands and gave him a hopeful smile. "It'll all come right in the end, honey. Now come inside and dry those tears."

He dashed his hand against his eyes as he followed her into the kitchen, angrily wiping away the tears that wouldn't stop falling. His father was nowhere to be seen.

"Dad's out with the menfolk," his mother explained, "having something of an intervention for Bob Weaver." She shook her head. "I let those babies down." She turned around and leaned against the kitchen counter, lost in thought. "When Nancy died, no one wanted to admit what Bob was like. No one wanted to admit that those kids were in trouble. And - and we told ourselves that you don't interfere with other people's kids. Your Dad kept telling me to stay out of it, to let the matter work itself out - how do little kids work out something like that?"

"I threatened to kill Bob a few times," Davis gave a short, bitter laugh. "Grace always defended him."

Patricia looked alarmed for a moment. "Killing someone like him isn't worth it. But I understand why you wanted to." She shook her head again. "Poor Billy. Even when he was dying, all he could think about was his Dad being disappointed in him. What that man did to his son. It's an absolute tragedy."

"I should have told the truth," Davis said ruefully.

"Honey, you spent most of your life seeing Grace and Billy being treated like punching bags," Patricia sat down opposite him, taking his hands in hers. "I think this is the one time where you felt you could actually do something for Billy. Helplessness is an awful feeling."

"It cost me Grace, all over again."

Patricia gave him a smile. "Honey, she just needs time. She'll understand."

"Would you?" Davis asked. "Would you understand someone leaving you over something so stupid?"

Patricia sighed. "Sweetheart, I'm not Grace. I haven't lived her life. I don't have her trauma burdening me. I think you need to understand why she reacted the way she did, and just give her space to work through what she now knows. You can't go back and change the past. All you can do is explain to her why you did what you did, when and if she's willing to listen. And if she won't forgive you, then you have to accept that too." She fixed him with her bright blue eyes. "You left because you felt guilty over something you didn't do, and told yourself for years that people would hate you for it. You didn't give anyone a chance to even process what had happened before you ran. And in the end, besides Bob Weaver, no one even blamed you. Fear drove you away, and it blinded you to everything, even your love for Grace."

Her words were hard to hear, but Davis knew she was right. He had made a choice to lie, to save Billy's honour.

That choice came with consequences. He had accepted for years that people might blame Billy's death on him, and he had cast himself out of the community, certain no one would be able to forgive him. He'd been so foolish.

And yet... The feeling wouldn't leave him alone.

"I think I should leave town," he said quietly after some time.

Patricia sighed heavily and shook her head. "Did you even hear a word I just said?"

"I hurt people, Mom."

"And you will continue to hurt people if you keep up and running off whenever things get hard." She leaned back in her chair and crossed her arms over her chest, giving a short, frustrated gasp of a laugh. "Seeing you two together, suddenly everything made sense again. You were happy again. You were *you* again." She looked away and bit the inside of her cheek, and Davis could see the tears welling up in her eyes. "Bob Weaver wasn't the only one who lost a son that day." She looked back at him as the tears began to overflow.

"Oh Mom -"

"You were *so* sad." The words tumbled out of her in an almost strangled scream. "You couldn't laugh, you barely ate. You had horrible, screaming nightmares. And then you were gone. I couldn't do anything. I was totally helpless, and then you were just *gone*." A sob escaped her lips. "You're my only son, Davis. My only child. And seeing you like this, again. Over this whole sad story, *again*." She reached across the table and took his hands, her eyes pleading with him. "The past needs to stay there, honey. It's never going to stop tearing us all apart if you don't just leave it where it lies. If you don't let Billy rest. If you don't allow yourself to finally have some peace."

"You could come with me."

The look of confusion and hurt on her face broke his heart. "I can't leave, not now, not after what's happened."

"Grace, there's nothing here for us."

"I'm here." She stared at him, bewildered. "I'm here, *Davis."*

"You hate this town."

"Every kid hates their hometown. I'm not a kid anymore, Davis." She shook her head, raking her fingers through her hair. "I don't understand this. I don't understand how you can just leave." She turned away, crossing her arms across her chest, her shoulders hunched. "I just don't understand how you can leave me here."

"Come with me!"

"No!" She spun back to face him. "You stay here!"

"I can't."

"Yes, you can. And if you loved me, you would."

"Don't do that."

"Oh," she scoffed, "I see. So it's your way or no way."

"I can't stay here. They all blame me for what happened."

"God dammit, Davis! The only person who blames you, is you." Her eyes narrowed. "Just say what you really want to say."

"And what is that?"

"That you want out. That's all. From this." She gestured back and forth between them. "From us. And this is just an excuse."

Her words cut through him like a knife. "How can you say that?"

"How am I supposed to think anything else?" She took a step towards him, then her mouth hardened, her jaw clenching, and she jammed her hands into her pockets. "Fuck you, yeah? Fuck you. Don't ever come back."

"Grace, wait." He hurried down the hallway after her. "Grace! Please!"

She pushed through the screen door, jumped down the porch steps and broke into a run across the yard.

"Grace!" He caught up to her easily, grabbing her arm. "Please, come on."

"Don't ever talk to me again, Davis." She was crying now. "I can't believe you'd leave me, when I just had to bury my brother. You're just like everyone else. All that talk, all that bullshit you spun me about it being us, forever. You're a fucking liar."

"Grace, please -"

"Fuck off. Enjoy Alaska." She ran down the road, and he stopped himself from following her. He watched her disappear around the bend, her red hair flailing behind her. He stood there, alone, willing her to come back. But she wouldn't. She'd made up her mind. She was gone.

Thunder rumbled overhead.

"I'm surprised to see you here," Sarah stood with her arms crossed, eyebrows raised. The cafe was mercifully empty. Davis didn't know if he could have handled another scene in front of anyone.

Davis attempted a smile, but when his face wouldn't respond, he merely shrugged. "She won't see me."

"No, I guess she wouldn't be interested in that right now." Sarah sighed, and dropped into the chair opposite him. "What the fuck, Davis?" She asked quietly. "What were you thinking? You honestly think Billy would have wanted this?" She rubbed her forehead. "I can't even begin to imagine what you went through. The - the trauma of listening to someone dying. Someone you cared about. I mean, holy shit." She shook her head. "But Billy wouldn't have wanted you to throw all of this away, for him."

"He begged me, Sarah." Davis took a deep breath. "The thought that his Dad would think badly of him… He couldn't handle it."

"But Davis -"

"Sarah, you know what he did to those kids." Davis interrupted her, frustration straining his voice. "We all knew. We all looked away. You helped Grace learn how to put on make-up to cover up her bruises for fuck's sake." Sarah recoiled like he'd slapped her and hung her head in shame, but Davis continued on. "I saw Billy at the school every day, hours before anyone else, training until he couldn't walk, because his Dad made his life hell if he didn't make the team."

Sarah looked like she was about to burst into tears. "Davis, we were kids, I don't think any of us knew just how bad -"

"I saw the cigarette burns on Billy's back."

Sarah's face crumpled. "Oh god."

"I am sick and tired of people questioning why I did this for Billy." He was suddenly furious. "It was the only thing anyone ever did for him. It was the only thing I *could* do for him. And it wasn't until he was fucking dead."

Tears filled Sarah's eyes. "I'm so sorry Davis."

He exhaled, feeling guilty for taking his anger out on Sarah. She was right - they'd all been kids, doing whatever they could to patch and cover what was happening. What power had any of them had to really step in? He reached over the table and took her hand. "I'm sorry, Sarah. It's not your fault." He took Billy's watch out of his pocket. "Can you see that she gets this? I don't feel right keeping it."

Sarah nodded, wiping a tear away with her hand. "You're leaving then? I had a feeling you'd be leaving town." She gave him a sad smile. "I wish you'd stay."

Davis opened his mouth to explain, but quickly closed it again. He'd explained enough, and he didn't feel like listening to yet another person try and talk him out of it.

"Where are you going to go?" She asked.

"Back to Alaska," he replied. "There's a fire crew in Fairbanks that needs folks. I got to know them pretty well while I was up there."

"When do you leave?"

"End of the week."

"Didn't Joseph offer you a job here?" She looked at him hopefully. "You don't *have* to go."

Davis shrugged. "Clearwater isn't the place for me. I don't want to hurt anyone anymore." He rose from his chair, and Sarah jumped up, throwing her arms around him.

"I'm so sorry, Davis." She said again. "I really hoped everything would work out for the two of you." She let go of him, and gave him a warm smile. "I hope I see you again one day."

"I'll be back," he promised, "one day." He turned and walked out of the cafe. He looked down Main Street, hoping to spot a small red car, or a head of shiny blonde hair. He saw neither.

Sighing, he walked to his truck.

Davis was packing the last of the kitchenware into a cardboard box when he heard the front door of the apartment open. His heart leaped into his mouth for a moment, but then he heard heavy footsteps and knew it wasn't her. He was mildly shocked when his father rounded the corner.

"Dad?"

Paulson stood, arms across his chest, gazing around the apartment at all the boxes. "So you're really going then?"

"Yes, I am."

"Running off again," Paulson shook his head.

"Dad, I really don't need to hear this right -"

"I think you do need to hear it." Paulson sat down at the dining table and gestured at the chair opposite. "Take a seat."

"Dad -"

"I said take a seat." Paulson looked angry, then looked up at his son, and his expression softened. "Give me a minute of your time, will you? We need to talk." His tone was almost pleading.

Davis sat down, eyeing his father carefully. Paulson sighed, playing with his wedding ring, and it was the only time Davis had ever seen his father display anything like nervousness. "Is everything OK, Dad?" He asked after a while, when his father had continued to remain silent.

Paulson nodded, sniffing. "I never told you how proud I was of you."

"When?"

"When the story came out with Billy. I knew you'd covered for him."

Davis raised his eyebrows. "How did you know?"

"You talked in your sleep after it happened, a lot. It always woke me." He gave a short chuckle. "You know I was always the one who woke up when you were a baby? Your mother would need waking, she was a real deep sleeper. So I would get up and bring you to her. Anyway, after the - the accident, I'd wake up when you called out in your sleep, telling Billy it would be OK, that you'd get him out. I knew you hadn't sent him into that house."

"I was stupid to lie," Davis said quietly.

"It was stupid of everyone to believe it." Paulson countered, the irritation on his face very obvious. "You didn't do anything stupid, you protected your friend."

"I lost Grace."

Paulson shook his head. "You made choices, she made choices." He leaned back in his chair, rubbing his fists along his thighs. "I watched for too many years. I told your mother to stay out of it, and thankfully she ignored me. Those kids didn't deserve what happened to them." His eyes flickered to Davis, then away again. "I beat Bob up once."

Davis looked at his father in surprise. "You did what?"

Paulson nodded, a self-satisfied smile crossing his face. "One night at Doherty's, he started on me, about you and Grace, calling Grace a whore. So I hit him. He was too drunk to remember it happening. I should have probably done it more often."

"I should have done more to help her." Davis shook his head. "I threatened to beat him up so often, to kill him even." His father gave a slight nod, and Davis knew his father had probably had rather similar thoughts at some time. "But Grace always defended him, wanted me to have understanding for the fact that she loved him. It used to drive me mad. I just didn't get it." He sighed. "I think I still don't."

Paulson shrugged heavily. "It's like being in a cult, son. Growing up in a bad family." He scratched his cheek thoughtfully. "By the time you realise that what's going on isn't normal, you have so much to unlearn. And having people tell you it's not normal, it's not good - it makes you cling to it harder because, well, who wants to hear that their family is wrong?"

"But Grace hated her father, she always wanted to leave."

"And then what happened when you said you'd take her away?" Paulson gave him a sad smile.

"But that was different." Davis felt strange talking so openly with his father. They'd never spoken to each other like this before. "Billy had just died and -"

"Do you think she would have left if Billy had lived?" Paulson interrupted him. "She said a lot of things. She could have left when you went to the academy, come with you for your training, and she didn't. She could have broken up with you at any point, and left on her own. And she didn't. And then when you wanted to leave, and had good prospects, she didn't leave. She stayed on, for years. Because she hadn't made the choice for herself yet."

She hadn't made the choice for herself yet. The words hit Davis hard. All those years that Grace had begged him to take her away. And yet every time they had a chance to go, she'd had an excuse, a reason not to go.

"Some people wrap themselves up in all the things that are wrong in their life," Paulson went on, gazing back out the window, "and then having to let go of that means no longer protecting that hurt part of themselves. I would know." He gave a short, bitter laugh. "I hated my old man. He was a bastard. Treated me like dirt. And what did I do? I did the same thing to my own son. And to my wife. Because it was easier to just do what I knew rather than try and fix myself."

Davis stared at his father in shock. "Dad, this is -"

"Not like me?" Paulson looked back at his son. "I'm too old to lie to myself anymore, son. I know I did you wrong. I know your mother deserved more. I could have done better, and I didn't." He leaned forward, his eyes lighting up hopefully. "But it's not too late for you, or for Grace. You're still young. And you can do better than we did. You can be different."

Davis shook his head. "I think it's too late for me and Grace, Dad."

"Well it certainly will be if you get in that truck tomorrow and drive away." Paulson snorted. "Alaska. Cold, dark. Lonely." He fixed his son with an earnest gaze. "Stay. Running away won't help."

"Dad -" He was tired of having this conversation with everyone.

"I know what you're gonna say, and I know why you're feeling what you're feeling. But what if -"

They were interrupted by the chirp and wail of a siren. They both listened as the familiar sound came closer then disappeared into the distance as the engine sped up the mountain road. "Storms rolled through last night," Paulson muttered, "must have started a fire somewhere." He looked back at his son and sighed. Davis could see his father's shoulders slump in defeat. "I can see I can't talk you out of this. But I want you to know - I just," he ran his hand over his head, "I just want you to be happy, son."

"I know, Dad," Davis didn't know what else to say. "But right now I just need space."

Paulson sighed again and nodded. "Come tonight for dinner, before you leave."

"Sure will, Dad. I just need to head down to the site office first to sign some paperwork."

Paulson turned and walked out of the apartment without saying another word. Davis stood alone in the apartment, surrounded by boxes, and with the creeping doubt setting in, letting him know he was perhaps making a big mistake.

Chapter Eight

Davis pulled up to the demountable site office, grateful that Craig's truck was nowhere to be seen. He had no desire for another showdown with his ex-boss, not today. Dark, grey clouds hung in the sky, and he could smell smoke.

Two of the workers were in the site office, one of them on the phone, and the looks on their faces as Davis walked in gave him cause for alarm. "Everything alright guys?" He asked tentatively.

They looked at each other, then back at Davis. "We can't get a hold of Craig." The man paused, and Davis waited for him to go on. "You see... Well, one of the feller bunchers shorted out yesterday. It had been on the fritz for a while but Craig just had one of the other guys rewire it."

Davis felt slight panic rise in his chest. Rewiring the equipment was a dangerous job, and equipment that was shorting out was a huge fire risk. "Why didn't Craig call a proper electrician?" He already knew the answer.

The other man shrugged. "It was going to take too long, and he didn't want to waste money. We all warned him. But you know he doesn't listen to us."

"He refused to hire another safety consultant after you left." The first man said, his voice strained with irritation. "It was all such bullshit."

"So what's happened now?" Davis asked.

"Craig told us to leave the feller where it was and move on to the next area," the first man replied, "but now one of the teams has reported smoke and they're really worried the feller has caught fire. Someone's out there investigating right now, but we can't reach Craig."

"Why didn't you call the fire department when you got the report of smoke?" Davis was incredulous.

The man looked at each other tentatively again. "We're just following orders." The other man said half-heartedly. "Craig didn't want anyone to know about the problems on the site. Any call for the fire department had to be cleared by him first."

"Right," Davis pointed at the first man, "you, call the fire department right now, and that's on my order."

"Yes, sir," the man was already dialling the number before Davis finished talking.

"You," Davis pointed at the other man, "you come with me and show me where this feller was left." He picked up two radios, throwing one to the man on the phone and tucking the other into the waist of his jeans. He turned and rushed out of the office, stopping at the shed outside to grab an axe, a chainsaw and a fire extinguisher. He threw them in the bed of his truck, then grabbed two gas masks as an afterthought. He climbed up into the driver seat, the site worker scrambling up into the passenger seat.

The man gave Davis directions up the side of the mountain to where the feller had been left, and Davis felt his throat tighten as the smell of smoke became heavier. Soon he had to close his window as a light veil of smoke became apparent between the towering trees.. *God dammit Craig*, he thought to himself, his teeth clenched. And then they saw it - flames licking at the tops of the trees beyond the next canyon.

"Oh fuck," the man gasped from the passenger seat. "That's miles from the feller."

"Which means we already have a huge fire on our hands." Davis replied, picking up the radio. "How are we going on the fire department?" He waited for a response.

"Fire department are on their way boss, over." Came the crackly response.

At that moment, Davis heard the sound of a chopper overhead, and he opened the car door to lean out. The smoke was becoming thicker as the wind shifted, and he hoped the fire was doubling back on itself and would burn itself out.

Within moments, the chopper roared past overhead, and Davis watched as it passed over the burn, dumping retardant on the rising flames. The smoke was still becoming thicker, and he closed his door, throwing the truck into reverse and turning around to head back down the pass road. If the wind was changing direction, he didn't want to get caught. They stopped a ways down the mountainside, and got out to watch as the helicopter passed over the burn again.

"I think they might have gotten it in time," the man said hopefully.

Davis nodded. "Yeah, thankfully."

"Craig isn't going to like this."

"Craig is probably about to wind up in jail." Davis countered, though he knew even as he said it that this wouldn't be the case. Rich men like Craig didn't go to prison. He'd pay a fine, sure. He might lose the logging contract. He might be forced to finally upgrade his equipment. But there would be no further consequences.

"Thankfully no one got hurt," the man continued.

"Yeah," Davis snorted cynically, "not this time." He looked down at his hands and saw his fists balled up, knuckles white. The urge to go out and do something was overwhelming. His body was primed to jump in. But that wasn't his job anymore, not here. He unfurled his fists and took a deep breath. The fire department had this under control, and there was no point sitting here and watching.

That evening his parents took Davis out to dinner at an Italian restaurant in Mammoth Lake, his mother claiming it was too hot to cook. As the sun hung low on the horizon, the temperature seemed to soar even higher with the promise of a steamy, sticky night ahead. The smell of smoke still lingered.

"I heard about the fire today," his Dad said as they waited for the appetisers to arrive.

Davis nodded, absently swirling the glass of wine in front of him around in languid circles. "It could have been a whole lot worse, thankfully the wind was in our favour."

Paulson snorted. "Your idiot ex boss is going to be run out of town on a rail."

"Good," Patricia said emphatically, downing her glass. "We have enough problems without that man setting the entire county on fire." She looked at Davis momentarily, as though she wanted to say something else, but at that moment the food arrived.

They made small talk as they ate, the light outside fading. Davis barely noticed the first fire engine speed past the restaurant. The second one he saw. The third made the entire restaurant stop and fall silent, as it flashed past the windows with the sirens blaring. Davis heard a beeper go off somewhere nearby, and one of the chefs ran out of the kitchen, throwing his apron aside as he bolted for the door and down the street. They were already calling on the volunteers.

"Oh no," Patricia had gone pale. Everyone knew what this meant. The patrons of the restaurant suddenly moved as one, and within seconds everyone had spilled out onto the sidewalk to see what was happening. "Oh god!" Patricia gasped.

The ridge was on fire. In the deepening night, the ridge glowed angry red, the plume of smoke an eruption of grey against the navy sky. Another fire engine raced past as they all stared up the mountain. Paulson turned to Davis. "We should get back right now." Davis nodded in agreement. A short time later they were flying up the mountain road, the glow to their left becoming brighter and brighter as they got closer to Clearwater.

The trees around them bent and shook as the wind picked up, and Davis heard his mother sniffle in the front seat. She was frightened. He reached forward and placed his large hand on her shoulder, which she gripped wordlessly. They all knew - this was very very bad.

It seemed the entire town had convened in the main street of Clearwater. An evacuation order was surely in place by now. Paulson pulled up outside the bar, where Davis immediately spotted Patrick with his daughter in his arms. Sarah was there with her husband and child, looking terrified. Joseph was giving directions in a loud voice, and people started to get into their cars.

Davis jumped out of the backseat of his parents' car and approached Patrick, who was strapping Kayley into her carseat. The little girl looked terrified as she clutched her pink teddy. "Patrick," Davis called out. Patrick turned and raised a hand briefly.

"We have to move, now."

"What's happened?" Davis asked.

"That fire down in the logging tract, the wind picked up and the embers started travelling." Patrick replied as he walked around to the driver's seat door. "Evacuation order is in place now, the wind isn't in our favour and the whole side of the mountain is on fire." He leaned over the roof of the car for a moment. "I gotta get my girl out of here. We're headed down to Mammoth Lake before the mountain road gets cut off. Let me know when you're safe, yeah?" Patrick gave him a weak smile and a nod, then got into the car, driving away in the long caravan of cars that was leaving town.

Davis jogged back to his parents' car, where Paulson had gotten out and was speaking to a few of his workmates. "Dad, you and Mom have to get out of here."

"Son -" Paulson began to protest, but stopped when Davis shook his head emphatically.

"Dad, I need to go and get my truck, then you and Mom have to go."

They screeched into his parents' driveway, and while Davis ran in to get his keys, his mother scurried into the lounge room. Davis knew what she was getting. She emerged with four photo albums and a jewellery box in her arms. The family treasures. The first thing she always packed up for fire season.

Back at the car, Davis leaned down to his father in the driver's seat. "Get down to Mammoth Lake with everyone else."

"Where are you going?" Paulson asked, without a hint of question in his voice. He knew where his son was headed.

"I have to help where I can."

Patricia was white as a sheet, but she nodded. "You take care, baby." Her voice cracked. "Let us know when you're safe."

Davis knocked on the roof of the car, and they drove off. He stood for a moment in the front yard, the smell of smoke oppressive in the air, and the distant roar of the fire carried on the wind.

It was happening again. He quashed the fear rising in his throat, and jumped into his truck, headed up towards the emergency response centre to help any way he could.

"Billy, talk to me."

Silence.

"Billy, you better talk to me. I know you're still there."

Silence.

"Billy. Billy! You better answer me."

Silence.

"Goddammit Billy."

"I'm here."

The crackling response came so suddenly Davis nearly dropped his radio. "I told you not to go to sleep. You better stay awake up there."

"It's so hot."

"They're almost here."

"No one's coming, Chev."

"Don't you give up now."

"Tell Grace I'm sorry."

"You tell her yourself. You stay awake, you hear me?"

"I'm glad you two will have each other."

"Billy, you're going to be fine. They're almost here."

Davis heard Tyler roaring into his radio, asking where the water plane was.

"Davis, look after her."

"Stop it."

"It's so hot."

"You stay awake!"

He looked over at Tyler, who merely shook his head.

"Billy?"

Silence.

"Billy?"

Silence.

"Billy answer me!"

Silence.

Two engines thundered past him as he approached the emergency response centre. It was too dark for the choppers to head out, but there was no way the ground crews would be able to do more than attempt to contain the fire. It had gotten too large. Davis gripped the steering wheel tighter as he navigated up the hill. The smell of smoke had become almost overwhelming.

He parked up besides the centre, and his phone beeped. A message from his mother popped up, letting him know the road to Mammoth Lake had been cut off and everyone was being diverted back past Clearwater and down to Devil's Hollow. He wrote back quickly that he loved her, then jumped down out of his truck, grabbing his heavy boots from the backseat, and hurried into the centre. He didn't know if he could do much good, but he was going to try.

Inside, Joseph and a few cadets were standing over a map, Joseph giving orders into his radio. Joseph looked up as Davis walked in, and gave him a curt nod. "Good to see you," he said.

"I wanted to see if I could help at all," Davis responded.

Joseph nodded and turned to one of the cadets. "Get a kit ready for this man." The cadet rushed off, and Joseph turned back to Davis. "It's bad."

"I know, sir. The road down the mountain has been cut off."

“Yes it has. We have to divert folks back to Devil’s Hollow.” Joseph rubbed his forehead. “Mammoth Lake have engines fighting on the other side to try and stop the front moving down that hill, but…” He trailed off. Davis had never seen Joseph like this before.

“Sir?” He asked after a few moments, surprised when Joseph looked at him with despair in his eyes.

“They’re getting worse, Chevalier. So much worse.” He shook his head and took a deep breath, gathering himself and straightening his shoulders. “Right,” he looked back at Davis, the staunch determination back. “I need you to take those cadets and prep engine four, we have volunteer crews headed in and I need an experienced hand to supervise them.”

“Yes sir.” Davis headed to the locker room where the cadet had placed his kit. He stopped short for a second - the cadet couldn’t have known. It was just a coincidence. But his kit was laid out in front of locker 14. The one they'd left empty, out of respect.

Billy’s locker.

Davis pushed away the flicker of foreboding in his chest and got changed into the blue shirt and thick cotton trousers, pulling his boots on. The cadet rushed past him with overalls and a jacket as Davis entered the engine room. The other cadets were already winding up the hoses, one checking the pressure gauges.

The siren blipped and wailed for a moment overhead. “Crew advise, Jolie and Devil’s Hollow are cut off. Crew advise, Jolie and Devil’s Hollow are cut off. Evacuees are being redirected back into Clearwater township.”

One of the cadets swore under his breath, and Davis felt his lungs tighten up. This was getting bad fast. "They're sitting ducks now." One of the others said, and Davis saw the fear on his face. These guys were young, and they were scared. They all had families down there.

Joseph entered the engine room with three volunteers behind him. "Chevalier, I want you to head down into town and manage the evacuees."

Davis nodded, directing the cadets into the engine, and heading out to follow behind in his truck. The glow from the fire dominated the skyline now, and the wind had picked up. Thunder rumbled - or was it the roar from the fire? It was hard to tell.

They arrived down in town, pulling up in front of the town hall. Davis spotted his parents' car as they drove down the side street, the engine pulling up by the playground on the basketball court. Davis parked up behind them. The town hall was crowded, and people were milling about the front on the lawn, people sitting atop their cars. Despite the number of people, it was quiet. No one was panicking. They'd done this before. They knew panic was futile at this point.

Thunder rumbled overhead again. "Is that - is that from the fire?" One of the volunteers, a boy of maybe 17, asked Davis. They both looked up the ridge, which glowed bright orange.

"It could be," Davis replied. "And if it is…" He trailed off. Both of them knew what that meant. If the fire was now large enough to cause a thunderstorm, it had broken lines and was out of control.

His hands were still black. He couldn't wash the soot off. The soot from his hair had clogged the drain. He stood staring at himself in the mirror. He was pale, the bags under his eyes were dark purple.

Suddenly there was a knock at the door. "Honey," his mother's voice came softly, "Grace is here."

He couldn't face her. But he had to.

He'd been there when Joseph had told her that Billy was gone. Grace had howled, fallen to the floor, clasped onto his arms, screaming. He had both their screams in his head now, preventing him from sleeping. And when he did finally sleep, he heard them in his nightmares too.

Now they had to go and see Billy's body. He didn't want to. He didn't want to know what was left of it. He didn't want to see the burns and the charred skin, and the smell... He lurched to the toilet and threw up.

"Honey?" Came his mother's voice again, tight with worry. "Honey, are you OK?"

He coughed and spluttered, wiping his mouth with a towel, sitting on the cold floor, trying to pull himself together. "I'll be right there." He replied, his voice raspy. The smoke, the damn smoke.

Grace was standing in the kitchen, looking tiny in a big black sweater, her red hair pulled back from her face. She looked like a child, small and scared. She threw her arms around Davis's neck, and he could feel she was shaking. "I don't want to go," she whispered. "I'm scared."

"I know, baby." He replied, holding her close. "I know. But I'm here."

Patricia picked up the car keys. "Come on, I'll drive you." She held out a hand, directing them outside. "Neither of you is in a state to drive."

They sat in the back together, Grace almost wrapped around him, still shaking. "I feel cold," she whispered. Davis put his arms around her, trying to warm her up.

The drive to Mammoth Lake went by far too quickly. He wasn't ready for this. He couldn't do it. He couldn't watch Grace do it. He felt sick again. Pull yourself together, *he scolded himself. He had to be there for her.*

They were ushered into a small room to wait, and after a few minutes the medical examiner called them in, a look of sympathy and compassion on his face. Grace walked ahead, Davis right behind her with a hand on her waist, letting her know he was there.

There was the gurney. There was the heavy sheet covering what was left of Billy. And there was the smell. Burnt flesh. Smoke. Davis took a deep breath through his mouth, trying to steady himself.

The medical examiner said something to Grace, but the humming in Davis's ears was so loud he didn't hear what he'd said. Grace nodded, and the sheet was pulled back.

She screamed. She fell back against Davis. He held her up, not wanting to look, but seeing the side of Billy's head. The dark curls were gone. There was just red, black, burnt. She turned and tried to put her arms around his neck, but she simply collapsed against him, screaming sobs tearing through her as she shouted her brother's name over and over again.

Billy.

Billy.

Billy.

"Davis?" Patrick's voice snapped him back to reality. He stood before him, the tiny figure of his sleeping daughter on his shoulder, and Davis could see how scared his friend was. "I thought you'd left?"

"Fire had other plans I guess." He could at least attempt joviality. They both knew how bad this could get.

Patrick gave him a weak smile. "Well I'm glad you're here." The little girl in his arms stirred, and he made soothing sounds, rubbing her back. "She'll only sleep in my arms."

"She knows she's safe with you," Davis replied. "Go and sit down with her somewhere, try and rest." They both knew no rest would be had, but Patrick nodded and headed into the town hall with his daughter.

Thunder rumbled loudly overhead, and lightning flashed above the glowing ridge. A few people in the crowd exclaimed, and a small child began to wail. The wind had picked up. Embers would start to fly in their direction before long.

"Ok Everyone!" Davis called loudly, standing on the short wooden fence in front of the town hall. "I need everyone to take shelter inside or in their cars right now, no one outside! We need everyone safe!" The crowd followed his instructions quickly. He turned to the cadets. "We need to get this engine ready to spray down spot fires, that wind is picking up and it's going to carry embers down the mountain."

The cadets quickly set about steadying the engine and connecting the hoses and the hydrant. They gave the town hall a precautionary hose down, and then they sat and waited.

Suddenly, a small red car came careening down the side street, coming to a screeching halt. Davis's heart leaped as Grace stumbled out of the car and ran towards him. "I can't find my Dad!" She screamed to no one in particular. Two of the cadets approached her along with Davis. "He's not answering his cell!"

Davis saw his parents emerge from the Town Hall, coming to see what the commotion was about. Patricia ran over to Grace, who was sobbing loudly now.

"Honey, what's going on?" Patricia asked as Grace continued to wail.

"Where would he have gone?" One of the cadets asked her. "Maybe he's inside?"

"Who?" Paulson asked.

"My father," Grace gasped.

Paulson shook his head. "He's not inside.

Grace shook her head adamantly, and grabbed on to Patricia's arms, her eyes wild. "He went down to the cabin this morning."

Patricia gave Davis an alarmed look. The cabin. The cabin down by the lake. "He'd not still be down there." Davis reasoned.

"He's not back. He's not at home. No one's seen him. And there's no cell reception down there." Grace sobbed against Patricia's shoulder.

Shit. Davis knew the way to the cabin. It was a tight, winding road, not easily accessible. "Grace, if he's down there -"

"The mountain roads are all cut off," one of the cadets said. "No one can get down to the lake anymore."

Grace began to wail again. The sound made Davis's blood run cold. He set his jaw and went to the cab of the engine. He grabbed two fire blankets, remembering he still had the gas masks and the fire extinguisher from the work site in the back of his truck.

He turned to the older cadet by the engine. "You're in charge," he informed him. "You keep an eye on those trees and the embers. Hose down anything that catches. You know what to do. Keep these people safe."

"Yes sir," the young man replied.

"You're not going to go down there are you?" Paulson grabbed his son's arm. Over his father's shoulder Davis could see his mother staring at him, mouth agape, tears streaming down her face. "Davis, look at me." Paulson's voice was low, measured. "Son, I know what this means to you, but -"

"I have to go down there Dad."

"You can't, this is crazy."

"The brush over there isn't too dense, the fire is on the mountain, not down in the valley," Davis assured him. "I know the way down there better than anyone, besides maybe Bob."

"He might not even be down there anymore!"

"We both know he's down there, probably passed out drunk and no idea what's happening." Davis threw the fire blankets into the back of the cab.

"Davis, please -"

"I'm going." Davis interrupted, meeting his father's gaze.

"This is madness," Paulson responded, his voice strained with desperation. "Son, I cannot let you go down there. Not for Bob Weaver."

"Dad, I am not letting anyone die on my watch again."

"For God's sakes Davis, this has to stop!" Paulson exclaimed, slamming his hands onto his son's shoulders and shaking him, his voice desperate. "You don't have to die to redeem yourself! This is not what Billy would have wanted! This is not what Grace wants! And I am not letting my boy go down there to die for a man like Bob Weaver. I am not losing you!" His voice broke on the last word, and Davis saw tears forming in his father's eyes.

Davis wrapped his father in a hug. He'd never done this before. "Dad, I need to go get him." He pulled back, and looked into his father's face. "This is what I do. Now look after Mom and Grace, and I'll be back before you know it."

Paulson took a deep breath, defeated, and nodded. "You stay safe."

Patricia and Grace were both crying now, Patricia shaking her head over and over again. "No, Davis, you can't."

Davis put his arms around both of them. "I'll be right back." He looked down at Grace, her face pale and tear-stained. He gave her a smile, then took off towards his truck. The time for talking was done. As he gunned the engine, he knew what he was doing was dangerous - foolish, even. But he couldn't let Grace down.

He had to get Bob out of danger.

The fire was no longer glowing orange but pulsing red on the horizon as he took the turn-off before the national park down the mountain. The entire side of the canyon was on fire, and no doubt most of the valley. It hadn't yet reached the road.

The road was not really a road, hardly more than a wide biking track, and his truck barely fit down it. The road was bumpier than he remembered it, the rain having washed away much of it over the years. He pushed on. The trees were bending in the wind that was blowing, and he knew he didn't have much time before it carried embers, and the fire, down the mountainside towards him.

The lake came into view below him, matt and black as it reflected the smoke spreading overhead. The shore on the opposite side was on fire. Lightning whipped and cracked in the clouds above the hellish glow. The fire was getting bigger by the second.

The road levelled out as it came parallel to the shore, weaving along the tree line. He rounded a curve, and he could see the cabin up ahead, an indistinct dark lump illuminated by a single dim lamp on the porch. Bob's white truck was parked next to it. He was still down here. *Stupid old fool,* Davis cursed him. Bob Weaver didn't listen to anybody, no matter what it meant. Davis only hoped that right now, Bob would listen to him.

He pulled up beside Bob's truck, jumping down from the cab and calling out to him. The air was heavy and smoky, and his words seemed to be swallowed up by it. Everything was loud and oppressively silent, all at the same time. He ran up onto the porch and banged on the door. "Bob! Bob we gotta get out of here!"

No answer.

He pushed the door open - it always stuck on the frame - and looked inside. The cabin only had one room with a small kitchenette in the corner. In the dim light cast through the windows from the porch, Davis could make out a sofa and a mattress on the floor. But Bob was nowhere to be seen.

He ran back down the porch steps, headed to the small jetty that ran out over the water into the lake, where Bob fished from. It was empty but for an open tackle box and a net beside it. *Where are you old man?* Davis began to wonder if Bob had, in a drunken stupor, decided to walk out instead of risking driving. He could be anywhere in the woods.

The hairs on the back of his neck stood up, and he intuitively headed to Bob's truck. Maybe, just maybe...

Sure enough, there he was. Bob was lying on the bench seat in his truck, mouth agape, drooling onto the worn leather seat. Davis yanked open the truck door. "Bob, Bob, you gotta wake up, we have to get you out of here." Davis shook Bob's shoulder, trying to rouse the wiry old man from his sleep.

Bob swatted at him but did not wake. He tried to roll over but failed as the bench seat was not wide enough to accommodate such a movement. Davis began pulling him from the cab. The fire on the opposite shore had spread, and was heading for them. "Bob, I swear to god, if I die down here because of you -"

"What're you doing?" Bob was suddenly awake as Davis pulled him from the cab. "Let go of me dammit!" He swung his arms behind him and hit Davis weakly in the chest. He stank of whiskey.

"There's a fire you old fool!" Davis exclaimed, pointing at the shore. "See? You're about to get burned up, and burned up fast by the smell of you."

Bob pushed him away as his feet touched the ground, swaying in a non-existent breeze and gripping on to the side of his truck. "I'm not afraid of a fire!" He yelled. "I'm not afraid of anything, and I sure as hell aren't going anywhere with you!"

Davis towered over the man, who cowered a little despite himself. "Your daughter is waiting for you, and I am not letting her lose anyone else. Do you understand me? Now get in the goddamn truck. We're going."

At the mention of Grace, Bob seemed to sober up a little, and stumbled after Davis to the yellow truck. "I was about to drive myself out of here when you showed up!" The man slurred as he climbed up into the passenger seat. "I don't even know why you're here."

"Because your daughter is in a panic and looking for you," Davis hit back, gunning the engine and throwing the truck into reverse. He saw the fire explode over the tree line on the opposite shore as he looked back, sending a glowing rain of embers across the lake. "Now, we have to move and we have to move fast."

The truck thundered up the path, and Davis was aware of a growing glow above them. He leaned forward, glancing up through the windshield, and saw tiny fires erupting in the tops of the trees. The wind was howling audibly, and the fire swung gracefully from one treetop to the next. It was right on top of them. Davis put the pedal to the floor, and the truck shot forward over the bumpy surface, throwing Bob around in his seat.

"Take it easy you asshole!" Bob scolded loudly.

"Shut up!" Davis replied, not taking his eyes off the road. "If you don't want to die tonight just shut up and let me drive."

"I don't care about dying!" Bob replied. "I'm not afraid of anything. After all I've been through -"

"SHUT UP." Davis's teeth were gritted.

But Bob wouldn't be stopped now. "I lost my sweet wife, my Nancy, and then my only son, and you want to talk to me about *fear*?" He drew out the last word, and a bitter, scornful laugh escaped his lips. "I've been through about the worst any man can go through. You wouldn't have a clue!"

"Bob, you really need to stop talking right now."

Bob cackled, and was about to start again, when Davis rounded the corner. Both men stopped. Davis felt the air leave his lungs.

The entire forest was on fire. Trees had come down onto the trail, flames leaping high. The wind howled and the fire roared. Out of nothing more than instinct, he threw the truck into reverse as the huge tree above them came crashing down, narrowly missing the hood. Bob screamed and swore in garbled panic, grabbing onto the door of the truck. Davis kept backing up, feeling as though he was barely outrunning the fire as it shot along the trunks and branches besides the trail.

"Hurry up you idiot!" Bob yelled.

"I told you to shut up!"

With a sudden jerk they hit the guardrail at the corner of the trail, and Davis swung the truck around to head back along the path to the cabin. They came to a halt, and Bob swung like a deranged monkey from the truck door, his feet barely finding the ground before he began to run for the cabin, but Davis called out to him. "Not in there! That's a tinder box!" He pointed to the jetty.

The two men sat down on the jetty's edge, watching the fire explode around them. Davis imagined this is what the depths of Hell would look like, if Hell were a real place. It felt surreal to be sitting in the middle of it, desperately hoping that this wasn't the end.

"What do we do now?" Bob asked, hiccuping pathetically.

Davis shrugged. "We wait. We hope the fire burns out, and we wait."

"We're trapped."

"Yes, yes we are."

Bob sneered at him. "I can't believe I'm stuck down here with you." When Davis didn't respond, he snorted. "I know everyone believes your little story about Billy. I don't." He leaned forward. "I know the truth."

"You know nothing." Davis didn't look at him.

"I know my son was a hero."

"Then you'd know your son would defy an order to save someone's life."

Bob spluttered. "I - I know my son would have -"

"Which is it Bob?" Davis asked, exasperated. "Either your son was a self-sacrificing hero who would go to any lengths to save people, or he was a lap dog. Which is it? Because you can never seem to make up your fucking mind." Bob stared at him agape, so Davis went on. "Billy *was* a hero, he *was* selfless. But he was also brash. He disobeyed a direct order because he thought there were still people in a house we knew to be empty. You made him that way, Bob. He was so desperate to please and to serve that it didn't matter what anyone else said."

"I loved my son -"

"Bullshit, you love the bottle and that's it," Davis hit back. "Men who love their children don't burn them with cigarettes. They don't beat them black and blue with a fucking baseball bat."

"I had to raise those kids on my own, you wouldn't have a clue how hard it is to be a father raising his kids on his own!"

"Oh, that's your excuse now?" Davis laughed bitterly. "You chose to abuse your kids. You chose to hit them, to hurt them. Now shut up before I drown you in this goddamn lake, old man."

Bob went quiet, and Davis looked out at the fire around them. The smell of smoke was oppressive. The lake was unnaturally still. It felt like the fire had sucked all the air out of the valley, and they were suspended in a supernatural vacuum.

"Why did you come down to get me?" Bob asked after a while. "You hate me."

"Grace loves you, and I love Grace." Davis replied simply.

"Grace is too needy and soft-hearted, just like her mother," Bob scoffed.

"You're the only father she's got and she loves you." Davis replied. "She really drew the short straw with you."

"At least I never left her alone."

Davis clenched his fists. "There's worse things than being left alone."

"She cried every night after you left." Bob said. "It drove me insane. The endless sobbing and weeping and carrying on. I couldn't stand it. I told her to follow you if it meant I finally got some peace from her goddamn theatrics. So she began to pack her things, bought a plane ticket."

Davis felt his chest tighten. *She was coming after me?*

"I knew it was serious then," Bob went on, lost in memory. "When I saw that plane ticket. And you know, I thought to myself, there's nothing worse than being alone. Nancy had left me, Billy had left me. Grace was all I had left. So, I had to make sure she'd stay."

"What did you do?"

Bob grinned maliciously, staring out at the lake, almost as though he'd forgotten Davis was there. "I took a little trip down the stairs, broke my hip. But it was worth it." He giggled to himself. "She was so worried and concerned. I was in the hospital for two weeks. And when I got out, she cared for me, just like her mother would have. And she missed that flight. The suitcases went back into the basement. And I knew I'd won. Or at least I thought I had." He rubbed his chin, musing to himself.

"Why? What happened?" Davis almost choked on the words.

"Just before that Hal fella showed up, she packed those bags again." Bob spluttered again and coughed, spitting into the lake. "She'd been to see your Mom, the soft-brained fool. Must have talked her into seeing you. She cried and cried, and then those damn bags were packed. She even packed her Mom's jewellery. I was going to lose her for good. And, well, that couldn't happen."

Davis could barely contain his rage. "What did you do then?"

"Well, I could always use another new hip," Bob laughed maniacally. "Silly old man like me, I lost my footing on those stairs again."

"You threw yourself down a full flight of stairs, twice, to keep your daughter away from me?" Davis asked incredulously. "You would hurt yourself just to stop her being happy?"

Bob seemed to remember who he was talking to, and turned on Davis. "She would have never been happy with *you*," he spat, his words dripping poison. "I used to think you were a real man, someone to show Billy what he could be. But I was wrong about you. You think being the high school quarterback makes you special? You're a dimwitted fool, a pretty boy with no brain and no substance. You parade around town in your fag shirts, pretending to be the big hero when you're just a fucking pussy!"

Davis burst out laughing. The insanity of the situation was clearly getting to him. "You're a sad, pathetic individual, Bob." He shook his head. "You're throwing yourself down stairwells to trap your child into a life of serving you, drinking yourself into a stupor every hour of the day, and you think you're better than the rest of us."

Bob blinked stupidly, and hiccuped again. Davis couldn't think of anything more pitiful than the drunk old man sitting before him. He gazed out at the fire.

As though a jolt of electricity had hit him, Bob suddenly sprung into action. "I'm not dying down here with you, you fucking asshole!" He ran and stumbled down the jetty and back to truck. Davis sprang to his feet, calling after him, but Bob didn't stop. He sprinted like one possessed, jumping into the cab of his white pickup and slamming the door shut.

"Bob you idiot, you're going to get yourself killed!" Davis called, knowing Bob couldn't hear him. He knew he should run after him, but he was suddenly paralysed. He couldn't will his legs to move. *She was coming after me.* The thought made his breath catch in his throat. *She was coming after me, and this sadistic fuck maimed himself to keep us apart.* Bob's depravity truly knew no bounds.

Davis watched as Bob began to reverse his truck, almost ending up in the sand on the beach. The old man haphazardly manoeuvred up onto the track, revved the engine and stalled. The truck shook as the engine died. Bob got out of the car, gave the tyre a jerky kick which almost sent him toppling over, then began to run.

"Bob, you fool!" Davis broke into a sprint as the old man headed for the flames. "You're going to die you fucking lunatic!" For an old, drunk man with two prosthetic hips, Bob moved fast. Davis coughed as the smoke filled his lungs, the fire now moving steadily down the track towards the cabin. "Bob! Bob, stop!" He'd almost caught up to him. "Bob!" The old man didn't slow down. Davis reached out and grabbed his shirt, the sudden backward jerk eliciting a garbled yelp from Bob's mouth, and they both toppled backwards.

Suddenly Bob was on top of him, his fists hailing down on Davis's face. "*You fucker*!" He screamed. *"You fucking fucker! You stole her from me! You stole the only person who loved me! Fuck you! Fuck you!"*

Davis shielded his face and bucked Bob off his chest. He landed on the ground with a thud and immediately rushed at Davis again. "Bob, enough!" Davis grabbed Bob's wrists. "We need to get to safety! You're going to get us both killed!"

"I want you to fucking die!"

Davis put both feet against Bob's chest and pushed him away, hard. The man flew through the air for a second, then landed flat on his back. Davis scrambled to his feet, ready to grab Bob in a headlock and drag him back to the jetty.

At that moment, the tree above them gave way. Davis sprang backwards, not fast enough to avoid a dead branch that smashed against his leg. He gritted his teeth as he dragged himself away, looking down and seeing blood soaking through the leg of his pants. *Fuck, fuck, fuck. Don't be broken. Don't be broken.* He attempted to wiggle his toes and cried out as hot searing pain shot through his shin. *Fuck, fuck, fuck.*

Then Bob started screaming.

Davis struggled to his feet, leaning on a stump. The fallen tree was burning, flames leaping into the air. Bob continued to scream. Davis limped forward, moving around the fire, trying to follow the sound of Bob's voice. "Bob, where are you?"

Bob's strangled screams continued. Davis circled around, suddenly seeing flailing white hair. Bob was caught under the end of the tree, flames beginning to creep up his clothing. "It's burning me!" He called, frantically swatting at his pants, sending flames travelling up his shirt.

Davis lurched forward, the pain in his leg almost overwhelming him with nausea. He had to get Bob out. He grabbed Bob's shoulders, the flames on Bob's shirt lapping up his own arms. He didn't even feel them, the pain in his leg was too intense.

Bob continued to scream as Davis kept dragging him to the shore of the lake, not stopping until he pulled the man into the water and the flames went out with a sickening hiss. Bob instantly fell silent.

The two men lay in the water as the fire raged around them. Davis raised his hand, and saw the skin on his arms was red raw. He looked over at Bob. The man wasn't moving.

"Bob?" Davis could barely get the words out. The smoke was too thick. His head began swimming.

You stay awake, you hear me?

Who was that? It sounded like Billy.

You stay awake. Don't you go to sleep on me, Chev.

Davis raised his head. The entire shore was on fire, all around them. He looked back towards the cabin, which was engulfed in flames now. "Billy?" He didn't recognise his own voice. It was small and hoarse. The smoke... The damn smoke....

Stay awake, Chev. Grace needs you.

The pain in his leg and his arms was so strong. He felt darkness pulling at the edges of his vision. He looked over at Bob again, reaching out. The man didn't move. "Bob, don't die. Bob, stay awake." He tried to shake him. There was no response.

Davis began to cough. So this is where he would die. He closed his eyes and Grace's face swam before him. "I'm sorry Grace." He whispered. He felt his lungs tightening. The water around him was cool and still. He felt a last breath leave his body, and thunder rumbled above.

Then there was nothing.

Chapter Nine

Beep. Beep. Beep.

Make that fucking beeping stop.

Beep. Beep. Beep.

What the fuck is that?

There was a cold, unpleasant rush of air in his nose, and his eyes flickered open.

Beep. Beep. Beep.

His mother was there. Why was she here? Where was here? She was asleep.

Beep. Beep. Beep.

Make that fucking beeping stop.

His arms hurt. His legs hurt. His chest hurt.

Beep. Beep. Beep.

What had happened?

Beep. Beep. Beep.

There was a tube in his nose. More cold air. He tried to flex his hands. They were wrapped in something. The movement hurt.

Beep. Beep. Beep.

His legs felt strange, like the didn't belong to him. He tried to wiggle his toes and winced as pain shot through his right leg. It felt heavy. What was wrong with it?

Beep. Beep. Beep.

His mother. She was there. Asleep. He tried to open his mouth to say something, but his tongue was dry. His throat felt like he had swallowed shattered glass.

His mother woke up. She saw his eyes were open. She rushed to his side. "Oh Davis!" She burst into tears. "Nurse!" She called, pressing the call button beside him. "Nurse! He's awake."

He tried to tell his mother to calm down, he didn't need a nurse. But his throat was tight. He couldn't get words out. He tried to squeeze her hand. "Mom," he rasped.

"I'm here, honey," she stroked his forehead, smiling, tears running down her face. "I'm here, oh my baby. I was so scared."

"Grace." He rasped. "Grace."

A young nurse with her hair pulled back in a ponytail came in. "Oh he's awake!" She exclaimed, smiling. She approached Davis's bedside. "Davis, can you hear me?" She asked. Davis tried to nod, but it hurt. She saw his attempts at movement. "OK, good. Do you remember what happened?"

Beep. Beep. Beep.

"N - no." Something about Bob.

"You were found down in King's Lake. You were very very lucky." The nurse turned to his mother. "I'll call for the doctor." She hurried out of the room.

Patricia leaned over him, gently stroking his forehead. She was crying. She looked pale and hollow. "Oh my baby boy." She sobbed quietly. "I thought we'd lost you."

A fire. Yes. There was a fire. And Grace was scared. Why was Grace scared?

"Grace?" Talking was agony.

"She's OK honey, we're all OK." Patricia assured him. "The fire didn't reach the town."

Bob.

"Her Dad...?" Davis looked at his mother.

Patricia shook her head. "You were so brave honey."

I went to rescue Bob.

"He... He died?" Suddenly he remembered. The trees and the flames. Pulling Bob's body to the water.

Patricia nodded. "He was dead when they found you both."

"The... the tree." Davis told her. "The tree landed on him."

"I know honey. There was nothing you could have done."

He felt a wave of grief he didn't expect. First Billy, now Bob. He'd tried so hard to save this family, to protect them, and he'd failed. He looked down at his body and saw both arms wrapped up, and a cast on his right leg.

"What happened to me?" He asked.

Patricia swallowed hard, and bit back tears. "Your right leg is broken, and your kneecap is shattered." She took a deep breath. "Both your arms got burnt very badly. They... They said..." She trailed off as sobs closed her throat.

At that moment the doctor came in. "Glad to see you awake, Davis. How are you feeling?"

Davis tried to shrug, but his shoulders refused to budge. "Like I was pulled out of a fire." He said flatly, and the doctor laughed.

"Good to see your sense of humour is still in tact." He took a light and shone it in Davis's eyes. "Excellent. Now, you inhaled a lot of smoke. Your chest probably feels like an anvil is on it." Davis nodded slightly, and the doctor continued on. "You were in bad shape. Your leg had a compound fracture and we needed to give you a new knee. With some physiotherapy, you should be back on track."

"And my arms?"

The doctor hesitated. "The burns are quite severe. We did what we could, but with the skin grafts you are looking at limited movement and significant loss in muscle mass. And there will be extensive scarring."

Patricia sniffled beside him.

"Will - will I be able to work?" Davis asked.

The doctor shook his head. "Your firefighting days are over, I'm afraid. With therapy you will be able to do desk work." He gave Davis a sympathetic look. "I'm truly sorry."

Davis closed his eyes, suddenly feeling incredibly tired. After a few moments, he heard the doctor speaking again. "I think we'll let him rest, this is a lot to take in." Davis didn't listen to anything else the doctor and his mother discussed. He lay there trying to move his hands, and being alarmed at how tight they felt, like they were bound with duct tape. This couldn't be it. This couldn't be how it ended.

After the doctor left, he opened his eyes and looked at his mother, who immediately sat back down next to him. "Can I get you anything honey?"

"How long was I out for?"

"A week, sweetheart. It's been a week."

Only a week. A whole week. So long and yet not long at all. "Has Grace been here?"

Patricia gave him a pained look and shook her head. "I don't think she can face it, sweetheart."

"Can you call her?"

Patricia got up. "Of course, honey. I'll be right back."

As his mother went out into the hall to make the call, Davis stared at the ceiling. Bob was dead. He was severely injured. He'd never be a firefighter again. It had all been for nothing.

Patricia re-entered the room to find her son asleep again, and was thankful she didn't need to explain to him that Grace had not answered her calls, and probably never would.

How he'd missed hot showers. The dressings had finally come off, and at first the skin had been so sensitive that anything hotter than tepid had sent a jolt of nausea into his stomach. But now, after a couple of weeks, he could finally manage a hot shower, and it felt amazing.

Three months had passed. The cast on Davis's leg was off, the pins removed. His new knee no longer felt tight and stiff and strange, and he was managing to walk again. Being able to stand had been an achievement in itself, and he'd been very nervous as he tentatively tried out the prosthetic joint. But recovery had been surprisingly fast. He'd lost weight, mostly muscle, which he was very unhappy about, but it felt good to be mobile again.

He looked down at his arms. At first the scars had horrified him. Angry, red and thick, they roped around his forearms like tentacles. The milky patches of skin graft looked alien at first. Now he'd spent some time in the sun they were no longer strange and white. The scars were still there, but his mother slathered them in rosehip oil every day, assuring him it would help.

He raised his arms to wash his hair, and winced. This still hurt. Lifting and bending his arms, and making a fist, those were things he still had to work on. He could lift a kettle bell, but as soon as it had to go higher than his chest, the skin caught and tugged, like it was too small for his bones. The doctors had assured him he would be able to return to the gym and doing weights before too long.

The smell of cooking met him as he walked out of his bedroom. Thunder rumbled outside. He walked into the kitchen to see his mother standing by the stove, his father behind her, Paulson's arms around Patricia's waist. She was stirring something on the stove, and they were both humming along to a song on the radio, swaying together. It was an unusual sight, but it made him smile.

Since the fire, his father had been a different man. He'd finally retired. He insisted on taking Davis to all his physiotherapy appointments. He'd bought equipment recommended by the physiotherapist to help Davis at home. He had Davis up every morning to do his exercises. He was attentive and caring in a way Davis had not expected.

"I'm not interrupting am I?" Davis asked as he took a seat at the table.

His parents turned and grinned at him. "This is the song we danced to at our wedding." Patricia said, gazing lovingly at Paulson.

"Best day of my life," Paulson said, stroking his wife's cheek. "Couldn't believe my luck, the prettiest girl in California wanted me."

Patricia blushed. "Oh you old fool." She gave Paulson a kiss.

"Hey, not in front of the kids!" Davis exclaimed, laughing.

Paulson chuckled and got a beer out of the fridge for himself and his son. "Can't believe we've been married 30 years."

"It's your anniversary?" Davis asked. He knew his parents had gotten married only a few weeks before his birthday, which was now coming up, but since they'd never celebrated their anniversary he'd never been sure of the date.

Patricia nodded. "Yes it is." She smiled dreamily. "My only regret is not being able to wear the dress I wanted because of my big old belly." She giggled and ran a hand over Davis's head. "Oh well, it was worth it."

"And quite the scandal." Paulson chuckled into his beer bottle.

"Well, happy anniversary." Davis said, clinking bottles with his father in a toast, and feeling a deep sense of contentment for his parents that he couldn't recall ever feeling before.

"How was physiotherapy today honey?" Patricia asked as she went back to her cooking.

"He's getting real strong real fast." Paulson answered for his son. "He'll be back to his old self in no time."

"Well, maybe a little longer than no time," Davis tried to sound light-hearted. "Getting back to being my old self is going to be -"

"You'll be fine," Paulson interrupted. "It's only been a month. You'll see. You won't know yourself come new year."

Davis detected something under his father's voice - a flicker of fear perhaps?

There was a knock on the front door, and suddenly Tyler was standing in their kitchen. "Hey everyone, sorry, your door was open."

"Oh not at all, Tyler, you're always welcome!" Patricia exclaimed, giving him a big hug. "Can I get you a beer?"

"Sure, Mrs C, that'd be great."

Patricia handed a bottle of beer from the fridge over to Tyler, and went back to her cooking. "Dinner won't be too long!" She announced as Paulson began to set the table for them.

Davis caught Tyler's eye and nodded towards the front door, and they went out onto the porch together.

"Needing to get away?" Tyler asked as they each took a seat on the loungers.

"It's their anniversary so they're like newlyweds."

Tyler laughed. "So, everything going OK?"

Davis considered his bottle of beer. "She still hasn't been by."

Tyler sighed. "She feels guilty, man."

Davis leaned forward, arms on his knees, and winced as pain shot through his leg. He leaned back in the lounger and regarded his friend earnestly. "I know I told you I wasn't ready to hear what happened. Well, I'm ready now."

Tyler took a long swig and sucked on his teeth. "There's really not a whole lot to tell." He rolled the bottle between his hands, and frowned. "But it was rough."

"I'm sorry it was you." Davis said apologetically.

"Part of the job."

"And I'm still sorry I put you through it."

"Chev, you're addicted to guilt." Tyler snapped. "I was doing my job. It wasn't easy to see you like that, it wasn't easy to pull Bob out of that water, the whole thing sucked. But I don't want you apologising to me for it." He took a deep breath, seeming to steady himself. "Sorry. I didn't mean to -"

"It's ok," Davis interrupted. "I've been where you are. And you're right."

Tyler looked up at the sky as lightning flashed. After a few moments, he began to talk. "When you didn't come back, Grace lost it. She was sure you'd died. Joseph sent the water planes out early, before sun up. They doused the valley. Most of it was burnt out already. We took the command vehicle down to find you. Took hours to cut through all those trees. I was sure I'd be coming down to find a dead body." He stood up and walked over to the railing, leaning against it with his back to Davis. "We finally got through, and got down to the lake. You and Bob were black, burned up, covered in soot and blood. Bob was starting to drift into the lake. He was dead. I could see it from up the shore."

"I think he was dead before I got him into the water." Davis said ruefully.

"Probably." Tyler agreed. "Medical examiner said his internal organs were basically mush. The tree falling on him most likely killed him." Tyler turned back to Davis, but didn't look at him. "We hauled you up and out of there. Grace was waiting up at the top of the trail with Joseph. She saw you and fainted. Just, bang, hit the deck."

Davis closed his eyes, and gritted his teeth. Poor Grace.

"She was sure you were dead," Tyler went on. "You were rushed off to the hospital. Grace came to, wouldn't talk to anyone. Your Mom called the next day and told us that you'd been in surgery. I tried to tell Grace, but..." He trailed off, and his eyes flickered to Davis. "She wouldn't answer her phone. And no one but Patrick has really spoken to her since."

"And Bob's funeral?"

Tyler shrugged. "She didn't want one. That asshole is buried in a box somewhere no one will ever visit him."

Davis sighed heavily. "Fuck it all to hell."

"I don't know what to do about her, man." Tyler said, his voice strained with worry. "Patrick tried to tell her to talk to you, and she just won't. She feels so guilty."

"She and I seem to have that in common," Davis mused, finishing his beer and placing the glass bottle on the table beside him. "I should go see her."

"Well you can't right now, she's gone to Wyoming."

"Wyoming?"

Tyler nodded. "Yeah, Sarah's aunt lives there and offered to have Grace come and stay. Fresh air and horses or something."

"Well that will probably do her good."

The two men fell into silence. The thunder continued to rumble overhead. After a while Patricia called them in for dinner. The evening passed by pleasantly, with Davis's parents telling funny stories from when they had met. Despite the laughter, Davis couldn't help but let his mind wander back to Grace. What was she doing? When would she be back? And when, if ever, would she ever forgive herself enough to talk to him again?

"Well, as I live and breathe!" Sarah exclaimed, and rushed at him. She stopped short and hesitated just as she reached him. "Am I going to break, crush or destroy anything if I give you a hug right now?"

Davis laughed. "Hugs are fine, just save the MMA bodyslam for after Christmas."

She threw her arms around him. "It's so good to see you out again." She looked up at him with tears in her eyes. "You're making me all emotional Chev!" They both giggled as she wiped tears away. "What can I get you? It's on the house!"

"Just a coffee thanks."

Sarah nodded and went behind the counter, taking the large pot of coffee from the machine. "So, are you driving yourself again?"

"Oh yeah, just had to wait to get myself a new truck." He pointed out the front windows at the shiny red truck.

Sarah gave him a little smile. "Her favourite colour?"

Davis nodded and looked down at his hands. "Have you heard from her?"

Sarah came and sat down at the table with him, placing the mug of coffee in front of him. "She's doing really well," Sarah told him. "She's called a few times, but she mainly talks to Patrick. Kayley misses her terribly, so..." Sarah trailed off and gazed out the window.

"Is she ever coming back?" Davis knew she didn't have an answer, but he posed the question all the same.

Sarah was quiet for a moment, then sighed. "She sold her Dad's house, did you know?"

"I did." His father had seen the For Sale sign go up, then swiftly go down again when a couple relocating from San Francisco had bought the house. They were doing a wonderful job renovating the place, but Davis didn't want to know what they'd have to do to get the interior up to scratch after years of Bob Weaver neglecting it.

"And she quit her job with the rangers."

This was some information Davis didn't expect, and he raised his eyebrows in surprise. "Why did she do that?"

Sarah shrugged. "She used up all her leave and then I think she didn't want to mess anyone around. She'd been gone a while. She's got the money from the house so she's OK for a while."

Davis took a sip of his coffee. "Did you know she was going to follow me to Alaska?" He'd not discussed this with anyone yet.

Sarah regarded him with surprise. "No, I had no idea. Who told you that?"

"Bob Weaver."

Sarah snorted. "Don't believe everything he says."

"Oh this I believe," Davis insisted. "He told me down on the jetty. Said he'd thrown himself down the stairs to stop her."

Sarah gasped. "You are joking."

"I'm not."

"That rat bastard." She shook her head. "You think you've seen him stoop as low as he can go and then he just pushes the bottom of that barrel into hell." She paused for a moment. "Grace wasn't by any chance considering going after you again a while later, was she?" She found her answer in the look on Davis's face, and gasped again, a bitter smile on her face. "He is just... *Was* just the most unbelievable son of a bitch out. Anything to stop Grace being happy."

"I don't know if I should tell her or not. If she ever speaks to me again that is," Davis said dryly.

She considered this for a moment, then shook her head. "I don't know. Would you want to know that your Dad had done everything possible to stop you being happy?"

"I don't know that that would come as a surprise to her to be honest."

"I don't know Davis," Sarah ran a hand through her shiny dark hair. "We need her to come back first, and when she does - who knows what state she'll be in?"

Patricia was hanging up washing as Davis pulled up in the front yard. He swung his legs down from the cab, landing a little too heavily on his knee, and winced. Was this ever going to feel any better?

"Oh hi honey!" His mother waved as the sheets flapped around her in the wind. "How was town? Gorgeous day!" The late Autumn breeze was fresh and the sky was brilliant blue. "I hope these sheets dry, it's gotten so cold all of a sudden!"

Davis helped his mother with the washing, then they sat on the porch together. "Mom," he began tentatively, "Bob Weaver said something to me, down on the jetty."

"Did he now?" Patricia raised her eyebrows.

"He said Grace was going to follow me to Alaska."

Patricia's face fell, and she sighed deeply. "Oh honey." She shook her head, and Davis could see she was trying to find the words.

"He said she came and talked to you about it, 3 years ago, before Hal came along," Davis went on.

Patricia opened her mouth and closed it again, clasping her hands in her lap.

"Is it true?" Davis pressed her.

"Yes it is." She admitted quietly.

"Why didn't you tell me?"

Patricia shook her head. "Because she didn't end up following you, I guess. It seemed like a stupid thing to tell you." She looked down at her hands, and Davis could see she was getting very emotional. "Grace came to me in a state. She missed you so much. She didn't know what to do."

"So you told her to follow me?"

"Yes I did, I told her you still loved her, I was sure of it."

"So why didn't you tell me?" Davis asked again.

His mother sighed again, and tears sprang into her eyes. "I didn't see that telling you she'd nearly followed you would do anyone any good. I didn't want you to be hurt all over again."

"I wish you had." He didn't want to get angry at his mother, but he couldn't deny that he was hurt. "I thought she hated me. I had no idea she still wanted to be with me. I might have -"

"Davis, you might have done a lot of things differently if you now was you then," Patricia pointed out. "But you made the choice to leave. I'm sorry I never told you, I really am. But I thought it would just hurt you. Some things we just don't need to know because they don't change anything."

"This changes everything!" Davis tried not to raise his voice.

"How does this change anything?" Patricia asked incredulously. "You're still here and hurt, Grace is still miles away in Wyoming refusing to come home, what has it changed?"

"It proves she still loved me!"

"Oh for Pete's sake, Davis, of course she did!" Patricia let out a growl of frustration. "You two, honestly, you're as bad as each other. Do you really think she ever stopped loving you? When she told me she was -" She stopped short and gave him a look of alarm.

"What? She was what?" Davis felt his pulse quicken. "What did she say?"

"No, no I can't tell you." Patricia shook her head emphatically. "She swore me to secrecy."

"Mom, please, if this is something I need to know -"

"Davis, I mean it, this will only hurt you more." His mother rose and hurried into the kitchen.

Davis followed her. "Mom, what did she say?"

Patricia backed against the kitchen counter, gripping it with both hands, her knuckles white. "No, I promised her."

"Mom!"

"No, I can't!"

"Tell me!" He bellowed.

"She was pregnant when you left, Davis!" Her hands flew to her mouth, trying to stop the words from tumbling out, but it was too late.

Davis felt the ground spin away from him. His eyes widened and he felt his mouth drop open. Blood rushed in his ears, deafening him. "She - she was what?"

Patricia sighed. "Oh honey." She bit her lip, as though trying not to cry. "My sweet boy, I'm so sorry."

Davis slumped into a chair at the kitchen table. He felt sick. "Why didn't she tell me?"

"Oh honey, she didn't know. She found out a few weeks after you left."

His eyes began to sting. His head felt full and heavy. "She was going to have our baby?"

Patricia sat opposite him, reaching across the table to take his hands, and flinching as he snatched them away from her. "Yes honey, she was. She told me she'd decided to follow you to Alaska when she found out. She started planning the trip and packing her bags. And then her Dad had his accident."

"His accident." Davis repeated flatly.

"Yes, he fell down the stairs and broke his hip."

"I know." He didn't want to tell his mother what he knew yet. This was all too much to take in. "So, what happened to the baby?"

"The day after her father's surgery, she started bleeding." Patricia said as tears began to stream down her face. "She lost it. I'm so sorry honey."

Davis felt the air leave his lungs. His baby. Their baby. It had died and Grace had to go through it all alone because he hadn't been there. Their baby. The baby he hadn't even known had ever existed.

"How far along was she?" Davis asked.

Patricia shook her head and shrugged. "I'd say 3 or 4 months, judging by the time you left. I'm not sure honey."

"She was pregnant, and I left." Davis put his head on the table in front of him.

"Davis, you didn't know."

His head snapped up. "Does it matter?"

"Of course it does! You would have never left if -"

"So it wasn't enough to stay for her but a baby would have done it?"

His mother couldn't stop crying. "Oh honey, it wasn't like that."

Davis shoved himself away from the table and ran outside. His knee ached, and he knew he should stop, but he needed fresh air. Why wasn't it storming? He'd never yearned for a storm before. But this glaring sunshine and clear blue sky was too much to bear, like a slap in the face.

He got to the fence, then stopped and turned back, then turned again to the street. He didn't know what to do. He didn't know where to go. He wanted to talk to Grace more than anything, but Grace wasn't there. She'd run away, just like he had, over guilt she had no reason to feel. *We're both fucking idiots*, Davis though to himself bitterly. How could two people mess up their lives this spectacularly, and still learn nothing.

He wanted to go for a long walk but knew his knee wasn't ready for that. So he jumped into his car, gunned the engine, then paused to get out his phone. He dialled Grace's number. He'd not called her, not once, he wanted to give her space. But now they needed to talk.

It went straight to voicemail. "Please call me," he pleaded into the phone after the beep, "Please, please talk to me." Not knowing what else to say, he hung up, choked back his tears, and took off for the national park.

"I thought I'd find you here."

Davis jumped at his father's voice behind him. He was sitting by the canyon, under a fallen redwood tree, watching the river rage below him. Paulson took a seat on the bench beside his son, stretched out his legs and sighed.

"Did Mom tell you?" Davis asked after a while,

"Not at the time," Paulson replied, "but she did just now."

Davis shook his head. "I can't believe she didn't tell me."

"Who? Your mother or Grace?"

"Both."

Paulson shrugged. "Grace was young, scared, alone. She was probably afraid of how you would react."

"This was *me*, Dad."

"The you that had just left and insisted Clearwater wasn't the place for him?" Paulson countered. "You had just done something Grace didn't expect, she was terrified. Not easy for a girl to tell a man news like that."

Davis looked at his father. "Was it like that for you and Mom?"

Paulson nodded. "Sure was. She was 21, she was so young, and I was so much older. Her family didn't like me, no one did. Maybe they were right." He gave a cynical laugh. "I still remember her face when she told me. She looked like she was bracing herself for a slap, it was awful. I never wanted to see her look like that again."

"But she did tell you."

"Grace was going to tell you too. It just... Well, it just had a tragic end before she got to."

Davis jumped up. "Dad, she has kept this from me for five years! Why didn't she ever tell me?"

"Are you angry she didn't tell you or are you upset she carried this alone this whole time?" Paulson stood and put his hands on his son's shoulders. "I know you're hurt. You've had all this happen and then you find out there was a baby and then there wasn't a baby. It's all been so much for you son, so much."

"Bob faked his accidents," Davis said flatly.

Paulson's eyes narrowed. "His falls down the stairs?" He sighed and nodded, his mouth in a hard line. "That old bastard. I should have known. He'd do anything to keep her close."

“I’m glad he’s dead.” Davis admitted.

“Me too, son. Me too.”

They sat back down and watched the river below in silence for a while.

“I’m glad you and Mom are happier,” Davis finally said.

“I just wish it hadn’t taken almost losing you for it to happen,” Paulson replied, a crooked smile on his lips. “I came into the hospital just after they brought you in, and you, uh -“ He choked up and cleared his throat. “Well, uh, I didn’t quite know what to do with myself. I’ve never felt more helpless or useless in my life. And your poor mother, she just, she broke down.” He put a hand on Davis’s shoulder again. “You’re my only boy, and I don’t know what I’d do if I lost you. Made me realise how much I had to lose, and how much time I’d wasted. It’s never too late.”

“Isn’t it?”

“No.” Paulson insisted. “It never is.”

Davis flexed his hands, feeling the scar tissue bind and hold back his fingers. “I don’t know what to do, Dad.”

“Give her time.”

“How much time?”

“As much as she needs. She’ll be back. Believe me, she will.”

The bar was quiet as Davis walked across the floor towards Patrick, who gave him a huge smile. “Well I sure am glad to see you here! Merry Christmas, my friend!" He put a glass in front of Davis and poured him a bourbon. "On me." He said, winking.

Davis had been trying not to drink much, but it was Christmas Eve. "Thanks, merry Christmas to you too." He took a seat. "Are you closing up early tonight?"

Patrick nodded. "Sure am, Kayley already laid out the cookies and carrots for Santa and his reindeer, and I have so many presents to lay out." He laughed. "And then my folks and Shelley's folks are coming over tomorrow. It'll be a good day." He poured Davis another bourbon as soon as the glass was empty. "And you?"

"My folks are at my aunt's tonight, I didn't much feel like going with them. Being festive feels, well, it feels a little strange."

Patrick nodded sympathetically. He looked up and waved at someone over Davis's shoulder. "Good evening sir!" Davis heard Tyler's voice.

"Why good evening my good fellow," Patrick's terrible British accent was back. "And merry Christmas unto thee. Does sir fancy a tipple?"

"Most certainly!" Tyler shrugged his coat off and hung it on the back of the barstool. "I come bearing news, gentlemen."

Patrick raised his eyebrows. "Oh?"

Tyler took his seat and leaned in, lowering his voice. "I just got word that an arrest has been made."

"An arrest?" Davis and Patrick looked at each other.

Tyler nodded. "They caught the guy who killed Hal Stephens."

"The guy with the Bentley?" Davis asked.

Tyler downed the bourbon Patrick placed in front of him and shook his head. "Nope," he rasped as the alcohol burned his throat. "The father of one of the girls Hal abducted."

"What?" Patrick and Davis said at the same time.

"Wait," Patrick began, eyes raised to the ceiling as though trying to recall a memory. "I thought those girls had run away from their families. Why would one of their Dads kill this guy?"

"Apparently the girl was being abused by her mother and stepfather." Tyler explained. "Dad's working out on an oil rig, when he gets back his daughter tells him what happened. Guy's an ex-Marine or something, tracked Hal down in LA. And boom. Got him."

Patrick exhaled heavily. "Holy shit."

"So who was the guy with the Bentley? How did he get the gun?" Davis wanted to know.

Tyler shrugged. "No idea. Maybe Hal sold it to him?"

"OK maybe, but the rest of it doesn't make any sense though," Patrick mused, crossing his arms across his chest. "Why would a guy in a Bentley pawn a gun like that?"

"I dunno man," Tyler replied. "It's all a crazy story."

"Does Grace know?" Davis asked suddenly. Patrick and Tyler both looked at him, then each other.

"Uh, I don't think so," Tyler said hesitantly. "Maybe for the best too, to be honest." He rose and shook both their hands. "Anyway, I gotta run, got family coming up tomorrow and I have to get the pad all cleaned up so my Mom doesn't give me hell. Merry Christmas!" He called to the few other patrons, who returned his greeting with a wave.

Patrick turned to Davis. "Well that was unexpected." He looked like he wanted to say something else, but seemed to think the better of it, shook his head and rang the bell by the bar. "Last call folks! It's Christmas and I got a little girl to get home to!"

One by one the others shuffled out into the cold Winter air, waving as they left amidst calls of "Merry Christmas!" Finally it was just Davis and Patrick left. Davis began to put the stools up on the tables as Patrick wiped down the bar and emptied the till.

"Thanks man," Patrick said appreciatively when they were done. He turned the lights out, and they left the bar by the back door. "Closing up on a night like this seems to drag, I just want to get home to my daughter." Snow had begun to fall outside, and their cars were covered in a light dusting. "Ah this is awesome, Kayley was wanting a white Christmas." Patrick smiled into the night sky.

"You're a really good father." Davis said suddenly, his voice strained with emotion.

Patrick looked a little surprised. "Thanks Davis. I do my best." He narrowed his eyes slightly, studying Davis's face. "Is everything OK?" Davis nodded, then dropped his chin to his chest, and began to sob. Patrick lurched forward, alarmed, and put hands on Davis's shoulders. "Davis, oh my god, what happened?"

"I'm sorry," Davis stuttered.

"No, no, please, don't apologise. What happened?"

"Grace was pregnant when I left." Davis cried harder. All the emotion he'd been keeping down, all the tears he'd wanted to cry for Grace, for their baby, but hadn't allowed himself to, came spilling out.

"Oh shit," Patrick stood perfectly still, holding Davis up as he wept. "Oh man. What happened?"

"She lost it. She was going to follow me to Alaska, and she lost it. And I didn't know. And I wasn't here." He collapsed against Patrick's chest, covering his face with his hands. For the longest time the two friends stood there, and Patrick just let Davis cry it all out.

Finally, Davis stood and wiped his eyes on the sleeve of his coat. "Fucking hell, I'm sorry," he mumbled. "How goddamn embarrassing."

"I'm your oldest friend, if you can't cry on my chest whose chest can you cry on?" Patrick joked, handing him a tissue. "And I mean, Jesus Christ, Davis. This is... fuck. This is heavy. I'm so, so sorry."

"You wanted to go home to your daughter and I start crying on you in the parking lot."

Patrick gave him a knowing look. "I think those two things aren't totally unrelated though are they? Christmas is a time for families. And, well, you get to thinking." He stamped his feet in the cold and looked up at the snow. "How did you find out?"

"My Mom told me," Davis replied, jamming his hands into his pockets to try and warm them. The cold was gnawing at his skin. "Grace had confided in her when she decided to come after me a second time, just before Hal came along. Before Bob Weaver threw himself down the stairs a second time to stop her from leaving him."

"A second -" Patrick stopped, realisation hitting. "Oh my god. Fucking psychopath."

"And I can't reach her, she won't talk to me," Davis said, feeling the tears rising and forcing them back down. He didn't want to start crying again. "She never answers her phone, she never returns my calls. And I don't know what to do. I don't know what to fucking do anymore."

Patrick sighed and put a reassuring hand on his shoulder. "I know this is easy to say, but let it go for now. Just, enjoy Christmas with your folks. Try not to think about it all. And, well, see what the New Year brings, OK?"

There was nothing else to say. Patrick was right, the only thing left to do was wait, and see if Grace ever decided to come back. "Merry Christmas," Davis said, trying to smile. "Thank you for letting me cry on you."

Patrick laughed out loud. "Anytime. Merry Christmas to you too."

Davis walked back to his truck. The snow was falling very heavily now. There would be a proper blanket of it tomorrow, and Kayley would get her white Christmas. For a moment - just for a split second - Davis allowed himself to wonder what kind of Christmas he'd be getting ready for now, had things turned out differently.

Perhaps he and Grace would be downstairs, drinking egg nog and wrapping gifts while their child - a boy? A girl? - slept upstairs, dreaming of all the wonderful things Santa was going to bring them the next day. They'd be about 4 and a half now...

The lump in his throat began to form again, but Davis was too exhausted to cry anymore. He gunned the engine, headed for home. The house was mercifully still dark when he arrived, and he headed straight for his room, stripping off his heavy clothes and collapsing into bed, welcoming sleep and the dreamless darkness that came with it.

The New Year brought many things, but it didn't bring Grace back to Clearwater.

A week after New Years, Patrick introduced Davis to his new girlfriend, Alison. She had been a few years below them in high school, and had just returned to Clearwater after living in San Diego for a while. They were both coy when Davis asked what had brought her back into town, and he knew it had to be Patrick and Kayley.

"It feels strange, Davis," Patrick said as they stood in the park in the low afternoon light, watching Alison and Kayley build a snowman together. "I thought after Shelley, there'd never be anyone else for me. And then Alison and I ran into each other last year, when she was back visiting her folks. And it just - I dunno. It just felt right."

Davis smiled. "I'm happy for you, man. You deserve it."

"Kayley's been missing Grace a lot, having Alison around has made it a lot easier." Patrick gave his friend an apologetic look. "Sorry to bring her up."

Davis shook his head. "Oh don't worry. It's been, well, it's been a long time. I sure as hell don't have a monopoly on missing her. Have you heard from her?"

Patrick hesitated, and Davis raised his hands. "Please don't feel like you have to tell me. If she doesn't want me to know -"

"No, it's not that." Patrick sighed. "She doesn't say much when she calls, just talks to Kayley really. But she did ask about you last week."

Davis cursed the butterflies that instantly sprang up in his stomach. "She did?"

"Yeah," Patrick replied carefully. "She, uh, she was worried about your injuries and how you were recovering. I told her, and she hung up real quick after that. The guilt, I think, it tears her up."

They didn't speak for a while, watching Kayley and Alison build the snowman up ever higher, Alison sacrificing her scarf for him. Davis watched the little girl squeal in delight, glad she had a new surrogate mother to care for her.

"So this," Davis asked after a while, "this is serious then?" He gestured to Alison.

Patrick nodded. "It sure as hell is. I asked her to marry me on New Years."

Davis couldn't help but smile. "That's fantastic, man!" He grabbed Patrick in a bear hug. "Congratulations! You sure aren't wasting any time!"

Patrick laughed. "Thanks! Planning a wedding in May, just something small."

"Does Kayley know?"

Patrick shook his head. "We wanted to tell her together in a little while. I did tell Shelley's parents though."

"Oh?"

"Yeah," Patrick replied, his voice catching a little in his throat, "I wanted their blessing. It felt - well, it felt right. They met Alison at Christmas, and they love her. It was important to us both for them to be OK with it all. And they were of course."

"Of course they were, they want you to be happy as much as anyone else."

"It still feels odd, Davis. Loving someone, but also loving someone else. Alison understands, she knows I'll always love Shelley." He inhaled sharply. "She insisted on going to Shelley's grave and laying flowers. She, uh, told her she would always look after me." Davis could see his friend fighting back tears.

"She's a catch alright." Davis said.

"That she is."

Clouds had crept in front of the sun, and snow began to fall lightly in the fading light. Kayley came running up to her father. "Home for hot chocolate Daddy? Ally and me are cold!"

Patrick scooped the little girl up in his arms and laughed. "For sure, my sweethearts! Let's go!" He turned to Davis. "Care to join us?"

Davis shook his head with a smile. "You guys go ahead, I need to go home and rest this knee, it doesn't like the cold much."

"Your magic knee?" Kayley asked, her voice hushed and wondering.

Davis leaned in. "The magic knee." He whispered.

Kayley giggled. "Bye Davis!" She called as she waved over her father's shoulder.

Davis watched them leave, enjoying the sound of their laughter, fading in the distance as the falling snow swallowed it up. He turned and walked back towards town, mulling over what Patrick had told him. Loving someone while still loving someone else.

He climbed up into his truck, wincing slightly as he bent his knee. The cold really did make it ache. He gunned the engine, the snowstorm beginning to build outside. The snowflakes blew against the windshield as he drove.

He would always love Grace, he knew that. She'd been his first everything. But perhaps that was where she would always stay. Always the first, never the last. Perhaps, after 6 months of no contact, he had to accept that she wasn't coming back. And even if she did...

The wind was truly howling by the time he got back to his parents' house, heralding an incoming blizzard. He killed the engine and sat in the dark truck. He looked up at the house, welcoming light flooding from the kitchen windows.

He felt as though his life had been suspended since the fire, since Grace had left. He missed working. He missed having his own place. He missed *living.* Perhaps his life had been suspended even longer than he even wanted to admit - since Billy's death, since leaving Clearwater, since he'd carried guilt and shame and lies for so many years.

The time had come to admit that enough was enough. It was time for him to move on. He'd given a lot of his life to this place - now it was time to find a new place for himself. And perhaps, the time had come to leave Grace here, where she belonged.

Perhaps it was time to move on from her too.

Chapter Ten

The snow had thawed entirely over the four days Davis had been gone, but the bitter cold remained, threatening to bring a fresh downfall with it. He stretched his legs as he got out of the truck, his knee protesting at the long drive from San Francisco back to Clearwater. He grabbed his bag from the backseat and let himself into the house.

"Hello?" He called out, putting his bag down on the ground.

"I'm in the lounge room honey!" Came his mother's voice. He wandered in and found his mother sitting cross-legged on the floor, surrounded by photo albums, a glass of wine beside her. She smiled up at him. "You made pretty good time! How was the flight?"

Davis threw himself down in one of the plush recliners, stretching his legs out in front of him. "The flight was fine, it's the drive back that's the killer." He said, rubbing his neck.

Patricia nodded as she took a swig of red wine. "It's such a long way, twice as long as the damn flight. And?" She looked at him expectantly. "How did the interview go?"

"It went really well," Davis allowed himself a self-satisfied smile. "They seemed very impressed that someone with my experience would be on their team. And they seem like a great company, very well-equipped and focused on conservation."

"Oh that's fantastic sweetheart!" Patricia seemed genuinely pleased. "And Seattle isn't quite so far away as Alaska!"

"That's true. Maybe you can even talk Dad into leaving town since there'll be no glaciers involved." Davis joked.

Yes, this was a good opportunity.

After deciding to get back to work, Davis had been unsure what to do. Joseph Keller had offered him an operations co-ordinator position, but Davis wasn't sure he could handle sitting in a fire station, watching the crews haul out, and not feel that it was just a constant reminder of everything he'd never be able to do again.

So he applied for consultancy work, careful to avoid anything like SNA. He'd found a position with a company in Seattle, focusing very carefully on working closely with the national parks and private conservation companies to make the parks safe and sustainable, without compromising the integrity of the natural environment and wildlife. They were impressed with Davis's background both as a safety engineer and a firefighter, and had invited him to Seattle for a proper discussion about the position after virtual talks had gone fantastically well.

They offered him a great package, excellent pay and benefits, and he had found himself wandering around Seattle and being in awe of just how beautiful a city it was. It was busy, for sure, but after the isolation of Alaska and the small-town living in Clearwater, he felt excited about living in a big city. He was very sure he would like it there, even if it rained a lot. And while he could see his mother was a bit sad about him leaving again, he told himself this time it would be different. He wasn't running away, he was starting a new chapter on his terms. He'd come back to visit regularly, they'd come see him - this time *was* different.

Davis heard his father coming in the front door, calling out a greeting, then heading down the hall towards them. "Good, you got back safely then." Paulson said as he saw his son sitting in the recliner, handing him a beer. "Blizzard meant to be blowing in tonight, so you got back just in time by the looks."

"Davis is taking the job in Seattle," Patricia told her husband, beaming. "They loved him."

"Of course they did," Paulson responded, giving Davis an approving nod, "you're the best of the best. They'd be lucky to have you."

"Thanks Dad." He still wasn't entirely used to hearing quite so much praise from his father, but he enjoyed it all the same.

"So when do you move?" Paulson asked, taking a swig of his beer.

"They want me to start in April, so about 6 weeks."

"I'll drive up with you and get a flight back," Paulson said, clearly not asking. "You'll need help moving your things, I don't want you hurting that knee after all your physiotherapy."

Davis and Patricia gave each other a furtive smile. "That sounds like a wonderful idea, honey," Patricia said. "Father and Son road trip!"

Davis laughed. "Sure thing, sounds great." He got up out of the chair, his knee aching as he put weight on it. "I need a shower after that drive."

"Not a problem honey, I'll go get started on dinner!" Patricia put her hands out for Paulson to help her off the floor, and Davis couldn't help but smile to himself as he heard his parents laughing together as he walked down the hallway.

Life was good. He felt like he had balance again, solid ground underfoot. Perhaps Seattle was exactly the new start he was looking for.

"Well you will have to come back for the wedding!" Alison announced, raising her glass in a toast over the table. "Here's to your new job! Congratulations!" She, Patrick and Davis all clinked their glasses, and Kayley happily raised her bright pink plastic cup for everyone to clink too.

"Thankyou," Davis gave Alison a big smile, "and I will definitely be back for the wedding."

"Damn straight you will," Patrick said, leaning back in his chair, "you are not being released from your Best Man duties for anything, not even some high-flying job in Seattle."

"I"ll come to Sedaddle!" Kayley announced. "What's in Sedaddle I'd like?"

"Well there's ferries, and a big tower called the Space Needle." Davis told her, folding his arms on the table. "And sometimes you can see whales in the water as they go from one home to the next."

"Ooh I like whales!" Kayley exclaimed, doing her best whale song impression and sending the adults at the table into peals of laughter.

"OK, Miss Priss, time for a bath!" Alison retrieved the little girl from her booster chair. "Let's go and let your Daddy and Davis have some man talk."

"Man talk, man talk!" Kayley chanted as Alison carried her up the stairs.

Patrick turned back to look at Davis, still smiling. "Ah, this is great. I'm happy for you."

Davis nodded. "Thanks, I was a bit worried no one would take me to be honest." He saw Patricks' questioning look, and held up his hands. "I'm not - well, I can't work really fast anymore. I'm not sure if I'll ever get back to where I was at."

"Hey, they hired you for your brains, not your hands." Patrick pointed out. "And the physiotherapy is going well?"

"Oh sure, it's helping a lot, and I know I'll get stronger. And in Seattle I'll be able to have more access to doctors and specialists. But, it still makes me, I don't know, I guess nervous sometimes. I'm still getting used to things being... different."

"I'm sorry, man." Patrick looked at him sadly. "I hate that you have to deal with all this."

Davis shrugged. "Hey, I'm here, right? I'm here and I'm alive, and that's what matters. As long as I'm alive it can only get better."

"That is an excellent philosophy to have." Patrick said approvingly, and the two men raised their glasses in a toast again. "And I am sure Seattle will be a great new start for you."

The doorbell rang, and Patrick went to answer it.

Davis could hear Kayley and Alison singing upstairs, and then there were thundering footsteps on the stairs as Kayley came pelting down to present her new pyjamas to him. "Davis, lookit! Unicorns!" She announced proudly.

As she walked towards the table she turned to look down the hall to the front door, where her father had gone. She stopped short, and did an excited little dance, hopping from one foot to the other. "GRACIEEEEEEEEEEE!" The little girl cried, barreling down the hallway and out of sight.

Davis's blood ran cold. Patrick rounded the corner back into the kitchen, a concerned and slightly shocked look on his face. "Grace is here." He said to Davis in a low voice. "I had no idea she was back in town." He turned back to the stairs, where Alison stood looking confused.

"Who's here?" She asked.

Grace walked into the kitchen, Kayley in her arms. Davis felt like his head was full of cotton wool. He couldn't move. She was there, in the kitchen, a green knitted beanie pulled down over her red - wait, red? - hair, wearing a long brown coat that was powdered with snow. She looked right at him and smiled.

"Hello Davis," she said quietly.

He couldn't speak. They all stared at Grace for a moment, Alison with confusion, and Patrick and Davis with shock.

Patrick broke the spell first, hurriedly taking Kayley from Grace's arms amidst excuses that it was bedtime, and ushered Alison upstairs. He cast an apologetic look over his shoulder at Davis as they went. Kayley began to protest, but her father soothed her as they walked, telling her it was time for bed and that she would see Grace tomorrow.

Then they were alone, in Patrick's kitchen.

She was there. She was back.

"You look good," Grace said after a while, sitting down opposite him.

"Thanks," Davis replied, not knowing what else to say and unable to stop staring at her.

"It's been a while." She lowered her eyes.

"Yeah it has. A long while." He hesitated. "Your hair - " For some stupid reason it felt like the most important detail right now. Her hair. Her long red hair. Why did it matter?

She laughed. "Yeah, back to natural. It was time for a change." She looked over at him, her big grey eyes soft, pleading. "I'm so sorry." When he didn't respond, she leaned forward across the table, reaching out but not quite touching him. She looked down at his hands, and alarm flickered across her face. "Oh god, Davis..." She trailed off, tears welling up in her steely eyes.

It was all too much.

With a lurch, he pushed himself away from the table, stumbling down the hallway and out of Patrick's front door, the icy night air hitting his lungs and causing him to gasp. He couldn't focus. He fumbled the keys to his truck out of his pocket, dropping them in the snow, bending to pick them up, cursing.

He heard her footsteps crunching through the snow, hurrying up behind him. "Davis, please, I'm so sorry."

"Grace, I can't do this right now." He couldn't look at her. He tried to unlock the truck, his fingers seizing up in the cold, dropping the keys again. "Fuck. Grace, please, I can't do this."

"Davis," she clutched at his arm, "please, please look at me."

He shook her off. "Grace, no. I can't do this."

She clutched at him again, her hands on his face, trying to turn him towards her. "I'm so sorry," she was crying now. "Please, please look at me! Just talk to me! I just want to talk to you!"

"Enough!" He bellowed, pushing her away. She stumbled back a step, her face tear-streaked, her mouth open in a silent wail. "Grace, just, enough!" He said again. "I can't do this right now."

"I'm so sorry." She repeated.

"Stop apologising!" He didn't want to yell. He hated yelling at her. He never wanted to yell at her again. But he couldn't stop himself. "Just stop! You disappear then show up again months later, throwing Sorry at me like it makes it all OK?"

"No, I know it doesn't, but I need you to know -"

"Know what, Grace?" He interrupted. "Know that you left me in a coma, know that you took off to Wyoming without a second glance, know that you suddenly reappear like you never left expecting what?"

"I needed space," she stammered, "I couldn't face it -"

"*You* couldn't face it?" His rage was spilling over. "*You* couldn't face my burns and my scars and my shattered useless fucking leg and my knee that's not even fucking mine? *You* couldn't face the endless therapy and my fucking job being taken from me? *You* couldn't face that, huh?" He laughed bitterly, shaking his head. "Well, how awful all that must have been for *you*, Grace."

"I'm sorry, I just want to talk!"

"*Now* you want to talk?" He asked incredulously, the cold air catching in his throat. "How many times did I call you, begging you to call me back, *begging* you to just talk to me? And you just ignored me? And now you come back and just expect me to, what, take you back?"

Grace shook her head, tears streaming down her face, her breath exploding from her mouth in thick puffs in the frigid night air. "I know I did the wrong thing, I know I shouldn't have left you, but I was so sure you were dead, and then they didn't know how badly hurt you'd be, and if you'd even wake up, and I just couldn't do it. I'd just lost my Dad and -"

"Oh, my condolences by the way," Davis sneered, "but I guess at least you now felt he couldn't hold you back anymore." He laughed bitterly. "Good old Dad dies and off you run, finally free. One thing he couldn't fake was death, I guess."

Grace's eyebrows knit together in confusion. "What do you mean, fake -"

"His hips, Grace!" Davis exploded. "His goddamn falls down the stairs, you honestly thought those were accidents? You are so goddamn naive! He did it to stop you from following me, which, while we're on the subject, was an amazing thing to find out all these years later."

She frowned. "What do you -"

"Following me?" He raised his eyebrows. "Deciding to follow me then letting me believe I was some monster who'd abandoned you instead of just fucking *telling me*."

She covered her face with her hands, sobs shaking her shoulders, and he regretted everything. This isn't what he wanted. He wished he could take it all back. He felt guilty. How could he be so mean, so cynical? He should comfort her. He should take her in his arms, dry her tears, talk to her. But the rage tightening his chest was stronger than any guilt he felt, and kept him rooted to the spot. The snow fell around them, the wind whispering through the surrounding pine trees.

Finally, and without another word, he retrieved his keys from the snow, climbed into his truck, and drove away. He cast a glance in the rear view mirror, and saw Grace watching him go, unmoving. She disappeared into the falling snow, and as Davis drove down the road, he wished more than anything that she had just stayed away.

That had been easier than this.

A soft knock on his door roused him from his sleep. He looked around the room, dazed. What had he been doing? His laptop was open beside him, real estate listings for Seattle on the page.

The knock came again. "Come in." He called, rubbing his eyes and willing himself awake. Why was he so damn tired all the time?

His mother came in, a mug in her hands. "I made you a coffee honey." She sat down beside him, handing over the mug and casting a glance at the laptop. "How's it going?"

Davis took a sip of the coffee and nodded. "Yeah good. There's a few decent places near the office."

"So you're still doing this then?"

He gave his mother a puzzled look. "Of course I am. Why wouldn't I?"

"I just thought..." She trailed off, and fiddled with her fingernails nervously. "You know, with everything that's happened, maybe -"

"Oh Mom," he sighed in frustration, "you cannot be serious."

"Have you tried calling her?" Patricia asked, something akin to desperation in her voice.

"No, I haven't, and I'm not going to." Davis got up off the bed.

"But Davis, she's come back, doesn't that mean something?"

"You know what?" Davis snapped. "It actually doesn't. I was in a coma and she stayed away. I was recovering from major burns and a destroyed leg, and she went to fucking Wyoming." Patricia winced as he swore, but he carried on. "She left when I needed her. I nearly died trying to save her father, I nearly killed myself trying to save her brother, and I am quite frankly done putting myself on the line for the Weavers. I am just done."

"Don't you think it's a little hypocritical to blame her for leaving?" Patricia countered quietly. "You left her when Billy died."

"I asked her to come with me, Mom. That's the difference. I blamed myself for leaving Grace for a long, long time. But she could have come with me. But her piece of shit father meant more to her than me or her own future. She's free of him now, so maybe she'll finally get up the courage to actually live her life." Davis turned and stormed out of the room. It was snowing heavily outside, and as he entered the kitchen Paulson came in, rubbing his hands together and puffing air into his clasped fingers to try and warm up.

"It's an absolute white-out out there." Paulson announced, stopping and observing his son's heaving shoulders with a creased brow. "You okay son?"

Davis shook his head as Patricia entered the kitchen. "It's nothing. Just -" he cast a glance at his mother. "Just trying to work some things out. About moving, you know?"

Paulson glanced from his wife to his son and nodded slowly. "Right," he said, and Davis could hear the distrust in his father's voice. "Well, anyway, I have some news from the chief of police." Paulson settled down at the table and Patricia set about getting him a coffee. "Bentley guy showed up."

Davis regarded his father with surprise. "He showed up? Where?"

"Well, he didn't show up in the sense of they know where he is," Paulson corrected himself, "but they did get some news on him. Car dealer in San Diego came across the wanted poster somehow, brother is a cop or something. Anyway, he sees the APB and says he's seen the guy. Traded a car in, a Bentley of all things."

"He traded it in?" Patricia asked incredulously, taking a seat at the kitchen table.

Paulson nodded. "He sure did. A few days after dropping in the gun at the pawn shop in Mammoth Lake. Traded it in for a Camry and cash."

"And then?" Davis asked.

"And then, presumably, made a break for the border." Paulson shrugged. "That's the last anyone saw him. The police back-tracked and it seems this guy was pawning off his valuables at every store he could down the coast."

"Do we know who he was yet?"

"Some drug dealer from up here in the mountains, operation got busted when he started dealing coke or something." Paulson took a sip of coffee. "Must have run for it before the cops could get his passport. APB went out when he was long gone."

The whole situation was becoming stranger and stranger. "So how did he get the gun from Hal?" Davis mused, rubbing his neck.

"Well, Hal probably sold it to him?" Patricia offered. "His assets were all frozen when the farm was raided, he would have needed the money."

"I suppose so," Davis replied, though something about it all still struck him as odd. His phone rang, interrupting his thoughts. He pulled it out of his pocket and saw Patrick's name on the screen. "I gotta take this." He said to his parents, heading back down the hall to his room.

"Hey man, how's things?" Patrick asked, his forced cheerfulness painfully obvious,

"I'm fine," Davis replied, "just looking at places in Seattle, getting ready for the move."

"Right, right." Patrick hesitated for a moment. "So, uh, Grace wants to talk to you."

Davis exhaled heavily. "Patrick, come on."

"Look," Patrick said quickly, "I know she caught you off guard the other night, and no one could blame you for reacting the way you did. It was, yeah, it was a lot. But she just wants to talk to you and work things -"

"OK, I need everyone to accept I am not going to talk to Grace right now." Davis interrupted. "For my own sanity, I need to close the book on that."

"I understand, I really do," Patrick said quickly, "you're hurt and you're angry and -"

"No Patrick, I am not hurt and angry, I am just *done.*" Davis interrupted emphatically. "I am just *done.* I don't want this anymore. I want it all to fucking *stop*. I'm trying to get my life back in order and I don't want to deal with this shit anymore."

"Come on man, this is *Grace* we're talking about." Patrick's tone became more terse. "This isn't some random person, it's Grace. She loves you and -"

"She couldn't even pick up a phone to talk to me when I was recovering from burns I sustained saving her fucking drunk of a father." Davis hissed down the phone.

"Hey," Patrick almost barked the word, "come on, she never asked you to do that. You went down there yourself."

"Right, so why the fuck is she crawling off to Wyoming if she has nothing to feel guilty about?" When Patrick didn't respond, Davis continued. "I know everyone has it in their head that Grace and I are some sort of Clearwater Power Couple. We aren't. Whenever we need each other, one of us splits. If that's love Patrick, then we should stay the fuck away and stop hurting each other." Patrick remained silent, and Davis sighed. "I don't know what else to tell you, Pat. It's over. Done. I can't do this anymore."

"OK," came the reply, after several more seconds of silence. "OK. I understand. I do." The line went dead.

Davis felt like his skin was ten sizes too small. The room felt oppressively tiny all of a sudden. He wanted to run outside and scream his lungs out. He wanted to punch the walls down. He sat down heavily on the side of his bed, put his head between his knees and breathed deeply to try and calm himself down.

I need to get the fuck out of this town.

He looked out the window at the blinding snow battering the window pane, and hoped and prayed the thaw came soon. He didn't want to stay in Clearwater a minute longer than he needed to.

Chapter Eleven

The nightmare startled him out of sleep. Davis lay flat on his back, chest heaving, waiting for the heat of the flames to subside. Rain pelted against his windows. It was still dark. His throat was dry and his tongue stuck to the roof of his mouth. He swung his legs over the side of the bed, sitting up and wincing as his knee protested against the sudden movement.

He reached for the glass of water beside his bed, and found it empty. He got to his feet, walking through the dark apartment to the kitchen. He filled up his glass, and took a long gulp. Swallowing hurt his throat. Since the fire he'd had problems, often waking up with a sore throat and chest. He was sure he was snoring. The doctors had told him he might have some issues, but no one could tell him how long they'd last for, or if they'd ever get any better.

Davis walked over to the glass balcony doors, and gazed out at the rain-soaked city. Seattle was great, and he liked it a lot. He enjoyed his new job, and his boss was very understanding and supportive of his employees. His colleagues were a passionate and engaged team, and he'd secured an amazing apartment with a view of the city and the surround beyond it. Life was good.

But the nightmares had returned, in a relentless stream that had almost made it impossible to sleep. He had begun to dread closing his eyes.

In his dream it wasn't always Bob that Davis was hauling from the flames. Sometimes the broken body was Billy's. Sometimes it was his mother, her beautiful big blue eyes staring lifelessly at the flame-red sky. Once it had been Patrick.

And then sometimes, it was Grace. Grace's red hair sticking to his burnt arms. Grace's skin making a sickening hiss as the water of the lake extinguished the flames that were eating her up. Grace's body lying limply beside him as he tried his hardest to stay awake, to fight the oppressive smoke filling his lungs and pulling him down, down into the darkness.

Just like tonight.

He walked back into his bedroom and sat down on the bed, knowing sleep would be impossible for some time. He picked up his phone to check the time - it was 2.47am. He would definitely be working from home today. Lack of sleep always made his breathing worse, and made his whole body ache. A trip into the office, through the rain, and sitting in air conditioning all day, was not what he needed.

Davis lay down and stared at the ceiling. Every time he closed his eyes, Grace's face, flat, lifeless, swam before him. He knew he shouldn't think about her - he'd spent the past 3 months determined not to think about her, and for the most part he'd succeeded. But after every nightmare, every feverish dream where he tried desperately to save her, despite knowing the outcome, despite knowing it ended with her dead in the lake beside him - his mind would wander, wondering where she was. What she was doing. How she was feeling.

She'd not shown up to Patrick's wedding the month before. Davis had braced himself for it, telling himself he could do it, he could cope; he was determined not to let Patrick down. But the night before the wedding,

Sarah had told him Grace had left town again, this time to see her maternal aunt in Oregon.

"She's gotten back in touch with her Mom's family since her Dad died," Sarah had said, rolling her eyes. "I mean, it's great that she has some family, but my god, where the fuck were they after Nancy died?" She'd shaken her head, and tutted in disgust. And Davis had felt the air leave his lungs as though he'd been holding his breath for a week.

The wedding had been lovely - Kayley had officially asked Alison to be her Mom during the ceremony, and there was not a dry eye in the house as the adoption papers were signed. Davis had never seen Patrick so happy, and he was sure Shelley would be thrilled her little family had found a new love, a new wife and mother, to watch over them in her stead. Seeing Patrick and Alison during their first dance, Kayley swaying alongside them and gazing up at her new Momma adoringly, had moved everyone to tears anew.

Coming back to Seattle on his own had not felt as terrible as Davis imagined. He had feared it would feel hollow and lonely, and that he would want to immediately go back home. Instead he had felt good, content, buoyed by the happy celebrations and the ease he felt at simply returning home for a visit. The old awkwardness was gone. But the feelings he had around not seeing Grace were complicated, a mix of relief and disappointment.

And the nightmares really didn't help.

Imagine her alive, he told himself. The therapist had told him to recall a time when the people he loved were alive, a time they'd been together, been happy, to cement that in his reality. Davis took a deep breath, and closed his eyes. At first, he saw Grace, limp beside him, her body swaying in the water of the lake. Floating away from him.

No, she's alive, he told himself. He conjured up her long red hair, her soft skin, her scent - *pears and jasmine, remember?* - and suddenly, he could feel her skin against him, warm, moving, and very much alive.

She was hot, every inch of her felt like fire.

Their bodies slid against each other, slick, bathed in sweat.

He buried his face in her hair, breathing her in.

Her hands grabbed his butt. "Harder," she moaned.

God - fucking - dammit. He opened his eyes, sighing heavily as his erection strained against the fabric of his pyjama pants. This probably wasn't what his therapist had had in mind. *You fucking idiot,* he scolded himself.

Now he wanted to call her more than ever. He wanted to check she was OK. He wanted to make sure the nightmares weren't some sort of bad omen, that she was in trouble. He picked up his phone, and brought up her number. *Don't do it, man.*

He knew he couldn't. He shouldn't. It was stupid. He had left her behind him. Why call her now? What was the point? *You're horny, that's all,* he reasoned with himself. *You're horny and you miss her and you're worried. It's not a great combination. Let it go.*

Suddenly his phone began ringing, and he was so startled he almost dropped it. His heart leaped into his throat when he saw it was his mother calling. It was 3am.

Something was wrong.

"Mom?" At first he didn't hear anything. "Mom?" He said again, feeling panic rising in his chest. A loud, heaving sob broke the silence.

"Davis!" Patricia cried. "Oh Davis -" She broke off.

"Mom, oh my god what's going on?"

"Davis?"

It took him a moment to place the soft voice coming through the phone. "Aunt Dora?"

"Yes, honey," came the reply. "It's me. You need to come right home. Your Dad's had a stroke. And the doctor's aren't sure he's going to make it."

The next flight to San Francisco left too late for him. Davis drove the entire 900 miles back to Clearwater, leaving almost as soon as he'd gotten off the phone with his aunt. He stopped only for gas, and to call his boss, letting him know there'd been a family emergency that he had to rush home for. Davis was incredibly grateful when the man didn't ask any questions, and just told him to take all the time he needed.

His mind raced as he drove. *Hold on Dad. Don't die. Please don't die.* The words he'd uttered to Bob, the plea he'd made lying in that lake - now he was making the same plea of his own father.

His aunt hadn't given him too many more details, she'd just told him that Paulson had come home early that afternoon from a walk, complaining of a headache. He'd gone to shower, and had collapsed in the bathroom. Patricia had found him unconscious. Davis couldn't even imagine how frightening it must have been for his mother.

He went straight to the hospital in Mammoth Lake, pulling up in the parking lot well after the sun had sunk behind the horizon. He rushed through the front doors, where a nurse regarded him sympathetically when he told her why he was there. She directed him to the intensive care unit, and Davis ignored the jolt in his knee as he ran down the seemingly endless corridors.

Most of the family had congregated in a tiny waiting room, and several pairs of sympathetic eyes met him as he burst through the doors. His aunts and uncles, some of his cousins - they all looked terrible, sad and drawn. His aunt Dora approached him, and even through his grief he wondered what his poor aunt must be feeling, seeing her little brother on his deathbed.

His deathbed. The words made Davis's stomach sink.

"Oh Davis, he'll be so glad to see you," Aunt Dora said sadly. "I hope he's still awake." She nudged him gently towards the doors of the ICU, where a nurse let him in, and showed him through to his father's bed.

Davis stopped short. His father - his strong, burly father - looked tiny and grey in the stark white sheets of the hospital bed. A tube ran into his mouth. The *beep beep beep* of all the machines Paulson was hooked up to sent a wave of nausea through Davis, as he remembered waking up in the hospital. Back when Paulson had thought he'd lost his only son.

Patricia sat beside her husband, holding his hand. Her face was bright red from crying, her eyes bloodshot. She stroked Paulson's hand over and over again. Paulson did not react. His eyes remained closed, his chest puffing up with each breath the machine beside him took for him.

"They said he won't last the night," Patricia said without turning around. "They - they said, it was a mass - massive stroke." Her breath caught in her throat, and she stroked Paulson's hand with more urgency. "He'd come home and said he had a headache. I told him to take a Tylenol and have a shower. I - I thought it was just a headache."

"Mom, you couldn't have known," Davis assured her, putting a hand on her shoulder.

"He'd been having so many headaches lately, we thought it was just the weather..." Her voice trailed off.

Davis sat down on the other side of the bed, looking down at his father's hand - the big strong hands, now lying limply, unmoving. "I wanted to say goodbye," Davis said quietly, reaching out to touch his father, and almost recoiling at the feel of his skin. Cold, smooth, something like stone. Like Paulson was already dead.

Patricia looked over at him. "Your name was the last word he said," she told him, before silent sobs began to rack her shoulders.

Davis stood up, and leaned over his father. "Dad," he said softly, "Dad, I'm here." Paulson's eyes remained closed. "Dad, I'm here, and it's OK. I'm here. It's OK. I'll look after Mom. You don't have to worry." He planted a kiss on his father's forehead, and his tears began to flow. He'd never kissed his father before. He laid his head against his father's forehead. "It's OK Dad. I'm here."

Paulson's chest rose suddenly, and a long breath hissed through the tubes coming out of his mouth. His fingers twitched, and Patricia gasped, grabbing his hand. "Sweetheart," she said urgently, jumping up and stroking her husband's cheek. "We're here, sweetheart, oh my love, we're here."

Davis felt he couldn't breathe for a moment, watching his father's face to see if he'd wake up. Paulson took another raggedy breath. And another. Then another. Then his face seemed to relax, all the tension going out of his cheeks. His chest sunk, and the monitors began to beep in a long, loud monotone.

"Oh no," Patricia wailed, "oh no, oh my love, no." She laid her head on Paulson's chest, sobbing. "Oh my love, no. No."

Davis sat down heavily, laying his head on his father's hand. There was no more movement in Paulson's fingers.

Patricia continued to wail.

Davis heard people enter the room, but he didn't raise his head from his father's hand.

The coffee in Davis's hand had gone cold. He stared at the sunrise, feeling numb. This was the first day of his life where he didn't have a father.

They had come to take his father's body down to the morgue after the family had all come to say their last farewells, and Patricia had wailed and screamed and refused to let go of her husband. After some gentle convincing, Aunt Dora had managed to lead her sister-in-law away, telling Davis she would take his mother home. Patricia had been too distraught to protest.

Davis had gone down into the morgue with his father's body, determined to be with him until the very end. He watched as they covered his father's body in a heavy sheet, and wheeled him in to the next room. Everyone whose path he crossed expressed condolences, grief, sympathy. He barely acknowledged any of them. He felt like a puppet, merely moving because he had to, some unseen force pulling the strings and forcing him forwards.

Now he sat on the bench outside the hospital, watching the sun rise, the sky turning shades of pink and purple and peach, knowing his father would never again see a sunrise, or a sunset, or have another cup of coffee, or read his paper at the kitchen table like he did every morning. Davis felt tears running down his cheeks. He tried to breathe deeply, but his chest was tight and heavy.

Someone sat down beside him, and laid a hand on his shoulder.

"I'm so sorry, Davis," Patrick said quietly.

"He was just - just gone." Davis said. "I wanted to say goodbye."

"He knew you were here," Patrick assured him, gently taking the cold coffee from Davis's hand and replacing it with a fresh, hot cup. "They know, believe me. He waited for you. He held on until you got here to say goodbye."

Davis took a sip of the coffee, not tasting it but being grateful for the warmth it imparted. "How did you even survive Shelley dying?" Davis asked.

Patrick sighed. "I nearly didn't, that's how." He replied. "I thought it would kill me. And I'd be lying if I said I didn't want to crawl right into that grave after her. But I had Kayley, and my parents, and I know that's not what Shelley would have wanted anyway. They want us to live. They want us to go on and live and be happy."

Davis began to cry, and Patrick placed an arm around his friend's shoulders. "Your Dad loved you," Patrick told him, "and you loved him, and he knew it."

"He always wanted to be a grandfather," Davis said shakily, "he wanted grandkids so bad."

Patrick kept his arm around Davis as he wept. The two men sat there like that, as the sun rose and the sky became bluer and bluer above them, for the longest time, neither one saying a word.

Patrick insisted on driving Davis home.

Paulson's truck stood in the drive, and Davis paused beside it, staring in the window of the cab. The truck his father had driven home two nights ago. Alive. Davis struggled to recall their last conversation. They had talked on the phone last week - hadn't they? For some reason he couldn't remember a single word they had said. It was all just lost in a haze.

Davis walked into the house, his family home, and it was oddly silent. No bubbling coffee machine, no smells of breakfast cooking. No Paulson at the table in the kitchen reading his paper. The house was cold and quiet and dark. He went to check on his mother, and found her bedroom empty. Aunt Dora must have taken Patricia back to her house. That was good, she needed people around her.

Davis found himself standing in the den, unsure of what to do with himself. He looked down and realised he was still wearing the clothes he'd driven down in the day before. He suddenly felt heavy and grimy. He went to his old bedroom. The bed was made, as it always was. A pair of jeans and a t-shirt he'd forgotten on his last visit lay neatly folded at the end of the bed.

He stripped off and headed into the shower. He stood under the hot stream of water for so long that it started to run cold. The sky had darkened, and as he dressed he heard thunder rumbling in the distance. The weather matched his mood.

In the kitchen, he put on the coffee machine. He wasn't even sure he wanted any. He knew he should probably sleep, he'd been awake for over 24 hours. But his brain was on autopilot, and putting on the coffee machine seemed like the most normal thing to do at that moment. *Mom and Dad would want a coffee right now,* he thought to himself, and stared at the machine as the coffee dripped down into the pot.

There would be a funeral to think about. He realised that he'd not packed any black clothes, much less a suit. He would have to ring his boss, and take more time off work. And then after all of that his mother would be alone here, in the house they'd shared.

Maybe he should ask her to move to Seattle with him? No, that was too soon. She wouldn't want to leave this house, not yet.

Maybe one day.

Maybe not at all.

He walked back into the den, taking a photo album from the bottom shelf of the bookcase. He flipped open the white cover, which cracked and protested. The photographs were from his childhood, he was maybe four or five? There he was, proudly holding up a fish, his wide smile gapped from his first lost baby tooth. His father sat in the background, fishing rod in hand, gazing at the camera, a small smile on his face.

That was probably as much as he allowed himself back then. Davis couldn't remember him smiling much.

Davis turned to the next page, to pictures of him starting school. Next to him, a grinning boy with curly dark hair and rosy cheeks proudly held up his small yellow backpack.

Billy, Davis thought mournfully.

In the background he saw Grace, her long red plaits hanging down her back, holding his mother's hand. He had a faint memory of that day - his father had taken the photograph, that much he remembered - and he was sure Bob Weaver had not been there. He recalled that Grace had been crying because she wanted to start school too, and Patricia had bought her a pink backpack as a consolation. Grace was standing with Patricia, gazing up at her with the same adoring gaze Kayley had given Alison at the wedding.

The following pictures were more of the same, school plays and Christmas parties. Davis hauled out another photo album; suddenly the past was a much more accommodating place to be, and he wanted to remember it all, to forget the present and immerse himself in memory.

This album was from his senior year in high school. A photo of Davis and Billy at track. Photos from football games. Davis being awarded Best in Play for the year. Then photos of the prom.

There was young Davis, in his tuxedo. And Grace, her hair swept up atop her head, wearing a blue dress, pinning a corsage to his lapel. And then him, tying a corsage to her arm. Smiling at each other. Young, in love. Hopeful. No idea of what lay ahead.

Davis shoved the album away. No. No. He didn't need that today.

He pulled out the album at the very end of the shelf. It was probably once white, but had yellowed over the years. The words "Our Wedding" were written across the front in gold lettering, which had almost completely chipped away. Davis flipped open the cover - and there were his parents. His mother, with a huge round pregnant belly, a flowing white gown draped over it. White flowers adorned her curly blonde hair. She was glowing, radiant, so very young. His father stood beside his pretty bride, smiling down at her proudly.

Pictures of his parents dancing followed. The family throwing rose petals. There was Aunt Dora, herself pregnant at the time with Davis's cousin Tiffany. She and Patricia stood side by side comparing bumps in one picture, Paulson standing off to one side laughing. His father was laughing. He looked so young, so *happy.* Davis had never seen him like that.

He turned the pages, more and more wedding photos following. He was about to put it away, when the last page flipped open as he went to close it. There was his father, holding a tiny baby with a mass of sticky blonde curls on its head, wrapped in a blue blanket. Paulson gazed down at the newborn, its tiny hand wrapped around his huge, stout finger. The love and awe on Paulson's face was evident. The next picture showed Paulson looking directly at the camera, his smile wide, holding up the little baby to show him off. Underneath Patricia had written "His Father's Joy - Davis, born 09/17/1992."

Davis felt the air leave his lungs, as though he had been punched. He felt a roar rising in his ears, and it took him a moment to realise the sound was coming from his own mouth.

"No!" He howled like a wounded animal, punching the wall. "*Why? Why?*"

Thunder rumbled above as the reply, and Davis wept until his body ached. His father, who had just started being a real father, a father that had spent Davis's whole life unable to express his love and pride for his son. Who had thought he'd nearly lost him, and insisted that it was never too late. Now he was gone, never to return, and it truly was too late. Paulson had been wrong.

Davis crawled up onto the sofa, exhausted, and welcomed the darkness that swiftly overtook him.

Davis stared at his reflection in the steamy mirror. He knew he should move, he knew he had to get ready for the funeral. But he couldn't will his legs to carry him out of the bathroom. Today was when it became real. Today they would say their final goodbye to Paulson, and he'd go into the ground, with Billy and Nancy and Bob fucking Weaver, and that would be it. The end of the man in the wedding photos, the end of the proud father holding up his newborn son.

He'd taken himself off to Mammoth Lake to buy a suit and shirt the day before, and he'd been so lost in his grief that he'd been halfway back to Clearwater before he remembered that he hadn't bought shoes. He'd turned around and spent another hour trying to find a shoe store and shoes that fit his enormous feet, and then on the way back from that journey he realised he hadn't bought a tie.

And suddenly it felt like the worst thing that had ever happened to him - that he would go to his father's funeral without a tie. He'd had to pull over, the grief made his body stiff and heavy and he couldn't focus on the road ahead of him. He wasn't sure how long he sat there, trying to breathe deeply, trying to fumble his way out of the numbness that overwhelmed him. Not even tears flowed any more.

He finally made it back home, where his mother assured him that his father had plenty of ties and that he wouldn't mind if Davis borrowed one. And the numb feeling came back all over again when Davis realised his mother still talked about his father like he was going to walk back in through the door at any moment.

"Honey?" His mother's voice came from the bedroom. When he didn't respond, she called out again. "Davis?" Her voice was hoarse from crying.

Davis pushed himself away from the bathroom sink, walking into his bedroom to find Patricia perched on the edge of his bed, dressed in a black skirt and blouse. Davis had never seen his mother wear black before, and she looked almost like a stranger, pale and tired. Her brilliant blue eyes were bloodshot from the tears that never seemed to stop. She looked up at him and smiled weakly, holding out a silver and dark grey striped tie in her hands.

"This is the most appropriate one I could find in your father's things," she said. "I can help you tie it if you like, I know your father never mastered it."

"Thanks Mom, I got it." He assured her, shrugging on his white shirt and buttoning it up before laying the tie under his collar and fastening it into a smooth knot. Patricia handed him his jacket and stood before him as he finished getting dressed.

"So, are we ready to go?" She asked weakly.

Davis nodded. "It'll be OK, Mom." He didn't believe the words as he said them, but he wanted to be strong for his mother all the same. She took a shaky breath, grasped Davis's hand, and they walked out of the house together.

One of Davis's cousins had come to take them to the church, and mercifully said very little as they drove down the mountain road into town. Davis could barely think through the numbness that had again settled on him. He felt as though he had blinked, and was suddenly sitting in the front pew of the church, next to his mother, whose tears had begun to flow again. The sight of his father's casket shocked him - how could someone fit into a box that small? His father had been a big man. Surely he wasn't in there.

The service passed in a blur. Neither he nor his mother felt able to speak, so Aunt Dora had volunteered to give the eulogy. Davis felt ashamed that he had let his father down, that he should have the strength to speak - fathers spoke at their own children's funerals, and yet here he was unable to speak at his father's. His mother had assured him that his father knew they loved him, and didn't need a eulogy to prove that. It didn't make Davis feel any better.

Aunt Dora spoke lovingly of her brother, of his love for his family, how he had overcome their childhood of poverty to build a home for his wife and son, of whom he was immensely proud. Patricia began to cry again, and Davis put his arm around his mother.

Soon enough, they were following the casket outside, watching it be lowered into the ground. Davis and his mother stepped forward to throw a handful of dirt down into the grave. Davis stared down at the box that held his sleeping father, then opened his hand above it, letting the dirt drop with a soft thud.

"Goodbye Dad," he whispered, stepping back from the grave and looking up, across the cemetery. It was a beautiful day. The sun shone, there was not a cloud in the sky and birds were singing in the trees nearby. There was no hint of a storm, no smell of smoke in the sky.

He thought he saw a figure standing in the distance, partially hidden by a tree. He thought for a moment that he saw flowing red hair, but decided it was his imagination.

Davis passed through the wake in a haze of disconnection. Patrick was there with Alison, Tyler came and gave his condolences. An endless stream of his father's friends and former colleagues, all giving him a firm handshake and a clap on the shoulder, assuring him that Paulson had been so proud of his son. "He talked about you all the time," Davis was told over and over.

After what felt like an age, the mourners began to leave, until it was just Aunt Dora and Patricia in the house with him. "Are you heading back to Seattle right away?" Aunt Dora asked Davis as they finished filling the dishwasher.

Davis shook his head as he started putting the food everyone had brought - it seemed like a year's worth of casseroles and tray bakes - into the fridge and chest freezer. "I'm not sure yet. My boss said to take all the time I need. I'm not sure what Mom wants to do yet."

Aunt Dora looked out the window onto the porch, where she had parked Patricia with a glass of wine. "I'm not sure either," she said sadly, "I can't imagine being here on her own will do her much good. But I don't think I can convince her to move closer to us, or to you for that matter." She sighed. "Patricia loves this house."

"Yes she does," Davis agreed, "I figure we all just need to give her time to decide what she wants to do."

Aunt Dora nodded. "Well, I might take her home with me again." She suggested. "Do you want to come down too? There's plenty of space for us all, and I think it would do you all good to not be alone."

"You go ahead," Davis said reassuringly, "I'll head down after you all once I'm done cleaning up here. I could use the quiet to clear my head."

Aunt Dora hesitated, but then nodded. "OK, you head on down when you're ready. Maybe we can have a barbecue! The weather is lovely!" Suddenly, her face crumpled a little and she put a hand to her forehead. "Oh dear, I can't believe I just said that."

"Hey, that sounds great," Davis said quickly, taking Aunt Dora's hand and giving her a smile. "It'll be great. Let's do that."

She returned the smile through tears, gave his hand a squeeze, and headed out onto the porch.

A while later he heard the car leaving the driveway, and Davis collapsed onto the kitchen floor, his legs spread out in front of him, his head leaning back against the cupboard doors. Would normal life ever feel normal again? He wondered if there would ever be a time when the sadness of losing his father wouldn't overshadow everything, when laughing or enjoying the sunshine or planning a barbecue wouldn't feel frivolous or somehow disrespectful.

We don't get over it, we get used to it. That's what his therapist had said about grief, about loss. Davis was sure a day would come when the grief and the numbness wouldn't occupy every fibre of his being. But today, it soaked into his bones and made him feel heavy and tired.

He heard a car on the gravel of the drive. A few moments later, quick steps sounded on the porch, and someone knocked lightly at the door. Davis answered it to Grace's tear-streaked face. Without hesitation, she threw herself into his arms. She collapsed against him, weeping. "I'm so sorry, Davis," she wailed. "I'm so sorry."

Davis held her, enveloping her, burying his face in her hair, breathing her in. He could taste the salt of her tears as he pressed his mouth into her cheek, feeling her warmth and her softness. It was the most natural thing in the world to have her here, to be holding her.

"I know I shouldn't be here," she sobbed, pulling back to look in his eyes. "I'm so sorry, I know I'm probably the last person you -"

He smothered her words with his mouth. He kissed her deeply, hungrily seeking her tongue out with his. She froze for only a moment, then wound her arms around his neck, and he lifted her up, carrying her blindly to the kitchen. They found their way to the counter, Grace's legs wrapped around his waist, the sundress she was wearing riding up around her thighs. They both grabbed at his shirt, undoing the buttons with clumsy, frantic fingers and discarding it on the floor.

Suddenly, Grace pushed against his chest with both hands. "Davis stop." She said breathlessly.

"Why?" He asked, pushing back against her hands to kiss her neck.

"This isn't how this should happen," she insisted, pushing back against him again and looking up at him with her big grey eyes. "You're sad, you're grieving, this is -"

"I don't want to think about it." He brushed his lips against hers, "I just want to be with you." He ran his hands up her thighs. "I need you, right now."

"No," Grace said softly, gently taking his hands and holding them in hers. "Stop."

"Don't you want this too?" He asked.

She gave him a small smile. "More than you can imagine. But not like this." She let go of one his hands to stroke his face gently. "I know you're hurting, but this won't change that."

Davis put his forehead against hers, and a deep, sighing sob escaping his throat. "I'm sick of crying," he whispered.

"I know."

"I'm sick of death."

"I know, baby."

"I'm sick of feeling so numb."

Grace put her arms around his neck and drew him close. Her sweetness and her smell and her soft skin enveloped him, and something unfurled in his stomach, like a knotted vine coming loose, and he sobbed into her shoulder.

"The numbness goes away, I promise," she said after a long time, when his sobs had subsided. "You'll start to feel again."

"I feel so pathetic, crying all the time," he told her.

Grace shook her head. "Oh baby, no." She squeezed him tighter. "Crying doesn't make you weak." She held his face in her hands and smiled hopefully. "Remember, you didn't want to be like our fathers? This is part of that."

"Why didn't you ever tell me about the baby?" More loss, more death. But he needed to know.

Grace closed her eyes for a minute and inhaled sharply. When she opened her eyes again, they were filled with tears. "I should have told you," she said quietly, "I wanted to, so many times."

"When did you find out?" He took a step away from her, leaning against the counter beside her.

Grace rearranged her dress, and sighed. "About a month after you left." She told him, not meeting his eyes. "I'd been feeling terrible, but I thought it was stress, grief, all of that." She shrugged. "I realised my period was really, really late. When the test was positive, I panicked. I didn't know what to do."

"Why didn't you just call me?" Davis asked, taking her hand.

She looked down at their entwined fingers and gave them a sad smile. "I don't know," she admitted after a while. "I spent weeks wondering what to do. I thought - I thought, I should tell you face to face. So I booked a plane ticket. My Dad had been awful to me, yelling all the time. I don't think he'd been sober a day after Billy died." She swallowed hard. "So, then, well, three days before I was meant to leave I - I came home and found Dad at the bottom of the stairs. He'd had -" She looked up at Davis, and the look on her face broke his heart. "I *thought* he'd fallen. I guess I was wrong, as always."

"I'm so sorry, Grace," Davis said. "I was such an asshole. I shouldn't have told you like that."

Grace shrugged. "It doesn't make a difference. I know my Dad - I know he hated me." She said the words very slowly, as though they were a very recent revelation, still taking shape. "He always hated us. He loved our Mom, he worshipped her. She was beautiful, wealthy, intelligent. The whole package. He only had us because she wanted children."

"He could have let your Mom's family have you," Davis said, trying not to let his hatred of that bastard Bob Weaver colour his voice.

"Sure, but then who'd clean the house and get the beers?" Grace asked sadly, trying to smile.

Davis shook his head. "So, when did you lose the baby?"

"The day after my Dad's surgery, I was sitting by his bed, and I - I had this pain, just this really weird, dull feeling." She stared out the window. "I went to the bathroom, and I was bleeding. I freaked out. I told my Dad I had to go and get something to eat, and I ran down to the emergency room." She bit her lip, and blinked hard. "They did a sonogram, and - and there was no heartbeat." Her voice broke on the last word, and a small sob escaped her. She looked at Davis with her dark grey eyes full of tears. "It was a boy." She whispered, and covered her face with her hand.

A boy, Davis thought to himself. *Our son.* He drew Grace close as she cried, holding her as quiet sobs shook her shoulders. The baby she'd kept secret, that she'd not been able to mourn with anyone. After she had just lost her brother, after she had just lost Davis - she'd lost her son, and been all alone.

"I'm so sorry Grace," he whispered, stroking her hair. "I should have been here. I should never have left you. I'm so sorry."

"The next day, when I went back to see my Dad, he yelled at me, asked where the hell I'd been, berated me for leaving him all alone." Grace straightened up and looked at him, stroking his cheek with her hand. "I should have come with you. I never should have stayed here." She put her lips to his, and she tasted sweet and salty. "I should have listened to you."

"My Mom said you were coming after me again," Davis said, his eyes still closed.

Grace sighed, her hand still on his face. "Yes. Just before Hal came along."

Davis opened his eyes, and looked at her. "What happened? I mean, what made you want to follow me again?"

Grace shrugged again, the sad smile back on her face. "I held Kayley." She said simply. "I went to the hospital after she was born, and I held her, and she was so tiny and sweet, and I saw Shelley and Patrick just so happy, and I - I just wanted that. I wanted it with you. But I didn't know, I just didn't know if you had someone else, if you'd even want to see me again. So I went to see your Mom."

Davis nodded, waiting for her to continue.

"She assured me you hadn't met anyone," Grace went on. "Her face, when I told her about the baby." Grace inhaled sharply. "She was devastated. She told me I should have come to her immediately." She shook her head. "I'm so stupid. Your Mom was the only Mom I ever really had, and when I really needed her, I told myself I had no one. Instead I defended my Dad and tried to convince myself he loved me." They sat in silence for a moment. "So, after speaking to her, I went and bought a ticket, and packed my bags. I was going to leave for good. I packed everything - Billy's watch, my Mom's jewellery, everything. I didn't want to come back. I wanted to be with you, forever, wherever you were."

"And then your Dad -"

"Yes," Grace interrupted, laughing bitterly, "yes, and then my Dad. I can't believe how naive I am"

"You loved him," Davis reasoned, "who would think he'd be capable of something like that?"

"Everybody, Davis," Grace said. "Everybody would think he was capable of something like that. Everyone, except me."

There was nothing else to say. Davis suddenly felt tired, heavy, the weariness of the day, the past week, suddenly sitting on his shoulders and threatening to drag him to the ground. "I need to sleep," he muttered against Grace's hair, and she nodded.

"I'll go then," she said, sliding down off the kitchen counter.

"No," Davis exclaimed, seizing her hand. "Please, just - nothing like before. I don't want to be alone." He drew her close, his arms around her waist. "I just don't want to be alone. Just - just lie with me?"

Grace nodded, stroking his cheek and planting a soft kiss on his lips. "OK. I'll stay with you."

They lay on his bed, as they had so many times before, all those years ago, as teenagers, and simply held each other. Davis stroked her hair gently, the afternoon sun casting shadows across the ceiling, and even as thunder began to rumble in the distance, he felt nothing but peace. She was here, in his arms. Alive. Breathing. They were together again. And for that moment, it was enough.

"So, what happens now?" Grace asked.

Davis stopped drying his hair and looked at her questioningly. "With -?" The word hung between them for a moment.

"Your Mom," Grace clarified, sitting cross-legged on the edge of the bed.

"Oh," he replied, the butterflies in his stomach subsiding only slightly. Davis hung up his towel and stepped out of the bathroom, pulling on a pair of sweatpants and laying back down on the bed, his arm behind his head. Grace turned immediately to snuggle in under his arm, and looked up at him expectantly. "I don't know," he answered after a while. "I haven't talked to her about it at all. I don't think she'll want to leave though. She loves this house, she's lived here for 30 years. With Dad." He emphasised.

Grace nodded. "She needs time."

They lay silently for a while, Grace stroking his chest.

"I thought," Davis began hesitantly, "I thought you meant -"

"Us," Grace interrupted. She sat up, leaning on one hand and pushing her long hair over her shoulder. "You thought I meant what was happening with us." She sighed and looked out the window. "I don't know, Davis. I don't know if either of us is in a state to make that sort of decision right now."

"I want to be with you," Davis said, running a hand down her arm. She looked at him and smiled, her fingers intertwining with his. "I mean it, Grace. This isn't grief talking."

"A few months ago you were telling me to go to hell."

"That was then." He insisted, frustrated and angry at himself for the things he had said back in Patrick's driveway. "I'm sorry for what I said back then. I was angry, and I was hurt. But I've had time, and I think -"

"You just lost your Dad, suddenly." Grace's voice wavered. "It's a hard, awful, sad time for you, and you're thinking about all the things you're going to miss out on, all the things he's going to miss out on. Being with me won't bring him back."

"It's not like that." Davis swung his legs over the side the bed, sitting up with his back away from her. She said nothing, waiting for him to continue. "What happened to make you leave?" He asked, looking over his shoulder at her.

Grace winced, and wrapped her arms around her legs, curling up into an almost protective ball. She shook her head. "I can't even tell you anymore," she said quietly. "When you went down there, as soon as you left I panicked. I couldn't believe you'd gone down there to get him. I wanted to drive after you and stop you, but your Mom wouldn't let me leave." She took a deep breath. "You didn't come back, and I - I lost it. I don't remember anything, except your Mom and I crying. I felt so guilty. Your Dad, he kept giving me this look - I remember you talking about the looks you got, after Billy died." She paused and bit her lip, blinking back tears. "It felt like how I imagine that would have felt. The guilt ate me up."

"I'm sure he didn't mean it that way."

Grace continued on as though she hadn't heard him. "The next morning, before the sun had even gone up, the choppers were out, looking for you. The entire trail had burnt out, it took them hours to cut through all the debris. And then, they found you - " she stopped, a small sob escaping her trembling lips, and she tipped her head back, staring at the ceiling as though she could make the tears stop falling. "You were covered in blood, you were barely breathing, it took them I don't know how long to find a pulse. They rushed you off to the hospital, and I just," she looked at him helplessly, and shrugged. "I'm so sorry. I just couldn't face it. I remembered Billy, and then I saw my Dad, almost the same, and it was too much. I'm so sorry, Davis. I'm so sorry." Her head dropped onto her knees, and her whole body shook as she sobbed.

Davis moved across the bed and pulled her into his lap, holding her as she wept. Of course she had run. Of course she had panicked. "It's OK," he whispered. She wrapped her arms around his neck. "It's OK, we're together now."

"Patrick called me to tell me you were in a coma, that your leg was shattered." She shook her head against his shoulder. "I couldn't, I just -" She moved her head away from his shoulder, and looked down at his hands, running her fingers along the scars the flames had left behind. "Do they hurt?" She asked quietly.

"No, not any more," Davis assured her.

"Is - is it hard to do things?"

"It used to be." He lifted his hands to her face. "But now, holding on to things is a lot easier."

She sobbed quietly. "I'm so sorry, Davis. You just lost your Dad, and I'm here crying my eyes out -"

"Shhh, enough." He wiped her tears away with his thumbs. "No more. I'm here. You're here. And that's all that matters. All that other shit, it doesn't matter anymore. We both made mistakes. But that's done now. I'm here. You're here." He kissed her tenderly, and her lips stopped shaking, her sobs finally subsiding. "I'm not losing you again." He whispered.

"Davis, you just lost your Dad, you're upset and -"

"No," he cut her off. "I'm not losing anymore time with you. I'm not wasting anymore time wondering and worrying if we're going to mess this up. My Dad, he believed we could make it work, that it wasn't too late for us. He told me that, it's never too late."

"I think sometimes it is," she said sadly.

Davis shook his head emphatically, still gently holding her face. "Only if we say it is. And I say, it isn't. I want to marry you. I want - I want to have a baby with you." She closed her eyes, her face crumpling. "I want *life* with you. Whatever that means. However it looks. I want *you,* Grace."

She opened her eyes, releasing a stream of tears down her cheeks. "I want you too."

"So, you'll marry me?"

She laughed incredulously through her tears. "Oh Davis, come on."

"I mean it."

She tilted her head to the side. "Stop it, you're crazy."

He smiled. "Maybe I am." He shrugged. "So, will you marry me?"

"Are you serious?" She asked, her eyes widening a little.

"Goddammit, Grace," he scooped her up, climbing off the bed with her in his arms, putting her on her feet and dropping down onto one knee in front of her. "Grace Julianna Weaver, will you be my wife?" He asked, clasping her hand in his.

Grace covered her mouth with her other hand, and nodded.

"Say it," Davis insisted, unable to stop smiling.

"You're crazy."

"I want to hear you say it."

"Yes," she gasped from behind her hand. "Oh Davis, yes." She threw herself down on him, her arms around his neck. "Yes, yes I'll marry you!" She kissed him tenderly, and he wrapped his arms around her waist, holding her close.

For the first time in what felt like an eternity, Davis felt sunlight within him. The numbness washed away. She was here. Alive. In his arms.

He didn't have to imagine it anymore.

"What is everyone going to think?" Grace asked as he stroked her hair, her head resting on his chest.

"I don't care," Davis said. He pulled her closer, enjoying the feeling of her naked skin against his. They hadn't made it to bed the first time they made love, too frantic and enthralled to even think of moving from the floor.

But the second time, they had taken their time with each other, moving slowly, deliberately, as though committing each other to memory. She was like coming home. She was perfect for him, in every way. Now they lay together, their skin cooling and the sunlight outside fading as dark clouds drew together.

Grace looked up at him. "I just don't want anyone to think this is all in bad taste, us getting engaged the day after your Dad's funeral."

Davis shook his head and stroked her cheek. "Anyone who knew my Dad would know this is exactly what he wanted." She looked at him, suppressing a giggle, and Davis laughed. "Ok, I mean *this* is probably not what he was thinking about. But the rest of it, yeah."

"Is your Mom going to be OK with it?"

"Grace, my Mom loves you. She's going to be thrilled."

At that moment, the front door slammed in the distance, and they heard someone walking down the hallway.

"Davis!" They heard Patricia's voice.

Grace's eyes widened and she jumped up out of his arms and off the bed just as the bedroom door opened.

"Oh!" Patricia exclaimed, her eyes first landing on Grace who hastily grabbed a t-shirt and attempted to cover up, then to Davis on the bed, who threw the sheet over himself. Patricia stood, frozen to the spot, for merely a split second, before she closed her eyes and backed out of the room. "Oh, god I'm so sorry!" She quickly closed the door, and then they both heard her start laughing. "I'll go put the coffee on, you two get decent!"

Grace and Davis looked at each other, and burst into laughter themselves. Grace tried to say something about showering, but was laughing too hard to get words out, she merely gestured at the bathroom door.

Once they were showered and dressed, they headed down to the kitchen together, where Patricia sat at the kitchen table, a smile on her face. Thunder began to rumble outside as they sat down together, and Patricia's smile became wider.

"So I take it you two have worked things out?" She asked.

Grace and Davis looked at each other lovingly, and Grace nodded. "We sure have." She said.

"I asked her to marry me." Davis told his mother, whose eyes widened for a moment, before they filled with tears.

"I'm so sorry about the timing," Grace said quickly, clearly alarmed. "I'm so sorry, Patricia. I know you just lost Paulson and -"

Patricia held up her hand. "Honey, no please, this is, oh this is so wonderful! Nothing would have made Paulson happier." She reached across the table and took Grace's hand. "He loved you, honey. He would be so thrilled to know you're going to be his daughter-in-law."

Grace gripped Patricia's hand and bit her lip, and Davis could see she was trying not to cry.

"Do you have a ring yet?" Patricia asked.

Davis shook his head. "Uh no, it was kind of, uh, spontaneous." He said, putting his arm around Grace's shoulders and kissing her on the temple. She leaned into him and sighed happily.

Patricia quickly rose from the table. "Oh, I'll be right back!" She said, and scurried out of the kitchen.

Grace looked at Davis questioningly, who shrugged.

Patricia came back a few minutes later with a blue velvet ring box in her hand, which she placed on the table in front of them as she sat back down. "Now, no pressure at all, but this was my grandmother's engagement ring," she said, opening the ring box. The platinum ring was set with a large elongated oval diamond, surrounded by smaller diamonds.

Grace gasped, and Patricia smiled, clearly pleased. "She was the only one who liked Paulson, who supported us getting married. She gave me this ring to wear until Paulson could buy me one." She took Grace's hand. "If you like it honey, and if Davis is OK with it, I'd like you to have it."

Grace covered her mouth with her hand and began to cry again. "Patricia, it's gorgeous." She turned to Davis, who took the ring from the ring box, and slid it onto Grace's left hand. It fit perfectly. "Are you sure?" Grace asked, gazing at the ring on her hand.

Patricia nodded. "Honey, nothing would make me happier than to see you with that ring on your hand." She rose from the table, walking around to them both. Grace rose and threw her arms around Patricia. "I'm so happy, honey." She said as Grace sobbed. She looked over Grace's shoulder at Davis and extended an arm to hug him as well. "Your Dad would be thrilled." She said again to Davis, and put her hand to his cheek. Davis felt a lump form in his throat and nodded.

Grace excused herself to wash her tear-stained face, and Davis and Patricia sat down at the table together. "I am sorry about the timing Mom," Davis said as his mother stirred sugar into her coffee.

She shook her head. "Oh honey, please don't apologise for being happy." She gave him an earnest look. "Life doesn't stop, even in the moments where we feel like it has. And I mean it, your Dad would be *so* happy." She took his hand. "*I'm* so happy. And I hope you and Grace are too."

Davis nodded. "I am. I mean, we are. So happy."

"So now we have a wedding to plan," Patricia said. "Where do you want to have it?"

"We hadn't really gotten that far," Davis replied sheepishly, and Patricia laughed.

"Yes, I had noticed." She giggled and blushed a little. "Not what I was expecting to come home to, but it's fine, it's fine. Good."

Grace walked back into the kitchen, and Patricia gave her a warm smile. "We were just talking about where you two would like to have the wedding." Patricia said.

"I guess maybe here?" Grace replied after a moment's thought. "Just something small in the garden? I'd rather do it here than have everyone travel to Seattle."

Davis gave her a surprised look. "You want to move to Seattle with me?"

Grace shrugged, smiling. "Where you go, I go."

"Of course," Patricia chimed in. "You two belong together. And a fresh start in a new city is just what you both need."

Davis took Grace's hand and raised it to his lips. "Whatever you want, babe."

Patricia clasped her hands to her mouth, fresh tears springing to her eyes. "I can't tell you how happy I am," she sobbed, rushing around the table to wrap them both in her arms again. "How utterly, wonderfully perfect."

Chapter Twelve

"Hey man, how's married life?" Patrick's face popped up on the screen, a huge smile on his face.

Davis turned the phone towards Grace, who waved from her spot on the couch, and scooted over next to Davis. "Hey, we're doing pretty good." She said, putting her head on Davis's shoulder. "How about y'all? Everything OK?"

Kayley popped up, grinning, a large gap in her teeth. "I lost a tooth and the tooth fairy brought me shiny money and I'm getting a baby brother or sister too!" She exclaimed.

Grace gasped as Patrick and Alison appeared on the screen behind their daughter, smiling. "Oh my god, you're having a baby?" She exclaimed.

Alison nodded. "We sure are," she said, gazing at Patrick lovingly. "I'm due in March."

"Congratulations!" Grace began to cry. "I'm so happy for you!"

"That's awesome, guys," Davis agreed. "Congratulations!"

"Thank you, thank you," Patrick replied, kissing Alison on the head. "We wanted you guys to know first."

"Well, we feel very honoured," Grace said, wiping the tears from her eyes. "Oh, how wonderful. I'm so happy." She began to cry a little harder, and excused herself.

Alison and Patrick exchanged a brief glance, and Alison took Kayley so Patrick and Davis could talk alone. “Everything OK?” Patrick asked.

Davis sighed. “Grace had another miscarriage,” he said sadly. “Last month.”

“Oh shit.” Patrick looked horrified. “I’m so sorry, we should have -“

“No, no, please, don’t apologise.” Davis interrupted. “You can’t have known. It was really early, we found out right after we got back from the honeymoon.”

Patrick shook his head. “Oh man, I’m so sorry, Davis. Do they know what caused it?”

“No idea. They did some tests and Grace is fine and I’m fine and they said we should be able to have a baby one day. Just - not this time, I guess.” Patrick began to apologise again, and Davis cut him off. “We’re so happy for you, really.”

“Thankyou,” Patrick said again, this time with a little less enthusiasm. “We’d wanted to ask you and Grace to be Godparents, but -“

“It’d be an honour,” Davis assured him. “Really, we would love to be.”

They spoke for a few more minutes before saying their goodbyes, and promising to see each other at Christmas. Davis leaned his head back on the lounge, closing his eyes. He was so happy for his friends, but keenly aware of the ache in his chest. He and Grace had lost two babies now. Would they every have the family they so longed for?

His phone beeped, and a message from Patrick popped up. *Didn't want to bring this up in our conversation, but thought it might interest you all the same. Take care.* Underneath the message was a link to an article.

And there was a mugshot of Bentley guy. As Davis began to read the news article, he assumed that perhaps Bentley guy had been shot. Confused for a moment, he scrolled back up and read the headline. "Wanted Drug Baron Found Dead in Mexico." Davis gasped, and read the article again.

Sure enough, it said Bentley guy - Jeffrey Billings, as he had been called - had fled the country after charges of possession and drug dealing had been brought against him. After being on the run for several months, he'd now been found dead in Mexico. The usual suspicions of cartel involvement were spruiked as the article went on, which didn't surprise Davis at all. A cocky rich boy thought he could take on the cartels and got himself into trouble.

He put his phone down and gazed out the glass doors onto the sound. The sun was setting, and a ferry was making its way towards Seattle. It was a peaceful scene.

After a while. Grace emerged from their bedroom, her face red. "Was Patrick OK?" She asked as she sat down and curled up in Davis's arms. "I feel so bad for leaving like that. They have happy news and I make it about me."

Davis shook his head and kissed her hair. "Don't be silly, they understand."

"You told them?"

Davis nodded. "I did. Patrick felt terrible."

"They weren't to know." Grace said.

"No, but they feel terrible for us all the same."

Grace went silent, running her hands gently along Davis's arms. His scars were less and less noticeable every day.

"Oh, by the way," Davis said after a while, "Patrick sent me an article. Bentley Guy's dead."

Grace turned to look at him, surprised. "Seriously?"

"Yep. Dead in Mexico."

Grace raised her eyebrows for a moment. "Jesus."

"Maybe he should have kept the gun instead of pawning it." Davis mused.

Grace smiled weakly, and rose to go to the kitchen. "Do you want a coffee?" She asked.

Davis got up from the couch and followed her, taking a seat at the breakfast bar. "Sure." He watched her as she got out the cups. "I still wonder why Hal sold the gun to him." He said, rubbing his chin. "It seems like such an odd thing to do."

Grace sighed, and avoided his eyes for a moment. "Well," she began, "you're the only one who's ever figured that one out." She looked up at him, and smiled at his puzzled expression. "Hal didn't sell the gun to Bentley guy."

"How do you know?" Davis asked.

"Because I did." Grace replied.

Davis raised his eyebrows. "You did?"

Grace nodded. "Yep."

"Why?"

Grace sighed, and leaned on her forearms on the kitchen counter. "After Shelley died, Patrick had a stack of medical bills. Just, drowning in debt. He tried so hard to keep himself afloat, but he just couldn't manage it. He asked for help, and we all did what we could, but he still needed over $75,000 to cover it all." She shook her head. "He was worried he was going to have to sell the bar, he wasn't sure how he was going to take care of Kayley, he was a mess."

Davis cursed himself silently again for not being around. He'd been in a well-paid job, he could have done more for his friend. Why hadn't Patrick called him? He knew the answer - pride - but felt angry at himself all over again.

"I had my trust fund," Grace went on, smiling bitterly, "or so I thought. I discovered that my father had drunk and gambled his way through Billy's first, and then through mine."

Davis shook his head. "What kind of fucking trust fund was that?"

"The trust fund of my mother," Grace replied dryly. "She adored my Dad, loved him, thought he was wonderful. Trusted him completely. More fool her, I guess." She looked down at her hands. "My Dad never wanted us. He only agreed to have babies because my Mom was desperate for them. She was beautiful, way out of his league, so he did anything she wanted. And then she died, and left us with him." She gave him a sad smile.

"I'm so sorry, babe," Davis reached over and stroked her arm.

Grace shook her head. "It is what it is. Anyway, so the trust fund was gone, and I didn't know what to do to help Patrick. And then Hal," she scoffed, "lost his mind because he thought I was looking to get the money to pay his goddamn lawyers."

"He what?" Davis asked incredulously.

"Yeah, his assets had been frozen and he needed money and of course he wasn't about to admit to his Dad what he'd been up to and what he needed money for, so..." Grace shrugged. "Anyway, when I told him the money was gone, he lost it. And that night, he split. I never saw him again."

"So where does Bentley Guy come into it?"

"He showed up two days after Hal left," Grace explained. "Said he was a business associate of Hal's and couldn't get a hold of him. He was driving this Bentley and wearing an expensive suit and huge Omega watch, and he just oozed that rich kid vibe. It was gross." She wrinkled her nose as though she'd smelled something bad. "He was such a smug asshole. Looked around my tiny apartment and couldn't stop grinning to himself. And then, well, then he saw the gun in the case on the mantle. He asked me if it was for sale, and in that moment I just thought, I hate this gun, I hate what it stands for and who gave it to me - so sure, why not?"

"How much did you ask for?"

"One hundred thousand dollars." Grace said, and laughed when she saw the look of shock on Davis's face. "Hey, I thought, money is nothing to this guy. He wouldn't care. And he literally just nodded, walked outside, came back with a briefcase filled with money, like something out of a mafia movie, and counts out one hundred thousand dollars, then throws in a another 20 grand and his business card and tells me to call him if Hal shows up."

"Holy shit." Davis leaned back in his seat and exhaled heavily. "So why did you report it stolen?"

Grace sighed. "That was my Dad. He came around and saw the gun case was empty, and flew into a rage. I told him Hal must have come back in during the night and stolen it, and my Dad was on the phone to the cops immediately." She rolled her eyes. "I didn't want to lie to the police, but I honestly never thought I would see that gun again." She shook her head and gave him a crooked smile "And then the police called me and told me Davis Chevalier had found the gun in a pawn shop in Mammoth Lake. I damn near had a heart attack."

Davis smiled. "I bet."

"But it was all worth it. It got Patrick out of debt, saved the bar, and meant he could look after his daughter without worrying about anything." Her face crumpled a little again, and Davis took her hand. "I feel so bad for not being happier for Patrick and Alison. He deserves it after everything he went through."

"Of course he does, and you *are* happy for them."

"I just - I just want that too." She said quietly, wiping a tear from her eye.

"Babe, of course you do." Davis gripped her hand tighter. "And we will. One day."

"What if we don't?" She asked him mournfully.

Davis shrugged. "I don't know. But I know we've withstood too much and gone through hell and back to be together, and somehow, someday, we'll have a family. We have as good a chance as anyone of having a baby, and until then, we just have to stay positive." He reached across the counter and put his fingers under her chin, lifting her face so she was looking at him. "Hey. I love you."

"I love you too," she replied, smiling.

They took their coffees out onto the balcony. The leaves on the trees below them were red. Fall was here, and it was becoming very cold. The rain was falling, and they wrapped up in a thick blanket on the love seat together, looking out over the Sound.

"I never thanked you," Grace said suddenly.

"Thanked me? For what?"

"For being the only person Billy could ever rely on."

"Oh Grace."

She turned to him, her eyes bright. "I mean it. Even though it meant you had to make a huge sacrifice, even though it meant you had to carry that guilt and that shame and that judgement, you still did it for him." She snuggled into Davis, and breathed in deeply. "I miss him."

"I know baby. Me too."

They stared out at the Sound as the light faded, keeping each other warm, and knowing that for now, having each other was enough.

2 Years Later

Davis sprinted down the hospital corridor, feeling like his heart was going to burst out of his chest. The nurse at the front desk recognised him as he came barreling through the doors, and stood up, pointing down the hallway. "Room three! Hurry!"

He'd gotten the call while he was at work, and things had gone much faster than he'd anticipated. He thought he'd have time. *Hold on, Grace,* he thought to himself. *I'm here, I'm here.* A lump formed in his throat as he remembered, for just a split second, thinking those words as he ran down the corridor towards his father, hoping and praying he was still there.

But this time was different.

Davis took the corner and kept running, thankful his knee no longer hurt. He skidded to a halt at the door and tore it open. The midwife at Grace's side beckoned him over to the bed, where Grace was red-faced as she bore down. "Quick, Daddy!" The midwife called. "You're just in time!"

Davis rushed to Grace's side and took her hand. "I'm here, baby, I made it." She gripped his hand, not saying a word. She took a deep breath and pushed again.

"Good," the midwife said encouragingly, "that's fantastic, Grace! I can see a full head of hair!"

"You can?" Grace asked weakly.

"I sure can, honey! Now, one more push and your baby's head should be out!"

Grace looked at Davis, and he gave her a smile. "We're nearly there, you'll be holding our baby in just a minute." He said, stroking Grace's forehead. "You're amazing, you're doing so well."

Grace smiled, then grimaced as the next contraction gripped her. She put her chin to her chest and bore down, her hand gripping Davis's ferociously.

"That's your baby's head delivered!" The midwife exclaimed, smiling up at them both.

Davis peeked down, and saw the tiny head, covered in sticky brown curls. Their child. Their child was almost here.

Grace gripped his hand again, and a scream tore from her mouth as she pushed once more, and their baby slithered out onto the bed. "Look Mama!" The midwife cried as she lifted the tiny purple baby onto Grace's chest.

Grace sobbed and pulled the baby close to her. Davis felt his face would crack from smiling. He stroked his child's face, soft and warm, like velvet. Grace looked down, then gazed up at him, her eyes full of wonder. "It's a girl, Davis," she said, through sobs and laughter. "We've got a girl!"

Davis kissed her forehead, and lay his head on the pillow, gazing at his daughter's face as she began to squirm and let out a long wail. Grace stroked the tiny baby's back with her hand. "Oh it's OK, little girl," she said soothingly. "Oh we've been waiting for you for such a long time."

"We sure have," Davis whispered, his voice catching in his throat. His daughter reached up and wrapped her tiny hand around his fingers, her skin purplish-white against his.

"Congratulations," the midwife said to them, beaming. "She's adorable. Do we have a name?"

"Willow," Grace said, not taking her eyes off the baby on her chest.

"Oh, that's beautiful," the midwife replied approvingly.

"My brother's name was William, and we wanted something to honour him."

"Well, I bet he's absolutely thrilled." The midwife responded. "He was looking down on you today, I'm sure."

Grace gazed at Davis lovingly. "They all were," she said to him, and stroked his cheek.

The next hours passed in a flash of weighing and measuring and admiring their fresh, new little person. Once they were ensconced in their room on the maternity ward, Willow found her way to her mother's breast, and fed for a long time, while Davis looked on, in awe of Grace and his heart feeling so full he thought it would burst.

"I think she's asleep," Grace said quietly after a while. Davis stood up from his seat beside the bed and gazed down at his daughter, whose skin was now beautifully pink. She looked peaceful in her mother's arms.

"I think you might be right," Davis whispered back. "You're amazing."

Grace leaned back on the pillows and gave him a tired smile. "Could you hold her while I shower?"

"Of course," Davis manoeuvred the tiny being into his arms, and she felt as light as a feather.

Grace winced as she moved on the bed, and stood up slowly and carefully. Davis held Willow with one arm and helped Grace up. "I'm OK," she assured him, "just feels like I gave birth to a bowling ball." She giggled, and looked down at the baby in his arms. "I can't believe she's here."

Davis gazed down at their child. "I know. She's so beautiful." He looked up at Grace. "Just like her mother."

Grace planted a kiss on his lips before gingerly making her way to the ensuite bathroom. After a few minutes, Davis heard the shower come on.

Davis looked back down at his daughter, who continued to sleep peacefully in his arms. He stroked her tiny hands with his finger, marvelling at how perfect each little mother-of-pearl fingernail was. The little girl stretched her hand and wrapped it around his finger again, and Davis felt tears forming in his eyes. "We've been waiting for you, for so long," he told her. "Me and your Mama. We thought we'd never get to hold you. And here you are."

The pregnancy had been hard for Grace. She'd been terrified the entire time. She hadn't told anyone until she truly couldn't deny it any longer, and even when each sonogram showed a healthy, thriving baby, she wouldn't allow herself to believe it was real. Davis had remained supportive, while trying not to give his own fears too much life.

And now, here he was, holding his daughter in his arms. "You're magic, my little Willow." He whispered as he walked his daughter around the room.

"Your daughter is behaving herself beautifully," he informed Grace as she emerged from the bathroom. "She hasn't made a peep."

Grace smiled and walked carefully over to his side, gazing at Willow lovingly. "Of course she hasn't, she's in the safest place in the world." She kissed her daughter's head, and the baby stirred slightly, smiling in her sleep. "I can't believe she's really here." Grace said.

"I thought I wasn't going to make it," Davis told her. "I'm sorry you had to go through most of it alone."

"She was in a hurry," Grace replied. "You left for work and I called Alison, and then I was going to have a shower, and my water broke as soon as I got in." She gave a small laugh. "So I panicked and rang the hospital, and they told me contractions should start soon, and as I was talking to the midwife, I had my first one." She shook her head. "And then it just went real fast. I was almost fully dilated by the time I got to the hospital."

"Well, little miss," Davis said to his daughter, "you certainly caught us out!"

Grace laughed and sat down in the armchair by the window. "She sure did." She tilted her head and gazed at Davis. "You look great with a baby in your arms."

"It feels pretty damn good."

"I want to have at least seven more," Grace joked, and they both laughed.

"Better get busy then."

Grace pulled a face and laughed again. "Maybe give me a few weeks." She shook her head and looked out the window. "Look at us Davis. Who would have thought those two messed-up kids from Clearwater would make such a perfect little creature, huh?"

"We did good," Davis said.

"That we did," Grace agreed, and they both went back to staring at their daughter. Davis was sure he would never tire of staring at the little girl's face.

"We should call your Mom." Grace said after a while.

"I will, real soon," Davis replied quietly, stroking Willow's brown curls. "I'm enjoying this, here, now, just the three of us."

"The three of us," Grace repeated, her voice cracking with emotion. She rose to lean against Davis's chest, and the looked down at their child together for a long time. "The three of us," she said again. "I love you." She kissed Willow's tiny cheek. "And I love you," she said, looking up at Davis and kissing him. "I've always loved you."

"I know," Davis replied. "And I'll always love you. Both of you."

Their daughter began to stir in Davis's arms, and her tiny face scrunched up as she let out a loud cry. Grace and Davis smiled at each other. "The rest of our life is going to sound like that," Grace joked as she took the baby from his arms.

"I can live with that," he replied. "She's worth it, every second."

"That she is," Grace agreed. "It's been a long journey, but what a prize at the end." The baby quieted as she heard her mother's voice, and Grace gently touched her nose to Willow's. "Your Uncle Billy would have loved you," she whispered, "and your Grandpa too. You have so much love around you, little one."

"A whole lifetime of it," Davis said, putting his arms around both of them, "a whole lifetime, and then some."

The baby wailed again, and Grace sat down to feed her.

Davis watched them both, the loves of his life, and felt deeply content. *You were right, Dad,* he thought, casting a gaze outside at the grey skies, *you were right. It's not too late for us. It's never too late.*

Printed in Great Britain
by Amazon